ELIC

THE ALPHA'S GAMBLE

GAMBLE

MISMATCHED MATES SERIES

Cover by Fiona Jayde

Published by Smoking Teacup Books
Los Angeles, California
ISBN: 9798857634462

Chapter 1

Throw the Dice

In my experience, private casino back rooms were plush, quiet oases, well stocked with top-shelf liquor, with absurdly attractive staff on call to cater to my every whim. Chairs so comfortable you could sleep in them, or even fuck on them—the staff really would cater to my every whim.

I shifted in my seat, plastic armrests creaking, trying to find an angle for my ass that didn't squish it against unyieldingly flat metal.

My mouth had gone so dry I'd have killed for even a lukewarm glass of nasty Vegas tap water.

My poker rooms had always been stocked with chilled Alpine mineral water.

New experiences were highly overrated.

Fuck this. All I'd done was mind my own business, doing my best to keep from getting crushed in between my overachiever little brother's single-minded drive to rule our family company with an iron fist and my parents' obsession with maintaining the perfect image of a wealthy, high-profile pack full of vigorous alphas. I'd simply wanted to be left alone to drink, fuck, and spend my time—and money—as I pleased.

My father's lies had put an end to that.

Cut off. My trust broken and used to pay off debts, not all of them even mine.

Well, to be fair, many of them were mine. But that had been what the credit cards were *for*, damn it.

I'd been left with nowhere to turn but the Morrigan casino, where I'd still had a line of credit and VIP status—at least until they'd apparently figured out, belatedly, that my situation had changed. Counting cards came as naturally to me as breathing. I should've been able to get ahead.

Fuck. An attempted deep breath that didn't go all the way down to the bottom of my lungs, and I had to stop brooding. It certainly wouldn't help me in here.

The metal table in front of me gleamed dully in the flickering light of the tube fluorescents overhead. Plain gray walls when I turned my head. Like a prison, or a police interrogation room.

At least they hadn't tied me up. Maybe they didn't have any restraints that would've held an alpha werewolf, or maybe they just knew they didn't have a good justification to treat me that way, the fuckers. They'd given me the suite and credit at the tables voluntarily. All I'd done was walk in the door.

The room didn't have a clock, and they'd taken my phone and my watch along with my other personal effects. Illegally, I was pretty sure, and I was going to have their asses for that…once I had the chance.

But it felt like hours since I'd given up shouting and banging on the door—which *was* strong enough to hold an alpha werewolf, it turned out. Maybe that explained the lack of restraints. I'd picked up the chair, meaning to beat it against the door too, but then set it down again. Where would I sit if I broke it? The dusty concrete floor? In jeans worth more than a month's paycheck for one of those fucking asshole goons who'd pulled me away from the cashier's window on the casino floor and taken me back here? Yeah, no.

Why hadn't I resisted them, caused a scene? I was cursing myself for that now, but at the time, I'd assumed a supervisor would be attending to my needs personally, somewhere more private, and had sent security to escort me safely to a back office.

And so they had, in a manner of speaking.

More endless time dragged past, and I tried again to find a comfortable position in this miserable excuse for a chair.

Finally, footsteps and voices filtered in from the hallway. One voice stood out, deep and commanding. A little involuntary shiver went down my spine. That didn't sound like some security peon with delusions of grandeur.

At least they'd finally realized I deserved the attention of someone with authority. Because anyone that voice belonged to had authority, I had no doubt of that.

The door opened, and three men stepped in. My nose twitched. My werewolf senses, the part of me that interpreted the presence of magic via instinct and smell and something I could almost taste on the air, went on high alert.

Most of the magic was coming from the shorter man on the left, a freaky-looking guy with a handsome face that was way too smooth and expressionless. A warlock, maybe, because I couldn't really place his scent, and he certainly wasn't a shifter.

And I immediately dismissed the second man. He had the trying-to-look-expensive-and-failing necktie beloved of middle management everywhere, and a faux-brass nametag with the casino logo on it. No one important wore a nametag.

But the third guy. Once my gaze caught on him, it stuck.

Everything about him screamed alpha, from his height and broad-shouldered build to his very faintly glowing eyes, and everything in between. And he had that presence. You couldn't fake it.

My father had tried to fake it for decades.

I'd been shocked when the truth came out. That he'd been using a shaman's magic to imitate an alpha's traits, covering up what he saw as his shame, and projecting all of his insecurities onto his sons.

Shocked. But not surprised at all. Because he'd never quite had it, that intangible quality that marked a shifter with the enhanced magic of an alpha. And with a couple of months since the revelation to brood over it, I'd thought of a lot of clues I really shouldn't have missed, like the way he'd always seemed to hate me despite how proud he pretended to be of his alpha son.

I'd thought that if I fit the mold he'd wanted me to cram myself into, he'd do more than give me money and shout at me.

That hadn't worked out well.

In any case, unlike my father, I was genuinely an alpha. But like him, I'd never had that *je ne sais quoi*.

This man had it. In spades.

He had a really nice suit, too. Dark gray Italian wool. And his tie passed muster.

His lip curled as he stared down at me out of cold, hard dark eyes.

Other than that, his face didn't give anything away.

"Do you know who I am? I demand to contact my lawyer," I said, the words taking effort to force out through air that felt congealed with tension all of a sudden. "I demand—"

The words died on my lips as the alpha had the gall to *laugh at me*, chuckling and shaking his head slightly. A lock of his dark brown hair fell onto his forehead with the motion. It should've made him look less intimidating.

It didn't.

"I know who you are. You're Blake Castelli, and you're not really in a position to demand much of anything." His voice matched the rest of him: deep, smooth, and cold, like glacier ice. "You're lucky the cops aren't here right now."

Sweat broke out along my hairline, but I kept my expression neutral through force of will. I could bluff; I did it at the poker table, and this wasn't any different—except that the stakes were higher. They couldn't prove I hadn't believed that check was good. In any case, it should've been. In a just world, it would've been.

"Counting cards isn't a crime," I said, as evenly as I could. And it wasn't like it'd done me much good, anyway, so they really shouldn't care. My luck had been shit enough to counterbalance any skill with numbers. Didn't they want to make money?

I ignored the little voice in the back of my brain that commented, in a dry tone that sounded way too much like my know-it-all brother, that if I couldn't pay up for the money I'd gambled on credit, they weren't exactly making a profit off of my losses on paper, now were they?

The middle-management guy cleared his throat, glancing nervously over and up—way up—at the alpha. "No, it's not a crime," he said. "But the check you attempted to cash was invalid. That's fraud."

"I've been a valued guest at this establishment for years!" The best defense was a good offense, after all. And they were being pretty damn offensive themselves. "You comped me and extended my usual line of credit, and now you're acting like—"

"Like you failed to disclose your changed financial circumstances and defrauded us twice," the alpha cut in, eyes flashing gold. "Once by taking perks you weren't entitled to, and twice by playing on credit you couldn't cover. And an attempted third time, when you tried to pass that rubber check. Anything you'd like to add?"

Shit. I straightened my spine, glaring the alpha straight in the eyes, feeling my own start to light up in response to the challenge, to my anger, to the urge to fight and then flee that rose up so strongly I almost choked on it.

"I'm not responsible for your poor business decisions," I snarled. "*You* comped me. *You* extended the credit. And who the fuck are you, anyway? You have no authority over me."

If I'd hoped my own alpha display, hands flexing with claws close to the surface and eyes glowing, would make this man back down...well, luckily my hopes hadn't been all that high.

His lip curled, and he stared down his nose at me like I'd been lying on the floor and whimpering instead of posturing. Fresh sweat broke out along my spine, and the golden light of his eyes seemed to shine right through me.

My father, the fake alpha, had always berated me for being an inadequate one, the hypocritical bastard. I'd seethed, and I'd pretended to submit, and I'd been so damn sure he was wrong. Not wanting to take over the family business, having no interest whatsoever in chaining myself to a desk in fucking Boise and arguing with the board for the rest of my life, didn't make me inadequate. It meant I had too much common sense to want to play my father's sick games the way my brother Brook did, to be our father's alpha proxy in business and everywhere else, too.

Of course, the way I'd gone about avoiding said desk and board of directors had been—in retrospect, because I'd had more time on my hands to be alone in my head lately than ever before, and I'd hated every fucking second of it—childish and cowardly. Alphas were bold, strong, in charge. They confronted their problems head-on.

Maybe it'd taken a shitty alpha to know one all along.

Because facing this guy down...I'd never felt so inadequate in my life.

Whimpering on the floor wasn't out of the question if he kept looking at me like that.

"Oh, I do indeed have authority over you," he purred, voice dipping even lower. "Declan MacKenna, at your service. I own this place, darlin'." Darling? Especially with the dropped *g*? And now that

I noticed, his voice had the very faintest lilt to it. Not quite an Irish accent, but something adjacent, just enough to go with his name.

Still condescending as ever-loving fuck, though, even with a hint of authenticity.

And a hint of familiarity. Had I ever met this man? I'd remember him. I'd definitely remember him, wouldn't I?

Or maybe I was remembering a Lucky Charms commercial and mixing it up with alpha porn. Who knew. I'd spent a lot of time drunk in my life.

Before I could muster the right words to express my outrage, my tongue thickening in my mouth, he went on. "Mr. Franklin, here," and he tipped his head toward the middle management stooge, "can have the police here within two minutes. They'll take you away, charge you for fraud, and hold you on bail that you can't afford and your family won't care to pay. I'll make bloody well sure of it. And if you think alphas do well in prison, think again. They'll put you in with all the other supernaturals, and you won't be the biggest and baddest in there, believe me."

"I'm a Castelli alpha," I spat, even though deep inside, I did believe him. In a general human prison population, I'd be the strongest and the most resilient. But the authorities tended to split the humans and the weaker magical species off from the real threats. I'd be seen as the latter. And I'd be no match for two or three alphas in a gang, or a couple of vampires.

If they went after me, anyway. But everyone had heard of the Castelli pack, right? We were one of the richest and most well-known in the country.

After all, my dad talked about it all the time…yeah. Shit. I was really, truly screwed.

I lifted my chin. MacKenna couldn't read my mind. "They wouldn't dare fuck with me. Not once they knew I was an alpha from the Castelli pack."

After a beat, he burst out laughing, cheeks flushed and eyes sparkling under the glow. It echoed off the concrete of the room. My own face went as hot as the surface of the sun. His two yes-men both smiled, shaking their heads.

Lightheaded and tingling, my hands clenching on the armrests with a horrid scritch of the claws that had crept out involuntarily, I had to practically bite my tongue in half to keep from screaming.

Laughing. This arrogant bastard, and his miserable peons, were *laughing at me.*

And I couldn't do anything about it. Because the son of a bitch truly did have all the power here.

He finally subsided, his laughter fading into a nasty, malicious grin.

"Sorry, Castelli," he said, with an emphasis on my last name that wasn't lost on me. "I was imagining you telling all those hardened criminals they had to leave you alone because of your blue-blood pack. I was being kind. Not the biggest and baddest? You'd be meat. *Castelli.* A pretty-boy rich kid like you? Fresh meat. Delicious. You'd be lucky to survive your first week."

My mouth went as dry as the desert outside this miserable little concrete box I'd been confined in. The way he was looking at me…as if I was meat to him, too. Nothing more.

"I'll pay back what I lost at the tables," I tried, the words scraping my throat raw. His eyes had caught and held me, and nothing existed but that dark, sinister glow. "I'll pay it all—"

"How do you propose to do that, exactly?" It wasn't MacKenna's voice. It was the third one, who hadn't spoken yet, his tone light but hollow, without any kindness in it. "Our background check shows you have no assets whatsoever."

"I'm sure we could come to some arrangement," I muttered, still looking at MacKenna, because I couldn't look away. And fuck that other asshole, anyway. He didn't deserve eye contact after interrupting me like that.

MacKenna smiled, a hint of fang showing. No smile in the history of smiles had ever been less friendly, and I stiffened my spine so I didn't throw myself back in my chair to try to get the hell away from him. I was a Castelli. Castelli alphas didn't cower, even when they were…meat.

"Maybe we can," he said after an endless moment of watching me, his eyes brightening even further. His scent had changed, gone darker, richer. Spicier and more overwhelming, his alpha pheromones pressing on all of my instincts. He was stronger. He knew it. I knew it. And my body and my magic couldn't deny it. I fought the urge to bare my throat, shuddering. "And this may not be the best venue to discuss it, after all. Castelli, a conversation with me, or the LVPD?"

I swallowed hard, and it did nothing at all to clear the tightness in my throat. Prison couldn't be that bad, I thought wildly. It couldn't be worse than dealing with this man.

But I'd come to Las Vegas on a gamble, after all, hoping my skill with cards would be enough to bluff my way through the line of credit I knew I couldn't pay for. The police, jail, all the horrors and indignities of the criminal justice system—those were known quantities. I mean, I didn't *know* what would happen, but I could take an educated guess. And none of it appealed to me. In fact, it made me want to run screaming.

Time to throw the dice.

"I'll talk to you," I managed to choke out.

And MacKenna's smile widened, showing way too much fucking fang for comfort. I'd made the choice he wanted me to make.

The LVPD suddenly sounded a lot better—but too late. He'd already turned away and put his hand on the door. "Bring him up to my suite," he threw over his shoulder, and strode out, leaving me alone with his minions.

The middle manager grimaced, eyebrows raised, and waved a hand at the door. Too-handsome guy's eyebrows drew together, the heated glance he threw after MacKenna and the quick glare he shot me giving me an unpleasant shiver.

My heart fell even further.

"Well, then, Mr. Castelli," he said, frowning a little, eyes still shooting sparks, "if you'd come with us?"

One of the security goons poked his head in the door and grinned.

I'd never wanted to claw out and rip everyone present to shreds more in my life.

Instead I got up, straightened my back and held my head high to try to preserve at least a tiny scrap of dignity, and let them escort me out.

Jail probably would've been better than throwing myself on MacKenna's not-so-tender mercies.

And in a few minutes, I'd find out for sure.

Lucky me.

Chapter 2

A Moral Debt

MacKenna had said he owned the casino, so I was a little surprised when the two security goons escorted me not to the very top penthouse of the place, but to a—still very expensive, of course—suite a couple of floors below that. The room I'd been given twenty-four hours ago, before they figured out what had happened to my finances, was a floor above this one, in fact.

Apparently MacKenna wasn't one for taking the maximum perks he could. *I* would have. False humility on his part? Or maybe he'd overextended himself financially and needed the income from the penthouse? Well, not like I could throw stones in that direction.

One of the goons opened the door, they all but shoved me inside, and the door shut behind me, leaving me alone in a spotless foyer with a huge, gilt-framed mirror hanging over an end table. I tried not to look, but I couldn't help glancing to the side.

No, being manhandled off the casino floor, left to stew for hours, and being interrogated and humiliated had not in fact left me at my best. Pale lips, too-flushed cheeks, and damp with sweat everywhere. My light blue eyes were even a little bit bloodshot despite my werewolf healing—no magic could completely compensate for the shitty, moistureless air in the bowels of a casino hotel. And my blond hair hung limp and bedraggled around my temples.

Fucking great.

I drew in a deep, shuddering breath and stepped through the foyer toward whatever lay beyond.

The luxurious vista before me had all the personality of a dentist's office, albeit a dentist who only cleaned the teeth of royalty or billionaires: several leather sofas, a huge screen on the wall, an elegant dining area, a cream carpet so pristine you could rub yourself all over it, a full bar stocked with—even by my standards—top-shelf liquor. No trace whatsoever of the man who presumably lived here: not a book, an item of clothing, or any personal touch. Beyond all of that, an expanse of windows displayed the whole Strip glittering and winking and flashing against a backdrop of mountains in the distance.

Fucking gods, it hadn't even gotten fully dark yet while I'd sat in that room. The setting sun still gilded all of it, just enough light for Vegas to become unearthly and impossible in its tacky beauty.

I'd had a room like this. I could've been lounging on my own sofa, pouring a drink from my own bar, getting ready for a night out at one of Vegas's most exclusive clubs. Or several of them. Surrounded by beautiful, laughing people, instead of here alone waiting for the next blow to fall…

And then I felt his presence, a flutter in the edges of my magical senses and a rich, dark scent in the air. MacKenna stepped out of a doorway off to the left, a glass of what looked like whiskey in his hand and an unpleasant smile twisting the corners of his lips.

He'd lost the jacket and tie, and rolled up his shirt sleeves to show a pair of muscular forearms with tattoos all over them under the brown hair.

My eyebrows went up. It took effort, expense, and magic to successfully tattoo a werewolf whose body was primed to reject anything it perceived as unhealthy. I'd never gotten any tattoos, knowing my father thought they made people look like lowlifes. But they'd always fascinated me. And they didn't seem to go along with the casino-owner-in-an-expensive-suit image. He had a past, maybe.

He'd also made a couple of remarks about my wealthy family background. A heavy, sinking sensation took over the pit of my stomach. If he had a past, if he had overextended himself buying this place, then…my attitude toward money, my past, would only make this worse.

"Take a picture," he drawled. "It'll last longer. Except that my people confiscated your phone, I assume?"

As a matter of fact…

"Yes, and they haven't given it back. Or my watch. That's Cartier. And you have the nerve to tell me I owe you money!"

His grin widened, and he took a swig from his drink and sauntered into the room, disposing himself in the corner of the nearest sofa. Taking his fucking time, while I seethed and stood there like a schoolboy called to the headmaster's office.

My every limb trembled with the urge to launch myself at him, claws and fangs out, and draw blood. Claw out his eyes, slash across his stomach, crimson splattering the black leather of the sofa and marring the perfection of that creamy carpet.

"I saw your watch," he said at last. "Next time invest a little more if you want something you can pawn later. That'd barely cover your bottle service from last night." Another swig. "I reviewed your bill. You drink like a teenager." A shrug. "A rich teenager. But I might be a little more sympathetic if you'd spent that much on Scotch instead of glow-in-the-dark vodka cocktails."

"I wasn't spending anything," I protested, furious. *Invest a little more?* What a hypocrite. He was the one living three floors from the top of his own casino! "It was a line of credit—"

"Exactly, you were spending *my* money, not yours!" He only raised his voice a little, but his eyes flashed and he bared his fangs and he—gods, the crashing wave of alpha rage and pheromones, almost a tangible thing in the air, and it hit me like a blow to the face.

I reeled back, stumbling a step before I righted myself, my whole body going hot.

I was an alpha. The strongest. The best. A Castelli. Except that I'd always had the impenetrable armor of a prominent pack, an endless bank account, more credit cards, my father's name and reputation.

And now I only had myself. No phone, no watch, no wallet. No one who'd take my call anyway.

His voice, smooth and deep again without a hint of emotion, cut through my confusion and whirling despair. "And now we're going to talk about how you will repay me, and the Morrigan, for the bar tab. And the suite. And the gambling losses. And by the way, you're shit at counting cards, if that's what you were really do—"

"I'm great at counting cards," I snarled, pushed beyond my limit at last. "And fuck you for—"

"I'm one more outburst from handing you over to the cops after all, Castelli. Watch your fucking mouth."

The absolute, imperative alpha command in his deep voice withered the words on my tongue and struck me completely, horribly, obediently silent.

Instantly.

As if I hadn't been an alpha at all.

I'd never been so ashamed in my life—and my family had really done their best to set the bar high.

MacKenna drained the last of his drink and set it down on the table with a clunk, leaning back into the sofa at his ease, knees spread in the universal posture of a man in command of the situation.

Those tailored trousers didn't have enough fabric to hide the bulge in the front of them.

He was half hard, it looked like.

A totally new type of shudder made my spine do a tango.

MacKenna was getting off on humiliating me. On having me in the palm of his hand.

And I could scent his arousal as well as see it, now that I was paying attention to it. Was that why my body had started to go haywire? Another alpha's powerful sexual pheromones wrapping around me, seeping into my body and my magic.

Making me react. Because my own cock had thickened. Not hard, not yet, but interested. Responsive.

Subjugated to his stronger shifter magic.

"Good," he said, startling me out of my horrified realization of the situation I'd gotten myself into. "I don't give a toss about your abilities or lack thereof when it comes to blackjack. I do care about your debt. And it doesn't matter how many watches you sell, or phone calls you make begging your family to pay me off. You're a criminal, I can prove it, and if you want to get out of that? Well, you'll be paying that off, too. Call it a moral debt, if you like."

I'd torn my eyes away from the front of his pants and forced them up to meet his, even though it went against every atavistic instinct I had to face him down with my body and my magic teetering on the brink of yielding to him already. Those deep, dark eyes, like black pits…nothing moral there, I'd be willing to bet. His expression didn't give anything away.

"A moral debt." I couldn't help the sarcastic twist I put on the words, even though playing it cool and pretending to be completely unaffected would have been a lot smarter. "Right. You mean black-mail."

Another casual shrug. "Call it whatever you want. But you owe me. And you're going to pay. Come here."

My hair felt like it was standing on end, and I stiffened my legs, rooting my feet to the floor.

No way would I move so much as an inch. He couldn't tell me what to do.

He shifted a little in his seat, spreading his knees a tiny bit wider.

And then he said it again, this time with a resonance in his tone that throbbed in my skull and made my eyes water. "Come. Here."

I resisted with every cell in my body, but it didn't matter. One foot moved, and then the other, MacKenna's alpha magic pulling on me like a rope tied somewhere inside my sternum. Did my own were-wolf magic reside around there? It felt like it. Like he'd somehow wrapped his own more powerful will around mine and *yanked*.

And yet he was still just sitting there, expression neutral, waiting for me to do his bidding.

As if this moment that was costing me everything, the last of my pride and my self-respect, meant absolutely fucking nothing to him.

One foot, and then the other, soundless on the plush carpeting.

I didn't stop until I stood between his feet, my legs almost brushing his. He had to tilt his head back against the sofa to look up at me. Shouldn't I have felt at more of an advantage, looming over him like this? But I didn't. I'd never felt so insignificant, so much at a disadvantage. Jail. Disowned. Fraud. *A moral debt.* He had me right where he wanted me, because he had all the cards that I'd always been able to play at will: wealth, power, *choices*.

"What do you even want from me?" I asked, even though I was starting to think I knew, and the pit of my stomach had clenched into a tight, churning knot. "And why? What—what could you possibly want from me? I'm an alpha!"

That last came out a wail, as un-alpha-like as a tone of voice could possibly be.

He had the audacity—and the cruelty—to chuckle, shaking his head at me, eyes faintly glowing. Mine were too, I thought, but I could hardly feel my magic anymore, it'd been so subdued by his. His scent had thickened even more, suffocating me: rich and powerful, a hint of sweetness underneath bitter darkness, like sugared Turkish coffee.

It was so unfair. So fucking unfair, that he had *this*, this innate power, when I couldn't even claim that after losing everything else.

He didn't only have power over me as the owner of this place, someone who could press charges or throw me out on the street, but as a man. That had been my last remaining worthwhile quality: being a real alpha, unlike my liar of a father.

Useless.

He considered me for an endless, agonizing minute, while I seethed and bit my lip and clenched my fists and felt sicker and sicker by the second.

MacKenna's lip curled. "You don't remember me, do you?" he asked at last. "I thought you were just bluffing and hoping I didn't remember, as if I'd forget. But you really don't fucking remember me."

That hit me like a thunderbolt, and my vision went sparkly for a second.

The familiarity in his voice…not a cartoon leprechaun after all. I nearly burst out laughing, my impending hysteria seeking any outlet it could find.

"Take your time," he said, with a dark, cruel edge to his tone. "Don't strain anything. I'll even help you out. We met almost ten years ago, at this very casino. In a private poker room. Ringing any bells?"

Ten years ago. I bit my lip hard, blinking to try to clear the spots away. All that got me was a fresh view of his hard, contemptuous, glowing-eyed face and the hint of fang showing where he'd all but bared his teeth at me.

That must have been one of my first trips to Vegas after I turned twenty-one, if not my very first. And that first time…the drinking had been the least of it. I'd been higher than my private jet's flight path on coke and X before I even took off from Boise. Remember him? I could barely remember my own name that weekend.

Little flashes, filtered through liquor and drugs and shame and denial …a girl I'd slept with, her laughing face as she put a thousand dollars of my money on a spin of the roulette wheel. A club, smoke and blue and pink lights.

The private poker room, and an incredibly hot guy with mesmerizing dark eyes who'd made me want…but he hadn't wanted me.

"Oh, fucking gods," I choked out, my knees going weak. "Fuck. *Fuck.*"

"And there it is." His grim satisfaction was laced with enough irony to sink a ship. "I'm honored you remember me after all. Out of all the lowly nobodies you've offered a wad of cash to suck your cock."

I stared down at him, chest heaving, extremities numb. Alpha werewolves didn't have strokes, or I'd have begged for an ambulance.

At this point, I'd have begged for the Las Vegas police.

But I had a feeling that wasn't on the table anymore.

"Of course, most of them probably took the money," he went on implacably, cold and hard and in control while I trembled and panted for breath in front of him. "And the ones that didn't, who knows what happened after that. I only know what happened to me." His voice dropped to an impossibly deep register, vibrating through me, almost rattling my teeth. "You told your casino host I'd hit on you. Made you uncomfortable. And I was out on my ass by morning. I guess I should be grateful you didn't accuse me of something worse. Either way, I couldn't get another job here after that. Blacklisted everywhere."

That…I'd done that? Little snippets of that night were coming back to me, freeze frames without context. The really hot guy.

MacKenna.

And then—I was angry. Hurt? Probably mostly hurt in my pride, that I'd tried to seduce him and he'd turned me down. Of course I'd offered money. That was only polite, right? Wasn't it? To make sure the people hanging out with me got something out of it? Like the girl playing my money at the roulette table. She'd been happy to fuck me and spend whatever I had on hand. Had I straight-up offered him cash for sex, or had that been his interpretation?

I didn't remember complaining to the host. That was gone, swept away in a haze of intoxication and sleep deprivation and distractions.

Besides…

"But you own this place now," I argued. Or tried to. He still hadn't moved, his head resting on the back of the sofa and his limbs sprawled. But I couldn't seem to raise my voice against the pressure in the air, a heavy, gathering tension like an electrical storm. His magic, building with his anger. At least I'd gotten to him the way he'd gotten to me. I refused to quail in the face of it, even though I thought I might throw up. I lifted my chin and stared him down. "You—obviously that was, I mean, embarrassing, but if you have the money to buy a damn casino, what did a stupid job matter to you?"

The kindling fire in his eyes was more than the glow of an alpha. That was rage, and my fists clenched at my sides as I fought the urge to run.

He might chase me.

And I wasn't any match for him. I might do some damage, but not enough to stop him from whatever he wanted to do to me.

Slowly, he lifted his head and sat up straight—and then he moved more quickly than I could follow, my wrists suddenly clamped in his hands. MacKenna yanked me down, and I stumbled to the floor, falling on one knee with the other leg twisted painfully under me. I bit back a yelp, but my cry died on my tongue anyway as he leaned down, his face only inches from mine, eyes flaring like twin supernovas.

"I earned every penny I have," he ground out, fangs flashing. "No one handed me a fucking thing. That job was my rent, my utility bills, food on the table. And my path to working my way up to something that was supposed to be mine. My grandparents built this place from the ground up, and my parents fucked it up and screwed the whole family—it doesn't matter. Fuck you, Castelli. You had everything. It wouldn't have cost you anything to act like a decent man. Instead, your stunt fucked me over for years. And now you're here, and I'm not inclined to give you any more leeway than you gave me. But I'm not forcing you. You can say no to paying me off the way I choose, and you get up and walk out that door. Tell your spoiled-brat sob story to Las Vegas's finest and see if they give a fuck. Last chance."

My arms shook in his grasp, and he tightened his grip until I could almost feel my bones grinding together. And fuck, but even when I pulled, I couldn't get loose.

I couldn't get loose.

When had I last tangled physically with another alpha? Not since I was a teenager, probably, and I'd been stronger…that time.

But MacKenna—he wasn't just stronger in terms of his negotiating position.

He was stronger, full stop.

And that combined with the machine-gun-bullets to the chest effect of his words had me gasping in shock. His grandparents? What the hell had he been doing with a menial job here, even if his parents had—done what, precisely? Spent too much money, probably. Made bad decisions. I had a vague recollection of someone who worked at the Morrigan telling me, years ago, about how the previous owners of the place had gone bankrupt, and that had almost certainly been MacKenna's parents. Gods, I could empathize with that, with having parents who cared more about looking rich and successful than about reality, but he didn't seem like he wanted to establish any common ground.

Quite the opposite.

Fuck, he was wrong about me! He was wrong, he was so fucking wrong, but how could I explain that to him?

And he claimed he wasn't forcing me? I didn't have a choice, no matter how much it amused him to pretend I did.

I could see the headlines now, whirring through my mind's eye like those newspaper montages in old movies.

Alpha Castelli Heir Arrested in Vegas.

Castelli Pack Embroiled in Scandal: Will the Family Business Survive?

Castelli Industries Stock Plummets as Blake Castelli Faces Fraud Charges.

At least this humiliation would be private, like all the ones that had come before it at the hands of my overbearing father. Once I'd…*satisfied* MacKenna—and the huge, intimidating bulge in the front of his trousers now only a couple of feet from my face clearly showed me how that would happen—no one would know. My brother, the company board. They'd never know. I could still try something else to get my life back in order and get what I deserved from my family.

But I wouldn't do it unless he spelled it out. Apparently I'd demanded that he blow me? Well, he could fucking come down to my level if he wanted me to submit to him.

"You have to say it," I rasped, wincing as his fingers twitched around my wrists, fresh pain blooming in ten points of contact. "Explicitly. If you're going to blackmail me, you should fucking say it."

At that, he threw his head back and laughed, a pleasant, mellow sound that grated on every single one of my nerves. "Blackmail you? As if you have any bloody moral high ground. You're facing the consequences of your own actions."

"Suck your cock or go to jail?" I spat, forgetting how determined I'd been to make him say it first. Damn it all to hell, now he could truthfully claim it'd been my idea, not his! But I couldn't take it back now. "That's not much of a choice."

He grinned, eyes gleaming with malice. "You said it, not me."

Damn it.

"Because you—you—fuck you, we both knew what you meant!"

"You said it first. Ten years ago, and tonight." Taunting. Cruel, so cruel, and I hadn't deserved this... "You're wrong about the bargain, though. The scope of it, anyway. Sucking my cock's just for tonight. You think one probably terrible blowjob's going to cover all your debts, financial and otherwise? Think again, darlin'."

Stung and furious, I cried out, "Terrible blowjob? You fucking—" And then I stopped dead, my own words ringing in my ears. "It's blackmail, and you're a sophist," I added weakly.

Because those should have been my objections from the start, not his opinion of my likely skills with my mouth. My leg hurt. My wrists hurt. And I was sprawled at his feet, barely able to pull in a full breath. That had to be my excuse for my brain going haywire.

"Oooh, ten dollar word," he drawled. "And I'm sorry to cast aspersions on your abilities, Castelli. I'm done talking about this. You're mine until I say otherwise. You'll do what I say, when I say, and we'll work out the details of how long you'll be paying me back once I see what you have to offer. If you're any good at it, maybe you'll be able to work it off in a few months."

"A few *months*?" I gaped at him, aghast. "This—I can't possibly owe you—you didn't even cash the check!"

"I'm going to let go of you, and you're going to open your pretty fucking mouth and take what I'm giving you. Or it's prison for you, Castelli."

His flat tone told me his patience had run out. The back of my neck prickled with sweat, and spots swam in my vision, nearly obscuring his harsh face and powerful body curled over mine, the fly of his pants with his hard cock behind it.

I couldn't go to jail.

Without a word, because I couldn't imagine anything I could say that'd make him have a little mercy, I struggled up enough to get my other leg under me and kneel properly between his feet.

I opened my mouth and waited.

I still couldn't remember most of that night when I'd apparently ruined his life, temporarily anyway.

But I'd remember *this* for the rest of mine.

Chapter 3

Playing with Fire

MacKenna lounged back into the sofa again, obviously trying to look like he couldn't give a fuck.

But he wasn't fooling me. His big body sang with tension, and the hands he'd taken from my wrists and rested on the cushions beside him had balled into fists. His chest rose and fell faster than normal respiration would account for.

The way his trousers seemed to be about to give way from the force of his erection clued me in, too.

Maybe that ought to be my way of making my fortune once I got free of MacKenna: a clothing line for alphas. *Guaranteed to stand up to the force of an alpha cock! Even when you're about to grudge-face-fuck someone you're blackmailing!*

I tried to choke back a hysterical laugh, but I'd forgotten my mouth was hanging obediently open, and it came out as a weird, strangled yelp.

MacKenna grinned at me, more like a shark than a wolf. Although his teeth would've done any predator, shifter or otherwise, plenty proud.

"Your hands and mouth are both free," he commented, still going for nonchalance—poorly. Well, I could hardly throw stones. I was about as nonchalant, kneeling here red-faced and sweaty and vibrating with apprehension, as a cat in a room full of rocking chairs. "I've already issued a clear invitation. Have at it."

An invitation I wished I could decline.

But that ship had sailed.

Gingerly, trying to touch the hard ridge of his cock as little as possible—and what I thought I'd accomplish with putting that off, I wasn't sure—I reached up and unbuckled his belt, undid the button, and tugged at the zipper with my fingertips. I looked like one of those pretentious assholes drinking tea with a pinky extended, the way I was contorting my hands.

MacKenna let out a scoffing sound. "It doesn't bite. I do, but my cock doesn't."

I glanced up from my horrified contemplation of his fly to find him gazing down at me avidly, jaw set and eyes gleaming with more than his alpha glow—although he went neutral again as soon as our eyes met, trying to hide his emotions. His lust probably should've frightened me.

But it didn't. It gave me a surge of confidence, a sensation of power, that I hadn't had since the door of that holding room locked behind me.

MacKenna held most of the high cards, but I had one ace to play: he wanted me. He might be doing this mostly for revenge, and to get his kinky kicks through subduing another alpha.

But he *wanted* me.

And I didn't want him.

Which put me in control…for a certain value of control, anyway.

Would it be playing with fire to try to use that advantage? Yes. I had no doubt of that.

Would it be immensely satisfying, though, to have him at my mercy? To play him the way he'd thought he could play me?

Also yes.

Doing my best to hide my newfound resolve, not too hard given how messed-up I already looked, I yanked his zipper down the rest of the way, the faint rip echoingly loud in the quiet suite. Alpha werewolf hearing magnified noises at the best of times, and this hardly counted as one of those.

His cock shoved through the gap, barely restrained by boxer briefs that were clearly fighting their best fight and losing. Had I imagined the slight hitch in MacKenna's breath?

It took both hands to pull the waistband down and over his cock until the underwear bunched up at his balls.

MacKenna had all the cock I'd have expected from an alpha—

and then some.

And then maybe some more. Gods, I hoped he never saw mine, because he had me beat by at least an inch, inch and a half, and my own didn't disappoint for alpha dick either.

So fucking large. A lot larger than…

A few disjointed fragments of memory whirled through my mind, and I went dizzy, reeling from it. A man leaning against a wall, not a shifter. A normal human who couldn't sense what I was unless I showed him.

His cock out, his harsh breathing, the hard floor of the club's back room against my kneecaps.

Just an anonymous cock, and an anonymous mouth, the hot rush of come down my throat and the shameful spill of my own inside my too-tight jeans.

I'd done this before. More than once? Maybe? Fuck, I might throw up. Flashbacks were supposed to be from PTSD, not from ill-advised almost-blacked-out sexual encounters.

But I swallowed hard and forced my eyes to focus.

That was good, right? I had some practice. Even if I couldn't remember what I'd done, or even if I hadn't done more than sloppily mouth the guy's cock until he came, both of us too drunk and high to care.

MacKenna would expect more than that.

Fuck.

I wrapped my hand around the base of his cock, right above the fabric of his boxer briefs. Gods, but it was hard, and it stiffened even more as I tightened my fingers, gripping him hard enough to be a threat without actually causing him pain; challenging him might be dangerous, but injuring him could be suicidal.

It didn't feel all that different from my own dick, with silky skin over a firm shaft, hot and pulsing.

That gave me the courage to tug up and then down, twisting my hand a little in a way I liked when I did it to myself.

MacKenna's soft grunt and involuntary-seeming, small upward jerk of his hips gave me the courage to lean in and set my mouth over his thick cockhead.

Salt. Clean, soap-tinged male musk.

And the spicy, sparking heat of an alpha werewolf's raw,

elemental magic. It all burst on my tongue like lightning, arrowing into my throat and down, lighting me up along the way, pooling in the pit of my stomach.

Well, maybe a little lower than that.

To my horror, I started to get hard myself, my cock stirring uncomfortably against the zipper of my jeans.

Another flash of another blowjob, adjusting myself so I didn't injure my dick.

I squeezed my eyes shut to try to blot out the memory and swirled my tongue around the head of MacKenna's cock, pressing my mouth down onto it, letting it bump into the roof of my mouth. There was no way I could take it any deeper than that, into my throat.

But then MacKenna made a sound. Something like a gasp, but trailing off into a growl.

I knew that sound; I'd made it myself when someone had me on the brink of coming.

Probably terrible blowjob. Yeah, fuck him and his sneering assumptions. I had him right where I wanted him, and I was going to blow his mind, not just his dick.

Drawing the deepest breath I could manage, I gathered up every bit of courage I had and aimed his cock toward my throat. All or nothing. I opened up as much as I could and forced my head down.

And down, and down, my throat spasming and my lungs laboring, eyes watering with the strain of it. My mouth had stretched as wide as it possibly could, saliva leaking out around his thick shaft. All my limbs went kind of distant, floaty, my attention narrowed down to the near-unbearable pressure of his cock filling my throat to bursting.

I swallowed convulsively, again and again, and my lungs felt like they were on fire.

But my cock throbbed in my jeans, agonizingly close to shooting off like a rocket. And for some reason I didn't gag. Maybe he was so far down inside me that my gag reflex had given it up as a lost cause? Or maybe alpha healing gave me a remarkable power of blowjob.

A half laugh, half moan of pain bubbled up with nowhere to go, and the gargling, choking sound I made around his cock sounded like a death rattle.

It should've turned him off. I knew it should've turned him off, if he had any decency at all. But his thighs pressed in against my shoulders, and I felt the heat of him as he leaned over me, compressing me into the space created by his body and enclosing me. MacKenna let out a low, reverberating growl, his cock swelled even more, and he shot hot come down my throat in pulse after heavy pulse.

I worked my throat frantically, pushing every drop down inside me.

The growl vibrated through me, seeming to blend with his orgasm and shake me from head to toe.

When the vibrations hit down lower, my stomach clenched and my balls tightened—and I came, helplessly, soaking the front of my underwear and my jeans.

He hadn't even touched me, not so much as putting a hand on my head to guide me while I choked on his cock. He hadn't used any force at all, and he certainly hadn't stimulated me.

The wet misery in my jeans was all my own doing, my own body's betrayal.

The moisture leaking out of my eyes probably looked like tears. If MacKenna thought he'd made me cry, on top of every other humiliation the last few minutes had brought me, I might have to jump out the window.

Hell, I might even survive it. Not that I cared that much as long as I could get out of his sight. Better a splattered pancake on the Vegas Strip than MacKenna sneering at me for having tears in my eyes and a wet spot on my clothes after he coerced me into sucking him off.

I started to pull off of his cock, my breath finally having given out completely, and my vision going dark—and then, horribly, my lips caught around him.

I was fucking *stuck*, and it was—he'd gotten—the fucker was *knotting my mouth*! Oh, fuck, I couldn't get away, the corners of my lips would split, I couldn't breathe, I couldn't—I flailed, hitting his legs, my own legs kicking…

And then MacKenna stuck a finger in each corner of my mouth and tugged, yanking his cock out at the same time, the knot popping out obscenely. The sensation of his not quite as huge cockhead ripping out of my throat and out through my mouth had me choking and coughing, reeling forward dizzily and landing with my forehead pressed against his upper thigh, my chest against the front edge of the sofa.

My throat ached and burned, the pain fading quickly as my natural healing took care of the damage done, but the sensation of being opened and filled and used was one that I thought might linger for a while, if not forever.

Yeah, I'd remember this.

Belatedly, I also remembered that I'd done that to myself—that I'd set out to take control.

And I'd proved that he wanted me, and that my blowjob skills were a few notches above terrible.

But part of that would've been remaining unaffected myself.

And I'd signally failed in that regard.

I panted against his leg, head still spinning too much for me to sit up, no matter how embarrassing it might be to have fallen into his lap.

A big, warm, heavy hand settled on the nape of my neck.

And for a second, one brief, horribly mortifyingly thrilling moment, I thought he was offering me some kind of help or comfort. The heat of him settled into my bones, soothing me, giving me the security of having an alpha taking charge and making everything all right—an instinct I couldn't control, even as an alpha myself.

He wrapped a hand in the overlong strands of my hair, tugging my head up without any particular gentleness.

"You're not done," he said, his voice a little rough, but not nearly as much as I'd hoped. I'd wanted him totally overwhelmed, dammit. Well, that had backfired on me.

Blinking up through still-wet eyes at his hard, implacable face, I didn't think the knotting had been involuntary, either. Most of the time, alphas could control that response—unless they were completely lost to the mating instinct, which clearly wasn't the case here.

My cock hadn't even wanted to knot. I usually didn't unless I was inside someone, and even then I could count on one hand the number of times I'd bothered. Getting away quickly usually trumped the take-it-or-leave-it pleasure of letting my knot expand, feeling it pulse in tight heat.

Apparently MacKenna didn't have the same relationship with knotting that I did.

Lucky me.

"What do you mean I'm not done?" I rasped, sounding like a ninety-year-old cigar smoker.

A thin, unpleasant smile teased the corners of his mouth.

"I didn't want to choke you to death. You're welcome. But my knot needs some attention, Castelli."

Some attention. His knot needed some *attention*? How fucking much more attention could I give the fucking thing, when I'd already had it crammed in my mouth?

I gaped at him, dumbstruck.

And then he wrapped his hand more firmly in my hair and pushed me toward his cock again, until my mouth pressed against his knot.

Attention. He wanted…

"Lick it, Castelli," he growled, pushing me even closer, until I had to open my mouth or let my lips get crushed between my teeth and his cock.

The last of the fight went out of me at that. I'd get it back, and I'd give him hell. You couldn't keep a Castelli alpha down for long, right? (Unless you held his head down and shoved it into an even more alpha cock, but details.) Fuck it. I'd already choked on his knot. The mechanics of dealing with his giant dick didn't bother me that much, really—it was mostly his nerve in thinking he could get away with treating me like this.

So I licked his knot. Mouth open, tongue curling around him, lapping at him like an ice cream cone.

His knot had a slightly different texture from the rest of his cock: even firmer, with skin stretched tight over the thickness of him. I knew how mine felt in my hand, but it'd never occurred to me to have someone lick it or suck on it, as I found I'd started to do when my tongue got tired. Not quite hard enough to leave a hickey, although a hickey on an alpha would heal almost within seconds. But enough to really feel the texture of him, to taste the salt of his skin and the tension under it.

MacKenna muttered something I couldn't catch even with my enhanced hearing. I tilted my head enough that I could glance up at him through my lashes.

Okay, that was more like it. The way MacKenna gazed down at me, avidly, like he'd never seen anything he desired more...I had him hooked. He might be forcing me into this, and I might be on my knees licking his knot like a fucking whore, but those dark eyes overlaid with a brilliant alpha glow, and his parted lips, and the flush along his high cheekbones—that all told a different story.

I watched him as I licked and nuzzled at his knot, alternating laving it with my tongue and mouthing over it. And he watched me, his hand still gripping me hard, fingers clenching and unclenching as my mouth moved on him.

After a while I almost forgot the discomfort in my cramping legs and the weirdness of my position sprawled in his lap. My hands rested on his thighs, and that started to feel natural.

It all started to feel natural. Like I'd fallen into some kind of fugue, existing only in the moment. When he finally tugged on my hair to lift my head away from him, I startled a little bit, blinking. Gods. What the fuck had I been doing?

I looked down at what I'd been doing. His cock had started to soften, and the knot was going down. It still looked absurdly large—and threatening, because I knew exactly how short an alpha's refractory period could be.

MacKenna took his hand away. And that startled me even more. I hadn't realized how much the heat and strength of his grip had been grounding me and keeping me from panicking.

"That's enough for tonight," he said, voice gravelly and low. "The master bedroom's mine. You can have the other. Someone will bring your things from your previous suite in a few minutes."

Relief washed over me. He didn't mean to keep me in his bedroom with him, then. Which meant he wouldn't be repeating this all night, and also meant I'd get some actual privacy, time alone to rest and freak out and plan and get my head on straight, probably not in that order. But maybe I'd come up with an order once I had a second to think.

I realized I still had my hands on him, and I jerked them back like his legs had burned me, clenching my fists against the lingering feeling of his heat against my palms. Getting up could possibly have been more awkward if I'd tried very, very hard, but maybe not. I'd need to brace myself on him. Fuck that. I used the floor instead, which meant bending down more, and then boosting up with my legs trying to give out on me…

And then I'd wobbled upright, and he'd slouched back into the sofa looking completely satisfied.

With the damp front of my jeans at his eye level.

Alpha senses were all sharper than other people's, and that included smell.

I could scent my own come.

And so, I had no doubt, could he. As well as see the darker stain on the front of my jeans where it had soaked through.

MacKenna smiled slowly, a bared-teeth grin, but the smile reached his eyes this time. They crinkled around the edges, and sparkled, and—fuck, it hit me like a punch to the gut. This was why I'd hit on him ten years ago. Because he was an unbelievably, almost unbearably attractive man.

I didn't wait for whatever caustic remark he might've made if I'd given him the chance. My cheeks had gone hot, and I knew my eyes probably looked like saucers.

Instead I fled, stumbling around the sofa and toward the doorway he'd come out of, which I knew from the similar layout of my own suite upstairs had to lead to the bedrooms. His low chuckle pursued me down the hall. I dashed into the empty bedroom and slammed the door shut behind me. And then I dropped my forehead against it, heart pounding, lungs laboring.

Maybe you'll be able to work it off in a few months.

Well, fuck me.

Literally.

Chapter 4

So Sue Me

Waiting for the other shoe to drop was fucking torture. I took a long, boiling-hot shower, shuddering as I scrubbed the dried come off of my groin and shuddering again as the vigorous rubbing started to get me hard again.

I gathered my suitcases from the hallway where they'd been left while I showered, and I got a pair of clean underwear, thank all the gods above and below. I didn't unpack any more than that. My stuff had an odd scent to it, as if whoever had packed it for me had been wearing an unusually offensive cologne. It made my nose tingle, and I shoved the bags into the closet and shut the door, hoping the smell would dissipate overnight.

And then I slept, for some definition of sleep, tossing and turning and waking up twisted into a pretzel.

When I dared to poke my nose out of my room halfway through the next morning, hunger finally winning over wanting to pull the blankets over my head and stay there forever, the suite was silent. The kitchenette yielded nothing more than an empty mini fridge running almost as loudly as my growling stomach, a fully stocked coffee tray (although MacKenna had left the pot dirty but empty, the asshole), and a few bottles of water.

Not even the nice kind. Plain bottled water, like from the grocery store.

What kind of self-respecting casino owner, even one who might be in massive debt, lived like this? Fuck.

In a fit of pique, I went back out into the living area and picked up the phone on the desk in one corner of the room. A quick glance through the folder next to the phone, and an almost as quick conversation, and about half of the hotel's room service menu was on its way to the suite. I slammed down the phone with a sense of petty satisfaction. Fuck MacKenna. If he wanted to neglect me, and keep my phone and watch and wallet—which had conspicuously *not* been returned with my other personal effects—then he could pay to keep me in a style slightly closer to what I'd been accustomed to.

My satisfaction wore off quickly, though, as I paced the suite like a caged—well, alpha werewolf. I'd spent a lot of time in hotels over the years, but I never got used to the way the windows didn't open. And MacKenna's suite didn't have a balcony or anything. The lack of any breath of a breeze, that feeling of cooled and processed air on my face, and the sense of enclosure had me more than on edge.

Especially since I had the distinct idea it wouldn't go great for me if I tried to stage an escape. The Morrigan had the normal complement of cameras for a casino hotel, meaning fucking everywhere. MacKenna would catch up with me. Even worse, he'd probably send his security staff to catch up with me instead of doing it himself, and I'd get to relive yesterday's humiliating experience of being removed from the casino floor.

No thank you.

Honestly, staying here waiting to suck his cock was better than that.

Because I was pretty sure it wouldn't be so bad next time. I mean, he hadn't even said anything about the fact that I'd come. And now I knew what it felt like to have his cock stuffed down my throat and his knot in my mouth. Licking and sucking on it after he'd come in me hadn't even been so bad, really, had it? I mean, not my favorite. Disturbing. And too submissive for my tastes (so to speak, haha, I fucking hated my own sense of humor sometimes).

But not worth being publicly shamed in order to avoid it.

Besides. He'd been so damn sure I'd give him a terrible blowjob, or that I'd chicken out.

Fuck him. Castelli alphas weren't cowards.

Except for my father, and he hadn't even been an alpha.

So fuck him too, twice over.

The knock at the door startled me out of my pacing and snarling, and I got myself together in time not to terrify the waiter who came in pushing the world's most laden room service cart.

All right, that was more like it. I had him set it up in the little dining area by one of the huge windows, tipped grandly on the receipt because that was just what you did even when you were broke, and sat down, opening my mouth to let him know that was all.

We both jumped an inch as the door rattled and slammed.

A moment later, MacKenna strode in from the entryway, sleeves rolled up and jacket bunched in his hand, with that lock of hair hanging onto his forehead again. He stopped dead when he saw me, eyes glowing faintly and cheeks flushed, scowling like I'd thrown the bowl of lobster bisque at him instead of simply trying to eat it.

"The hell is this?" he demanded.

Part of me, a large part, wanted to dive under the table. "It's my lunch," I said as evenly as I could manage.

The waiter's nervous throat-clearing interrupted whatever else I might have said. "Mr. MacKenna," he quavered, sounding like he might be joining me under the table with his arms over his head. I couldn't blame him. He smelled like a shifter, and with two alphas in the room, one of them furious and the other on the point of murdering everyone if he didn't eat soon? Yeah, that would make even a human, let alone someone who could detect the gathering magic with his shifter senses, want to run away screaming. "I'm so sorry. Um. The order was placed from your suite's phone. We didn't mean to—"

"It's fine," MacKenna said, tearing his eyes away from me with a visible effort and focusing on the waiter. And then MacKenna—smiled. A genuine smile. One that made his eyes crinkle at the corners in a way that anyone would've found devastating, and by the waiter's body language, leaning a bit toward him, his own eyes widening…he wasn't immune. Was *this* MacKenna's type? This skinny little dark-haired guy with a button nose? "You got an order, you brought it on time and efficiently, good work. Tell the kitchen it all looks delicious. You can head back down now. Let me just see that receipt for a second."

My mouth had dropped open, and I snapped it shut with a click, my fists clenching at my sides. I gaped at them as the now-beaming and eyelash-fluttering little jerk who'd brought my food handed over the receipt. Seriously? All these smiles and nice compliments for some random employee who'd just been doing his job? And I wasn't allowed to *eat lunch* without getting glared at and intimidated?

"Oh," MacKenna said, his brows furrowing as he looked down at the receipt. "Fine." He handed it back. "That's all, thanks."

"Thank you, sir," the waiter purred, and he headed for the door. Swaying his hips? Definitely swaying his hips. That was so unprofessional I couldn't believe it. But MacKenna wasn't looking. He'd turned back to me, scowl fully in place again, and my eyes flashed to his like they were magnetized.

"You know," he said into the ringing echo of the door shutting behind the asshole waiter, "I'm going to add your three appetizers, two entrees, and three fucking desserts onto the bill you've already run up with me."

Okay, no. Fuck him. I stood up, dropping my spoon with a splatter of (really delicious-looking, just like MacKenna had said, dammit) soup and kicking my chair back with a thump.

"So sue me for having a sweet tooth, MacKenna. If you're going to—"

He took a single step forward, and it was enough to shut me up, the words withering on my tongue. Because the flash of his eyes and the way he flexed his hands, claws obviously almost popping, was nothing compared to the sudden thickening of the air around us, the almost physical weight of his alpha power.

MacKenna sucked in a deep breath, obviously getting himself under control.

That was even more intimidating. Alphas had a reputation for going off half-cocked for a reason; we didn't usually have the best control of our instincts and our emotions.

But MacKenna had been able to turn off the alpha anger in order to flirt with the waiter. He could rein it in now. He had control.

And that made me nervous as hell.

"I don't need to sue you," he said, his voice almost passing for normal and calm, but with a faint undertone of menace. "I could just call the cops and have them take you away, and they'll use their own damn lawyers. And I wouldn't sue over your sweet tooth, no matter how expensive it is. But if you think you're going to get away with this kind of petty bullshit, think again. I'm not going to sue you. I'm going to fuck you until you scream."

He was going to… "What?" I demanded. "Until I scream? Alphas don't scream, what the fuck are you talking—" And then I stopped abruptly, my brain screeching to a halt along with my mouth as what he'd actually said caught up to me. I'd focused on the screaming part, and overlooked the… "The fuck do you mean you're going to fuck me?"

MacKenna stared me down for a second. "Take your hands off your hips and stop yelling, you look ridiculous." He shook his head and walked away, moving toward the bedrooms. He shot back over his shoulder, "I'm going to fuck you because that's why you're here. Screaming's up to you. My room, five minutes."

And he disappeared into the hall, leaving me gaping at the empty doorway.

Fuck me. With that huge alpha cock. And that huge alpha knot, probably, since if he'd knotted me when I sucked him off, he'd definitely knot my ass.

So maybe I'd had a couple of experiences sucking dick. And maybe that wasn't the most alpha way of having a sexual encounter.

But getting fucked wasn't anything I'd ever thought I'd do. Stupidly, I'd assumed and hoped that MacKenna would limit himself to putting me on my knees. Because you didn't fuck other alphas, right? Right.

Stupid, stupid, stupid.

What choice did I have? I glanced down mournfully at my now-cold soup and the rest of my extravagant meal.

Wistfulness turned to rage.

Fuck his five minutes.

I charged across the room and toward his bedroom, barreling down the hall fueled by righteous indignation.

He'd shut his bedroom door, and I wrenched the handle so hard it came loose and then kicked the door, letting it thwack into the wall.

MacKenna turned around, casually dropping the shirt he'd had dangling from his fingers to the ground. He didn't look surprised; of course he didn't, because he'd heard me coming. His hearing was as good as mine.

I, on the other hand, probably looked gobsmacked.

Fucking Christ on a cracker, but MacKenna was ripped. Even for an alpha. How the hell did he keep a body like that working as an executive? And the tattoos weren't limited to his arms. One particularly intriguing work, that could've been some kind of scaled dragon or other monster, wound along his ribs, magic or simple artistry causing it to appear to ripple and gleam. The tail disappeared under his dark whorls of chest hair, making me wonder if it wrapped around one of his nipples.

Tattoos didn't look good on everyone. I'd met a guy once who could've camouflaged himself by standing in front of a gas station bathroom wall.

But on MacKenna, standing there half-naked and powerful…

I swallowed hard and dragged my gaze back up to his face, only to find him regarding me steadily, one eyebrow raised.

I'd meant to bang the door open and come out swinging, verbally speaking, and his nudity had taken the wind right out of my sails. Damn him.

"I'm not sure how many times I need to suggest you take a picture, Castelli," he rumbled at me, sounding half amused and half annoyed.

"I still don't have my phone," I snapped, managing to get my brain to work again after a beat. "And I didn't expect you to be—it hasn't been five minutes!"

"It only seemed polite to take a shower first," he said. "I've been working."

Polite. To me. That didn't compute.

I let out a scoff, and then crossed my arms for good measure. "Yeah, you've been so fucking polite so far. Whatever. Take your shower. I, on the other hand, am going to finish my food. Because if you're adding it to my 'tab,' as you put it, then I'm not going to pay for it without getting to enjoy it. Are we clear? Oh," I added, remembering my disappointment, "and you can take the soup right back off the tab. It's already cold."

"There's a microwave in the kitchen."

For a moment the power of speech deserted me. "Microwave— lobster bisque—what kind of monster puts *lobster bisque* in a *microwave?*"

MacKenna stared, barked a laugh, and shook his head, his eyes gleaming. Not glowing. Just gleaming. He really had amazing eyes, dark as ink. Mesmerizing.

"I guess I'm that kind of monster," he said with a shrug. Gods. And I thought I'd plumbed the depths of his depravity. Blackmail, coerced blowjobs, knotting my mouth—and now this? "Fine. You have ten minutes instead of five to eat your ridiculous sampler buffet. And after that, I'm coming to get you."

Something about his tone suggested he didn't mean he'd step into the living area, politely inform me the time was up, and usher me into his bedroom like a gentleman.

I lifted my chin. "You can try, if I haven't finished that cheesecake yet."

I spun on my heel and strode out, his low laughter echoing behind me.

Fucker.

I was going to enjoy the *hell* out of that cheesecake. After I'd had the rest of my meal. I'd compromise to the extent of saving the flourless chocolate cake and the apple tart for later, and he'd better be fucking grateful.

If he tried to make good on his implied threat, he wouldn't find me as passive as he had last night.

My bravado stood on shaky ground, and I knew it. But a few bites of the filet had me feeling a lot more ready to stand up to him.

The sound of the shower in the back of the suite helped. Knowing where he was, and that it wasn't next to me, helped a lot.

But then the shower shut off and I heard him moving around in his bedroom. The ten minutes had to be almost up.

I felt him there without needing to look. He'd come into the room silently, but his presence raised my hackles. Defiantly, I took another bite of mashed potatoes without acknowledging him, and then glanced at him out of the corner of my eye as he sauntered through the living area—wearing nothing but a towel wrapped precariously around his waist. Little rivulets of water ran down over his massive shoulders, trickling over his pecs and biceps. His hair gleamed, slicked back with water but already starting to wave at his temples.

MacKenna had legs like fucking tree trunks.

His third leg was almost as big, at least in my fevered recollection, but for now the towel was keeping it safely out of sight.

No tent in the front of the towel. So the anticipation of fucking me didn't get him all that hot and bothered, huh? Well, fuck him sideways. I'd make him work for it.

My own cock felt heavier than it had a minute ago, and that pissed me off even more.

Slowly, without acknowledging him in any way, I cut a piece of the salmon I'd moved to after polishing off the filet, and I put it in my mouth even more slowly.

MacKenna didn't react.

Another bite, and the back of my neck started to prickle. He wasn't standing behind me, more like off to the side, but he could still watch me fully while I could only glance at him. And I didn't want to do that too much; I was ignoring him, damn it! His gaze only weighed on me more heavily as the seconds ticked past. The salmon had practically melted in my mouth when I started eating it, and now it stuck in my throat.

Movement out of the corner of my eye made me jump, and my fork skittered on the plate with a cringy screech. A breath of a sound could've been MacKenna's low laughter. I forced myself to put one more bite of lemony rice in my mouth as he crossed the room and settled himself on a sofa, putting his phone down on the coffee table in front of him. I hadn't even noticed him holding it—but of course a dick like him would have something to keep track of the time. It wasn't the same sofa he'd been on the night before, but the one at right angles, putting him across from me instead of in my peripheral vision.

The fucker wanted me to have to see him.

He stared me in the face while my breath stuttered in my chest, and my hand shook a little as I tried to capture a bit more of the rice.

And then he tugged at his towel, letting it fall to the sides and reveal his cock, now half hard and lying against his thigh.

I refused to meet his burning dark eyes, but I couldn't help staring at his cock for a second.

Okay. I could do this. He wasn't dragging me to the bedroom. He wasn't doing anything at all.

So a naked alpha who basically owned me for the moment was watching me eat lunch, with extreme prejudice, from halfway across the room.

So what.

My side salad. I still needed to eat that before I started on the cheesecake.

Moving the plates around tipped my hand, though, because they clinked against each other and I cursed as I almost dropped one.

MacKenna wrapped his hand around his cock and started to stroke.

I dropped the plate with a thunk and clatter after all, a few croutons tumbling off and pattering on the floor.

"Don't mind me," MacKenna said pleasantly. "Eat up. After all, you're the one paying for it."

My spine tried to slither away and hide, and in the process my whole body gave a shudder. Fuck. That did not sound good.

But I'd agreed to this. Jail would be even worse, right? There'd be people watching me eat there, too. And the food wouldn't be five-star. No cheesecake in jail. I had to hold onto that thought to comfort me through whatever MacKenna would do next.

At least I had cheesecake.

With that in mind, I hurried through the salad, eating it only out of stubbornness, and then shoved the dish away in favor of the silver platter holding my three desserts. Well, not real silver, obviously. It would've been if MacKenna had any taste or style.

And clearly, I was grasping at straws to distract myself from MacKenna's hand moving steadily along the length of his cock, the stroke of his thumb over the head, the glow of his eyes as they rested on me without a moment's respite.

Gods, this cheesecake was good. Everything I'd ordered could've taken pride of place in any of the best restaurants I'd ever patronized, in fact. The first bite melted on my tongue, smooth and creamy and sensual.

I licked a trace of it off my lips, and as I did, I glanced up.

And found MacKenna's eyes fixed on my mouth.

My own cock throbbed almost painfully in my jeans. His stood straight up now.

I didn't want him, I didn't, but the force of his desire—and apparently I'd been wrong about him not being too eager, he'd just been biding his time, and that was so much more hair-raising than if he'd thrown me over his shoulder—had me squirming in my chair, my whole body on alert and responding helplessly.

Fuck that. Alphas were never helpless. Making him work for it. That's what I was doing. Taking control.

Obviously.

I forked up more of the cheesecake, slipped it into my mouth, and let out a little moan, pulling the fork out slowly and chasing it with my tongue.

MacKenna's jaw worked, his eyes glowing brighter.

The last bite of cheesecake went down, and I set my fork on the plate carefully without so much as a clink to give away the racing heartbeat that'd set my limbs vibrating. Everything tingled.

"All right," I said. "I'm done. For now."

Without letting go of his cock, MacKenna leaned over and poked his phone with the other hand. "I gave you ten minutes. You took eighteen." He glanced up and grinned at me, giving his cock another leisurely stroke from root to tip, the flushed cockhead shiny and mesmerizing as it disappeared between his long fingers. "You're paying for that too. Get in the bedroom and strip, Castelli."

Chapter 5

Eight Minutes

The walk to the bedroom felt endless. All the stalling and attempted mind games (which I'd lost, and the clenching in the pit of my stomach and the sweat on my spine made that abundantly clear) had distracted me from the reality of what we were going to do.

But I didn't have any distractions now, not with MacKenna practically breathing down my neck and the doorway of his bedroom looming in front of me.

His bed loomed even larger when I stepped through. I'd been a little taken aback by his impersonal lifestyle, the way he didn't splash out as much as he could have with little luxuries even when it would've made him more comfortable, but his enormous bed made me reevaluate. It had to have been brought in custom; maybe they'd even had to remove part of the wall.

More than big enough for two alphas.

And it looked sturdy enough to hold up to the force of an alpha fucking an alpha, too, with its heavy dark wood frame. No footboard, though.

The better to bend you over with, my dear.

His crisp white sheets and plain black duvet cover screamed the same lack of personal touch as the rest of the place, in contrast to the bed itself. Interesting.

And there, I'd distracted myself again.

Good for me, except that MacKenna said from right behind me, "I don't have all fucking day, Castelli," and I jumped. And then, as if he'd read my mind, he added, "Strip and bend over the foot of the bed. I need to get back to work."

"Well, aren't you a silver-tongued romantic," I muttered without thinking.

His laugh cracked like a whip and made me flinch, my shoulders tensing.

"Maybe I am, darlin', and maybe I'm not going to bother with you. You'll never find out, I promise you that. Strip. Bend over. Stop wasting my time."

MacKenna had gotten that tone again, the one he'd used a couple of times last night. The one that told me all too clearly that his patience had hit its limit.

Pushing him had been working for me so far, though, if only because it made me feel like less of a push*over*. So even though his voice felt like it scraped my spine raw, I still didn't hurry to obey him. It'd make it worse, I knew that. Whatever he meant to do to me, it'd be so much worse the more I pissed him off.

But it was like that feeling I got when I rode a motorcycle way, way too fast, or waited a few extra precious seconds to pull the release on my parachute when I went skydiving.

A rush. Fuck. Teasing MacKenna was giving me a *rush*.

It made sense, I thought wildly as I pulled my T-shirt over my head and let it dangle from my fingers for a moment, subtly flexing my back muscles as I did. It made sense, because no souped-up sports bike could compare to an aroused, angry alpha with a grudge. At least in terms of potential for grievous bodily harm, which seemed to be my bag, now that I thought about it. I kept my back to him, knowing I'd lose my nerve if I had to look at him.

Besides, the longer he went without seeing my semi, the better. I wished I could stay totally unaroused. Show him how much I hated this. But his magic and his pheromones had wrapped themselves around me like a choke collar. No other alpha had ever overmastered me this way, on an instinctive level that I couldn't begin to fight. I'd always been on even ground, at worst.

But MacKenna had a fundamental power to him that would've overmastered just about anyone. At least I wasn't special.

And I certainly wasn't special to him. Just someone he wanted to fuck, and not even because of anything desirable about me. The opposite.

My cock still didn't soften at all, even from that lowering

thought.

It made undoing the button and tugging down the zipper of my jeans a little more challenging, and I ended up struggling with it, making the process even slower than I'd intended.

MacKenna walked across the room, moving away for a minute and rustling something behind me, and then he stepped closer again. I knew not because of his silent returning footfalls, but because the heat at my back intensified. My skin prickled with awareness, hot and tight. At last I got a grip on the zipper with my sweat-damp fingers and pulled it all the way down.

Fuck this. If I couldn't strip slowly and maintain my cool, and do it elegantly, I should get it over with. Doing it slowly and clumsily would just make me look, well, clumsy. And nervous.

So I shoved the jeans and my underwear down in one go, grateful that I hadn't bothered with socks or shoes when I got dressed. Cool air hit my now-naked ass. Was MacKenna looking? A low, almost subsonic growl raised my hair, everywhere. Even my pubic hair felt like it'd straightened and stood to attention. Yeah, he was looking. My ass muscles clenched. I hadn't meant to do that.

Another growl, louder this time.

My heart had started to beat triple-time, vibrating down to the tips of my fingers and the soles of my feet.

Yeah, I really didn't want to actually be grievously bodily harmed, no matter how much the possibility of it tended to trip my trigger during recreational activities. And if I dragged my feet any more than I already had, MacKenna might snap.

I took one more second to step out of my clothes, kicking them to the side.

My lungs wouldn't let me hold a deep enough breath. Lightheaded and with black spots spinning in my vision, I leaned down and braced my hands on the mattress. I'd hoped for close to a ninety-degree angle, since the bed was kind of high.

No such luck. I had long legs for my height, and my ass stuck up in the air like I'd spent an hour finding the perfect angle to make myself look like a slut. My overlong hair hung in my eyes. I tried to blink it away and failed. My arms wouldn't give out for hours, alpha strength and all, but they trembled anyway, from nerves rather than any kind of muscle strain.

And the weight of MacKenna's gaze, and the pressure of his magic and the heat of him, rested on me like a ton of bricks.

The faint whistle of something moving quickly through the air alerted me just in time for my whole body to tense up—which only made the cracking, stinging impact of his hand against my ass that much worse.

Pain bloomed instantly, and searing heat, my balls swinging from the force of it. I pushed up, furious, my hands leaving the bed. "What the fuck, MacKen—"

His other hand in the center of my back shoved me right back down again, and this time I landed on my face with an *oof*, mashed into the fluffy duvet and choking for breath. Another smack, this one even harder and centered perfectly, the sting of it making me clench helplessly. His hand lingered, stroking a circle over the center of the pain, one finger prying between my cheeks.

"What the fuck are you doing?" I demanded, muffled by the bedding, twisting my neck to get some air and try to see him. I couldn't move, he had me pinned, and the angle of my body gave me no leverage at all, with my toes scrabbling at the floor for purchase.

"Eighteen minutes," he said, voice as calm as if I'd asked him what the weather looked like tomorrow, and not why the fuck he was spanking me like a disobedient brat. "I allowed you ten. So that's eight minutes you need to pay for."

"Eight—ow, fuck!" His hand lifted and came down again, this time on the left. The vibrations tunneled into me, lodging somewhere south of my sternum.

And my cock dug into the bedding, harder than ever, the pain somehow transmuting into stimulation, and I hated—*crack*, and another wash of burning humiliation, my ass jiggling and then clenching tight, exposed the whole time for him to do anything he wanted to.

"Fuck, MacKenna, stop, this isn't part of the—fuck!"

"That was five," he said, this time slightly less calmly. But it didn't matter. I was worked up enough for both of us, writhing under the weight of that hand in the center of my back. "Anything's part of the deal if I say it is. And here's six."

I squeezed my eyes shut against the burgundy starbursts exploding in my vision, but it didn't help at all. The duvet cover rubbed against my lips, and I chewed on a bit of it, tugging it between my teeth and trying to focus on that.

"I really should be making you count them. Maybe next time. Seven."

This time his hand came down so roughly and so fast it made me moan, panting into the bed and quivering.

I'd thought pain didn't bother me. I'd never been afraid of it, anyway.

But it turned out that it mattered a lot what kind of pain it was, and how it was given to you.

And it mattered even more that my erection hadn't died down at all. If anything, every jolt of MacKenna's hand slapping my ass hardened it more, drew my balls up tight and aching, their swinging motion tugging on something deep inside me.

It mattered that this wasn't something I'd chosen, like that time I'd eaten shit on a Ducati going ninety and stripped half the skin off my right side and broken a couple of limbs. I'd rolled around and groaned and cursed, stripped off what was left of my riding leathers, staring glassy-eyed at the mingled blood and cherry-red paint streaked all over the asphalt until I healed enough to try to stand up.

That had hurt more than anything I'd ever experienced before or since. A lot worse than MacKenna spanking me, even though he wasn't going easy on me, letting his alpha strength out to play.

This still…hurt *more*, in a way I couldn't make sense of even without having to put it into words. It cut at the very core of who I was.

An alpha. A man who made my own decisions. Someone who never had to answer to anyone for anything—okay, except for when my father or my brother had scolded me for spending too much money, but I pretty much ignored that anyway—let alone for *taking eight minutes extra to eat my fucking lunch.*

My own harsh breaths echoed in my ears. I opened my eyes. The final blow hadn't fallen. Gods, that was so much worse than simply feeling the pain of it: waiting for it, the skin of my ass on fire, flinching in anticipation of flinching again when he struck.

"That was seven," I managed hoarsely, and then wanted to hit myself in frustration without waiting for him to do it. So fucking stupid. What if he'd miscounted and thought he was done? "Fuck," I muttered.

MacKenna laughed. "I thought I'd save the last one for when you could really appreciate it."

For when I could really...a click and a soft squelching sound told me what he was using his right hand for, now that he'd paused in spanking me with it. Lube. He'd stepped away from me while I undressed, and he'd gotten a bottle of lube.

Slick fingertips stroked down the crease of my ass, from the small of my back down to my balls. I squirmed away involuntarily, clenching even more—both useless gestures, because MacKenna shoved his fingers between my cheeks and found my hole unerringly, his index finger prodding against it with irresistible force.

I'd never been penetrated. The press of his finger had me gasping, clawing at the bedding to try to get away, stiff cock trapped horribly in a fold of the duvet and pushing down painfully with every motion.

I tried to resist anyway, and I held my muscles as tight as I possibly could.

He shoved inside, only up to the second knuckle, a couple of inches of finger.

But it felt like he'd torn me open. Not because it hurt; it only hurt a little bit. Because he'd breached me. He had a part of him inside my body.

His cock down my throat and choking me hadn't felt this intimate, even though that had technically been inside me, too. But I'd had cocks in my mouth before.

MacKenna didn't move his hand at all.

After a moment I stopped moving too, hyperventilating into the bed and staring at the opposite wall, trying to regulate my breathing and my racing heart by focusing on the shadow cast by the nightstand. Perspiration coated my skin, clammy and awful.

"First time?" His voice didn't give much away. Maybe if I'd been able to see his face, like I had when I sucked him off and his eyes had shown me something more...but he was only a voice, relentlessly unmoved. "You're going to need to relax a little, Castelli. I'd have thought a party boy like you would've had something up your ass before now."

Well, now he'd given something away, and it was sardonic amusement, bordering on contempt.

I preferred no emotion at all to that, thank you very much.

"That's not my kind of party," I choked out.

MacKenna chuckled and pushed his finger in the rest of the way. "We'll see about that."

He started to work it in and out, bending it to stroke my insides as he moved.

It was excruciating. I couldn't escape it; I couldn't move away, or twitch him off of me, because he was embedded in me. And the more the pressure built, as he brushed over too-sensitive flesh, the more he stimulated nerves I hadn't even realized could send sparks up my spine like that, and the harder my cock got, until it throbbed almost painfully with the need for a hand or a mouth, anything.

Quiet whimpers and moans echoed in my ears.

Mine.

Those sounds were coming from me. My skin had shrunk too tight. My cock ached. MacKenna twisted his finger and pressed down, hard enough to make me cry out.

And then he yanked his finger out, tugging on everything he'd touched, and I moaned again, louder, claws itching at my fingertips and starting to prick holes in the duvet cover.

His hand came down on my ass, a vicious, full-strength blow, sudden burning pain transmuting into a shock that went straight inside me, right to where he'd been working me over.

Every muscle in my body went rigid. My cock pulsed, my back bowed, and I screamed my orgasm into the bed as I shot into it, rubbing frantically against the duvet.

I collapsed, limp and shaking, claws sheathed in the bedding.

MacKenna leaned down over me, not quite touching, his heat making my sweat-slick skin break out in goosebumps. His breath brushed over my ear. "I'll add the quilt to your tab, Castelli."

Gods, I hated him so much. I *hated* him. So he'd lost his job ten years ago when I complained about him, big fucking whoop. That didn't justify doing this to me, making me come when he spanked my ass and fingered me. I'd never felt less like an alpha.

Never felt less, period.

"It's a duvet, you ignoramus," I whispered into the item in question. "Not a quilt. Or can you only pronounce 'quilt'? Fuck you."

"Christ," he rumbled, and straightened back up again. "You're unfuckingbelievable. Fine. Duvet," and he said it with an exaggerated French accent that made me cringe. Asshole. "Either way, you're paying for it. And you're doing it now."

Chapter 6

You Can Tell Me How It Feels

MacKenna didn't bother telling me what to do next. Maybe he realized I had all the coordination and motivation of a wet noodle.

I didn't resist as he put his big hands on my inner thighs and shoved my legs up and apart, splaying me open with my upper body and my face still mashed into the now-ruined duvet and my ass in the air.

When he touched my ass, I flinched involuntarily—expecting another hit, no matter what he'd said about counting to eight.

"Fair's fair," he said, reading my fucking mind again, the bastard. Was I that transparent? Not that I'd ever put much effort into hiding how I felt. I just carefully felt only things I could show. Those weren't exactly the same thing. And MacKenna had me so off-balance that I couldn't curate my emotions anymore. They were coming faster than I could handle, and not controlled at all. "No more spanking. Unless you ask me nicely."

I bit my lip and kept any words that wanted to escape safely inside. I might've started begging if my mouth had opened. Not for more spanking, obviously. But for him to stop. He'd knelt behind me on the bed, his legs touching mine, the heat of his skin soaking into me, nearly burning.

And I knew what came next.

MacKenna would be coming next.

I'd come first, and fuck my life for that.

But the fucking came next. And a finger wouldn't compare. Panic started to seep in around the edges of my orgasm- and anger-numbed inability to think clearly.

Not that MacKenna gave me time to freak out properly, or to try to think, for that matter.

He wrapped one hand around my hip, and with the other he pushed my ass cheeks apart, his cock nudging in between. The slick tip—and at least he'd bothered to add more lube—pressed against my hole.

It felt a whole hell of a lot bigger than the opening it meant to breach. Like a battering ram with more girth than the width of the castle gates.

Panic won over inertia and my attempt not to sound, well, like his cock panicked me.

"That's not going to fit!" How cliché could I be? Would I be clutching my pearls and lamenting my lost virginity next? Accusing him of ravishing me?

Or possibly crying.

That was a lot likelier, given the hot prickle in my eyelids.

Fuck.

To my shock, MacKenna stopped moving, letting his huge cockhead rest against my hole, wedged awkwardly between my cheeks. That probably felt really fucking good for him, actually. A flash of the last time I'd fucked a guy passed through my mind. I didn't do it often, since it wasn't my favorite sexual activity, but yeah, that'd felt great, that moment when I was about to get inside him.

So maybe MacKenna was just savoring the sensation.

"Fuck, you're tight," he said. "But it'll fit."

Yep, savoring, not sympathizing.

I could appeal to his better nature. He had to have one, right? He'd started to push a little, the cockhead beginning to stretch me open. I had to shuffle my knees on the bed and brace with my chest, trying to ignore how damp and flushed and weirdly bent in various directions I'd gotten, how ridiculous I must look, how pathetic.

"You have to know how this feels, come on," I—whined. I couldn't deny it. I was whining, and squirming, and my claws were stuck in the fucking duvet and I couldn't get them out. "You're too big!"

His hand tightened on my hip. I clenched up more, even knowing how counterproductive it would be, because I couldn't fucking help it.

"I have no idea how it feels. I don't have any interest in getting fucked." Right. Because most alphas didn't get fucked, with the exception of female alphas…and those got fucked like they were fucking *you*, anyway. And now, also with the exception of me. "You can tell me how it feels, if you like."

With that, he thrust forward, burying what felt like a whole limb inside me. I didn't tell him how it felt.

Not with words, anyway.

I screamed, a long, drawn-out wail that put paid to any alpha posturing I ever wanted to engage in again.

MacKenna's hips slammed into my ass as he buried the last few inches of his massive cock inside me. Gods, no one could possibly enjoy this, and I felt like the world's biggest (okay, second biggest, my cock wasn't as huge as MacKenna's) prick for all the times I'd ever done this to someone else.

Panting, moaning, drooling onto the bed, splayed out and impaled so deeply I couldn't draw a breath, couldn't even feel my own heartbeat outside of where it pounded around that massive thing lodged inside me…I'd been conquered. Forced to submit.

And something in me—the only thing I had room for besides his cock, it felt like—finally gave up the fight. He'd mocked me and blackmailed me, put me on my knees, knotted my mouth and then made me lick his knot like a whore, taunted me and spanked me and now fucked me so hard the headboard slammed into the wall over and over again violently enough to dent it.

He'd mastered me. My body knew it. My brain had to accept it. And my own alpha magic had already rolled over and shown its belly, fucking traitor.

So I stopped even trying. I took his cock without any resistance, allowing myself to open to him, my legs spreading wider of their own volition to make room for him. My face was shoved into the bed over and over, but I only turned my head enough to avoid suffocation. He used me like a rag doll, a passive object to pound into, rearranging me to fit him.

And when the stretch and the burn and the bouncing, jolting force of it started to turn into irresistible heat building behind my balls, I didn't fight that either.

Every thrust stoked the fire, and every withdrawal left me

empty, wanting. Alpha refractory periods were short, and my cock started to fill again, fueled by the aching neediness where the thickness of his cockhead and the girth of his shaft rubbed over that spot I'd never known to aim for when I fucked other men.

Oh, gods. I really was the hugest prick, even if MacKenna had a couple of inches on me.

In me. He had all his inches in me, and I could picture that whole length sliding out all slick and thick, and then slamming back in. I could picture MacKenna, arm muscles tense and bulging as he held me in place, broad chest and shoulders sheened with sweat, the glow of magic overlaying the intensity of his black eyes. Gilded jet. Fixed on me, staring down at where he'd split me in half on his alpha cock.

That did it. One more powerful thrust, and I came again, soaking that poor fucked-up duvet a second time and moaning through it, clenching so hard around him that he let out a grunt of pain.

My head swam so much that the impossible stretch of his knot swelling inside me nearly flew under my radar for a second.

And then it hit me. So fucking big, and I knew what a knot looked like, I knew what *his* looked like, but the idea of it buried inside me…he came, in hot bursts, filling up any space he hadn't already taken up. The pressure made my eyes water.

Not tears, dammit. Watering. I squeezed my eyes shut and tried to ride it out.

He let out a low, growling groan and pressed even deeper, getting his knot all the way in. Tying us together.

Fuck. Tying us together.

MacKenna leaned down over me, and the change in angle pushed his knot even more firmly against my inner flesh, sending a quivering aftershock of orgasm winging along every nerve. If he kept that up I'd have another one, or something close. The fabric under me was already plastered, wet and clammy, to my stomach and my cock. If I came again I'd be lying in a swimming pool of come.

That image made me gag, and I lost another moment to swallowing down my nausea.

When I swam, so to speak, back to the present, I still couldn't focus on anything but the throbbing pressure of MacKenna's knot—and the suddenly very painful tug as he moved.

"Ow! Don't—" I broke off, too breathless to finish, desperately trying to shove myself up in order to follow his motion and keep his knot from ripping me apart.

"Hold still, and I won't hurt you," he said. I huffed a laugh with the last of my oxygen. A little late for a promise like that. "I need to move us onto our sides. I can't lie on top of you or kneel here for half an hour. Just let me turn you."

Fine. His show. I went limp again and bit my lip and winced as he lowered himself down on top of me, a heavy, hot weight that blanketed me from my neck to my feet. Would this have been comforting if he'd been someone I liked and trusted? Maybe. But as he'd told me, I'd never find out, so it didn't matter.

His muscular arm wrapped under me and clamped around my waist—and was that the faintest hesitation, as he discovered the wet spot?—and held me against his chest as he carefully rolled us both onto our sides.

My claws had retracted at last somewhere along the way. I stretched out my cramping arms with a sigh of relief. He slid his other arm under my head, giving me no choice but to pillow it on his bicep or break my neck trying to hold it up.

Which left me cradled in MacKenna's strong arms, our legs tangled together, his breath ruffling my hair.

And, of course, his knot stuffed in my ass.

Wouldn't do to forget that little detail.

Not so little detail. Huge detail, in fact.

I shifted uncomfortably, and he hissed and yanked me even tighter to his chest. Moving around didn't feel great for me, either, so I subsided with poor grace.

Silence, except for the faint hush of the air conditioner and, annoyingly, an occasional drip from the direction of the bathroom. Either MacKenna needed a better maintenance guy in this place, or he was one of those assholes who always left the faucet on a tiny bit. That drove me nuts.

He microwaved lobster bisque, so nothing would surprise me at this point.

That and the blackmail, obviously.

But the almost total quiet gave me time to regroup, finally, and to run through the last few minutes in my mind.

Wait a second.

"What do you mean, 'for half an hour'? Your knot went down in five minutes last night."

He shrugged, and I dipped up and down with it like a boat floating on an ocean it couldn't begin to control. Gods, this was too intimate to bear. His chest hair tickled my back. His hand rested against my sternum, splayed there and holding me close. Even without enhanced senses, I'd have been surrounded by his heartbeat, his warmth, his rich, spicy scent, the texture of his skin. With my enhanced senses, it all overwhelmed me.

"I didn't have my knot inside a very tight, virgin ass last night," he said. And then he paused. "Was that actually your first time getting fucked?"

"Of course it was," I snapped. "I'm not exactly crazy about the idea either!"

Another pause, this time much longer. His arm tensed around my waist, stealing a little more of my breath.

"That wasn't the impression I had," he said finally, his tone carefully, insultingly neutral.

I realized this was the first time he'd commented on how much my body had responded to him, to his touch and his rough handling and his dominance. And I'd have much preferred it if he'd mocked me for it rather than acting as if he didn't even care enough to sneer at me. As if my reaction to him was beneath his attention, even as he held me in his bed with his cock still in my body.

"I didn't think you noticed anything past your own knot." He went even tenser, and I added, "Bodies respond to physical stimulus. That doesn't mean I liked it."

"Do you want me to prove you wrong, or do you want to admit you're wrong right now and save us both the trouble?" Heat rushed to my cheeks and I went stiff in his arms. Admit I was— But he cut off my gathering tirade by saying, "You know what, never mind. I don't care if you liked it or not. I didn't injure you, and you agreed to do this. Beyond that, I don't give a fuck about your feelings or your virginity or anything else about you."

Something about that pinged my radar, and I tried to figure out what. Protesting too much? Why would he even bother to say that about proving me wrong in the first place if he didn't give a fuck?

But the hormones flooding an alpha after he knotted were so powerful, maybe he couldn't follow his own train of thought any more than I could.

After a moment, he added, "I'm glad you didn't like it, actually. That makes this easy. You're just a fuck toy. And that's all I want from you."

If I'd been able to get up and walk away, maybe I could've kept my stupid mouth shut. But I was stuck there, and biting my tongue when I wanted to say something insulting had never been my strong suit. Just ask my brother. Brook would've told anyone who asked, and probably a lot of people who didn't ask, what an asshole I was.

Also stupid.

Although he was wrong about that, I thought. I wasn't stupid. I simply had the bad habit of acting like it, see exhibit A: my mouth running when it shouldn't.

"If you wanted me so much, why didn't you just suck my cock when you had the chance ten years ago? Then none of this would've been a problem."

His body went so rigid against mine he could've been carved out of granite, and his hand flexed against my chest in a disconcerting, about-to-pop-eviscerating-claws kind of way.

"I didn't want *you*, and I still don't," he ground out, his emphasis on *you* very clear. "I want you to pay for being an entitled, smarmy asshole. And I want a hole to fuck. You think you were so irresistible, Castelli? Drunk and high and barely coherent, stinking of liquor, throwing your money around, hitting on anyone who held still long enough, making absurd demands and expecting everyone to cater to you? Get real. No one fucked you, no one even smiled at you, unless they were getting paid for it. And getting paid wasn't nearly enough for me to touch you with someone else's dick that night. Let alone touch yours."

I stared at the wall, keeping my eyes wide open and unblinking. If I closed them, if I gave them a chance to, they'd start leaking, I knew it. I could feel the moisture right there, all ready to gather and fall.

Fuck.

Fuck, fuck, fuck.

Every word had hit harder than the last.

Because I'd never really thought about it from the perspective of any of the people I'd hired or tipped to…cater to my absurd demands, to put it in MacKenna's words.

I wanted to deny it. At least in the privacy of my own head, I longed to refute it.

But the naked contempt in his voice crushed any efforts in that direction. He really felt that way about me. And I hadn't treated him any differently than I had any other service-y type of person I'd ever had following me around in a hotel or a casino or a club, cleaning up after me and bringing me what I wanted and looking pretty for me.

Except for the whole getting him fired thing. But I still couldn't remember that, and I knew for a fact I'd never done that before or since. If someone didn't do their actual job correctly? Yeah, maybe. But not for turning me down for an extra.

Anyway, that wasn't really me. I'd blame the drugs, except that I doubted MacKenna would accept that excuse. He couldn't spank and knot a baggie of X.

Me or not me, that was how he'd seen me. And if I'd given him that impression even before I got him fired, then that was probably how the other staff had seen me, too.

Had they all hated and despised me all these years? I was kind of charming, right? I knew I was. Who didn't like a tall, handsome alpha?

MacKenna, apparently. He preferred twiggy twinks with seductive hips. Or at least he was willing to be nice to them, and wouldn't waste so much as a single kind word on me.

I wanted to curl up and cover my face and pull a blanket over my head. Get in the shower and stay there, sit on the tile with my forehead resting on my knees for a week, or at least until the water ran cold.

But I couldn't. I had to lie here perfectly still with MacKenna's knot in me and the rest of his body surrounding me.

The pressure of his hand on my chest started to feel like a ten-ton weight. I couldn't breathe. The wall had gone all blurry and dim.

This was what I got for being a smart-ass. For asking a question I should've known I wouldn't like the answer to.

Panic bubbled in my chest, filling all the space that should've been occupied by oxygen. I had to get away from him. I had to. But his knot still showed no sign of getting any smaller.

Somehow, I managed to keep it all inside: shame and shock and sudden doubts, my desperation to escape and be alone. I clamped my teeth down on my lower lip to make sure no more idiocy got out of my mouth.

We lay there, both of us tense, both of us completely silent, until at long, long last his knot shrank down to almost the size of the rest of his cock. MacKenna loosened his grip around my chest. It didn't help much with the hard lump that seemed to have taken up residence in my sternum. Without a word, he started to pull out of me, his knot popping free and the rest of his cock sliding out.

That felt bizarre all on its own.

But the sensation of hollowness he left behind felt infinitely worse. My body had gotten used to having him in there, even if I hadn't. And the thought of how my ass must look, open and used, especially since I could feel his come trickling out of me the moment he withdrew…MacKenna could see me like that.

He'd seen it, and he'd remember it, and now that was what I was to him.

Not just a hole to fuck, but a thoroughly fucked hole. He might not even want me anymore, for whatever value of "want" he'd assigned to me, now that he'd turned me from an anal virgin into his wet, slutty thing.

And then I'd be willing to bet he'd have no qualms at all about handing me off to the cops and never thinking about me again.

MacKenna paused for a moment, his hand still on my hip, his body not touching mine anymore, but still so close. Looking at my ass, I knew it, because I could feel the weight and heat of his gaze like a physical touch.

Yeah. I closed my eyes and breathed as deeply as I could, willing it to be over.

And then it was. He let go of me abruptly, rolled off the bed, and strode away. I peeked from under my lashes in time to see him disappearing into the bathroom.

"That's all for now," he called back over his shoulder, and then he shut the door.

I dragged myself off the bed and lurched down the hall to my own room, trying to ignore the sensation of his come slicking my thighs long enough to make it into the shower.

I stayed there for a long, long time.

And if some of those tears finally made their way out, the shower washed them away before I had to acknowledge them.

Chapter 7

Uncanny Valley Territory

Sleeping off the spanking and the fucking and the knotting and the hideously disconcerting personal revelations took me a full twelve hours.

Unfortunately for me, those twelve hours started after my shower, which meant they ended when I popped awake, panting and with my heart racing from a dream I couldn't remember, and fumbled for the clock on the nightstand—which told me it was 3:27 AM. I flopped back on the pillows and blew out a long breath, flexing my fingers to get my incipient claws under control. Whatever dream I'd had, it'd almost pushed me to shift. I hadn't shifted fully in a long time. That might have been part of the problem. Maybe I needed to run.

Like that was going to happen, in the middle of a city and stuck here at MacKenna's beck and call.

But on the other hand...I eyed the clock again. Now it read 3:28 AM. Time sure did fly when you were having fun.

Fuck. It wasn't like I was a prisoner, right? And Las Vegas was a 24/7 kind of place. A lot of the nightlife would just be getting into its full swing at this hour.

Not that I had the money to enjoy it. I didn't even have the money for penny slots.

But that didn't mean I had to stay in this suite forever, and right now I couldn't stand being there. I'd been worried about leaving yesterday, but now MacKenna had to be confident that I wasn't going to run. I mean, I'd already let him knot me. Why try to get away now, when I no longer had anything to lose? And I didn't have to go far.

I could get some fucking fresh air—or something that would pass for fresh compared to the endlessly processed air in this building. The Strip didn't exactly smell great, especially to a shifter, but at least it'd be outdoors.

I forced myself to turn on the light, get washed up, take a piss, and get dressed without any particular caution. Not like I was slamming things around or anything, but dammit, I didn't need MacKenna's permission to go for a walk. Besides, he might never know I'd been gone. I'd come back before he woke up in the morning. Just a couple of hours of wandering to clear my head. Besides, I couldn't even bring myself to care what he thought. The desire to get out had built to an unbearable itch under my skin.

The silent suite lay dim and shadowy as I emerged from my room. Not a sign of MacKenna anywhere—but of course, there wouldn't be. He seemed to treat this place more like a hotel room than any of his guests did, and nothing like a home. Did he even have one? Or did he just hiss at people from under a bridge when he wasn't here?

I hadn't even had the time yet to think about what MacKenna had told me—or let slip out in the heat of his anger, more like—right before he'd put me on my knees. His grandparents had built this place. And then his parents had…what exactly? Screwed up. Gone bankrupt. And honestly, maybe the details of their failure didn't even matter, because the results were the same: he'd somehow ended up working here as a lowly peon, getting fired, and then turning around and buying the place. Which meant he'd come up with hundreds of millions of dollars in the meantime. It made me wildly curious about those missing years of his, and also about his attitude toward the Morrigan in general. I'd have thought he'd feel more at home here, if it had been the family business.

On the other hand, I wasn't really equipped to understand his feelings, period. How at home had I ever felt at Castelli Industries? If the business had gone belly-up or been bought out in a hostile takeover, would I have devoted my whole life to getting it back?

Not a chance.

My stomach growled threateningly at me, pushing my musings about MacKenna out of my mind. After twelve hours, my alpha metabolism was ready to eat my own internal organs. Without much hope, I stopped by the kitchen—only to find my abandoned chocolate cake and apple tart in the mini fridge. I stared down at them for a second.

MacKenna had put them away in the fridge, not thrown them out or eaten them himself. He hadn't even done something petty, the way I might have, like taking one bite out of each.

Something clenched in my chest. No, not following whatever line of thinking might lead from there.

So I ignored it, devoured the desserts, and headed out.

The door opened with the annoying clunk of the lock that all hotel room doors seemed to do, and it shut behind me with a heavy snick.

That was the moment, of course, that I remembered I had no key card, no phone, and no wallet.

Well, fuck me sideways.

Screw it. I was out of the suite. The tastefully pale blue and gray hotel hallway stretched out before me, a corridor to freedom—at least temporarily.

I didn't sprint down it to the elevator, but it was a close thing. My palms got all damp and clammy and my heart rate picked up. Like I was being chased. But the elevator came quickly after I'd punched the call button five or six times, and its ding had me grinning like a fool.

When the doors opened on the main lobby, the hubbub of voices and the more strident and insistent dinging of slot machines hit me like a wall. Lights. Noise. Air movement. People! People who weren't MacKenna!

I made it through the hotel lobby, busy even at this time of night, by dodging drunken, staggering guests and hotel staff rolling luggage carts and carrying trays of drinks, or hustling off to whichever of their demanding patrons had summoned them.

Yesterday, one of those demanding patrons would've been me.

Today I was practically invisible. One of the employees shot me a perfunctory smile and nod as I stepped aside to let her pass, since she was carrying a box that looked too heavy for her. I could've lifted it with a couple of fingers, alpha strength and all. But she rushed by, and the weird impulse to offer to help didn't seem like it would've been appreciated, anyway.

I'd been coming to the Morrigan for ten years—obviously, given my history with MacKenna, and that was clearly my first mistake—and it'd undergone some changes. It'd been your typical tarnished-tinsel Vegas hellhole then, had gotten shabbier and shabbier over the years, and now appeared to be in the middle of something of a makeover.

MacKenna must have only become the owner very, very recently. That probably accounted for my brief residence here as a welcome VIP; the paperwork hadn't gotten sorted out yet, and I was still on the books from the previous management.

Well, I'd almost gotten away with it. Shitty fucking luck. But not all of MacKenna's changes were bad, I had to grudgingly admit. The staff universally wore black pants, black shirts, and surprisingly tasteful red vests, not too cheap-looking and tailored differently to fit the women without being turned into corsets. The previous owners, whoever the hell they were, had put all the female staff in these tiny electric-blue skirts that would've been embarrassing for one of the ten-dollar hookers you could find a few blocks away from here. The girls had all looked so uncomfortable I couldn't even appreciate the view. They seemed a lot happier with the new uniforms.

And the carpets were new, and clean, and the place smelled less like a festering ashtray stuffed into someone's armpit and then half-heartedly washed with a bottle of vodka and a dirty rag.

With the nearly unlimited budget I used to have, I could've chosen any fancy place at the newer and more upscale end of the Strip. But I'd picked the Morrigan on that first visit. Something about it called to me, and I followed my instinct. Maybe because it'd always been a more supernatural-centric establishment than some others. They had a higher than normal proportion of shifter employees, for one thing.

And after that, I'd kept coming back, because of something that most people didn't know about me, something I hid almost fanatically: I was kind of sentimental.

The Morrigan was where I'd popped my Vegas cherry, the place I'd learned how to play blackjack, where I'd gotten my first legal drink. And the Morrigan had been my casino, my hotel, my Nevada home away from home, ever after.

Now MacKenna had popped my real cherry in the Morrigan.

What sweet irony.

Ugh. I stepped out onto the Strip after running the final gauntlet of penny slot machines and a set of double glass doors, and immediately looked up at the sky, sucking in the deepest breath I'd ever taken. No stars, of course. Mere celestial objects couldn't compete with a billion mega-powered LEDs glaring up and drowning them out. But real sky, nonetheless.

And real air, even if it came with mostly car exhaust and the stink of unwashed streets and the pervasive stench of booze and boozy sweat that no shifter's nose would've been able to tune out.

A white stretch limo pulled up, vomiting out a gaggle of young women in dresses so short I couldn't help ogling for a second, one of them with a veil-thing precariously dangling from the side of her hair.

"Oooh!" one of them called out, giggling and stumbling into her friend and shooting me a wide smile. "Want to come up to my room?"

The rest of them burst into laughter.

If I still had my own suite, I'd have invited them up to it. Sent down for a bartender to come up and make everyone fruity cocktails for what was left of the night and all morning. Maybe gotten a private party room with a DJ.

For a second, I considered accepting her offer, even though I didn't have anything to bring to the table but myself. MacKenna hadn't made me promise to be only his fuck toy. I could be this pretty blonde's fuck toy for a couple of hours while he was sleeping, right?

But even if I could've gotten away with it, and I probably wouldn't, the way he'd fucked me had left its mark. I wore his possession of me like a brand no one else could see. If I fucked her, I'd be thinking the whole time about how his cock had filled me yesterday. Every flex of my ass when I thrust inside her would engage muscles I'd never had a reason to think about much—before MacKenna.

I gave the bridal party a smile and a wink. Probably not my best work, but an effort all the same. "You're out of my league, ladies. Have fun tonight. And congratulations!" I added, smiling again at the sloppy bride-to-be.

I made a break for it, heading down the sidewalk, followed by their friendly catcalls.

As soon as I'd turned my back, the smile fell off my face like a too-heavy mask. Shit. This was my life now. Making up excuses to get out of having fun and sleeping with attractive women, in case it pissed off my blackmailer.

Those girls wanted me. Or at least one of them did. They saw something appealing in me. Why didn't MacKenna?

I needed a drink, and a cigarette, and to maybe go jump off a bridge.

The far north end of the Strip, where the Morrigan guarded the border between glitzy Vegas and seedy Vegas, didn't have much to offer. A parking lot across the way half full of construction trucks. A guy with an armful of strip club flyers slogging his way wearily to the gods knew where. In the distance, the lights and the clubs and the very expensive good times.

I ended up wandering down the block and then turning right, heading off of Las Vegas Boulevard and along a lonely, dusty side street past a diner and a cluster of the most horrifyingly run-down beige apartment buildings I'd ever seen. Those were on the other side of the street. On my side, I had the back of the Morrigan and its dumpsters, delivery bay, and earsplittingly obnoxious…loud things. Condensers? Air filters? Whatever. They were loud. And huge.

A dour-looking man in overalls, maybe maintenance, had leaned up against a wall to smoke a cigarette, thumb flipping at the screen of his phone.

A second later he'd let me bum one and I'd taken up my own position against the wall, staring dourly in my turn at the condenser-things since I didn't have a phone of my own to scroll.

Honestly, I didn't miss my phone that much. I mean, I did, in the sense that I felt like I was missing a limb. But I didn't in the sense that I couldn't think of a single person I'd want to communicate with, or whose lives I'd want to be caught up on. And the news could go fuck itself.

The maintenance guy dropped his cigarette butt and vanished around the side of the building. I took a long drag and gazed up at the pinkish-white glare that was all I could see of the sky from here.

"This doesn't seem like your natural habitat." The light, neutral voice startled me so badly I flailed, fumbled my cigarette, caught it, cursed as it burned me, and managed to wedge it between my fingers again, all while spinning wildly to see who the fuck had spoken to me.

It was the fucking weirdly handsome guy, the too-smooth one MacKenna had with him when he came to interrogate me. The one who'd stunk of magic and had given me the glare of death. His short dark hair was slicked back, his bland black suit neat as a pin. Four in the morning, and he looked like a cut-rate Ken doll who'd just started his nine to five. I hadn't heard or smelled him approaching. Getting snuck up on like that had my hackles up so fast I was almost growling.

"The fuck do you want? And where the fuck did you come from?"

He took a step closer, smiling slightly, eyes glinting pale in the reflected glare of the sky and the spotlights across the loading dock. He was approaching me from the same direction as the maintenance guy had gone, so there had to be a staff entrance or something over there. But I hadn't noticed him before he spoke. And I couldn't smell him at all, even now that he stood near me; he had to be masking his scent and his magic.

I resisted taking a step back and forced myself to hold my ground. I wasn't scared of this guy.

Even if his plastic smile and opaque eyes gave him all the charisma of some kind of creepy sci-fi replicated human that didn't quite pass as a real person. The hour and the lighting didn't help.

"It's my business to keep an eye on Mr. MacKenna's assets," he said. "This isn't somewhere you should be, Mr. Castelli."

Completely putting aside his categorization of me as one of MacKenna's "assets," the fuck?

I took a long drag on my neglected cigarette, aiming my exhale in his direction. The smoke parted around him like the Red Sea. Gods, I hated magical assholes.

"Not sure what's wrong with the back of the hotel," I said finally. "It's quieter back here."

It wasn't, really, what with the machinery chugging away. But at least it didn't have any people. Until this fucker came along, anyway.

"That's it precisely," he said. "It's vulnerable. You're vulnerable. Not everyone has the same vested interest in Mr. MacKenna's well-being as we do." His teeth flashed in the odd light. Normal human teeth, white and even. They still made me shudder.

That and the weirdness of that statement left me speechless, thank gods, because I had the sudden feeling that talking to this man was *dangerous*. I couldn't explain it. I couldn't justify it. He was half my size, and the magic he'd shown so far—hiding his scent and his magical nature from a shifter, making cigarette smoke move away from his face, being super quiet—didn't rise to the level of a direct threat. And he had to work for MacKenna, right? Since he'd been in on my interrogation the other day. Not that I automatically thought someone working for MacKenna couldn't be a threat to me. But if I was one of MacKenna's "assets," then taking this guy at face value…he'd be looking out for me, like he said. At least making sure I didn't get killed or something.

And I knew, in an instinctive way I couldn't shake, that he wasn't looking out for me. Not at all. He was threatening me, although…why? He hadn't been happy when MacKenna decided to deal with me personally rather than having me arrested. That had been obvious. But would that really be enough to make him dislike me as much as I'd started to think he might?

He hadn't moved a muscle while I stared at him, so unnaturally still it pushed him even further into uncanny valley territory—and that was coming from a werewolf who was literally not human but close enough to pass, himself.

Another drag of the cigarette bought me time and gave me a reason not to say anything. *Not everyone has the same vested interest in Mr. MacKenna's well-being as we do.* Irony? He had to know I wasn't MacKenna's biggest fan, right? Or was he implying something about how much he had invested in MacKenna?

Fuck, I hated weird, creepy people who stared at me, and I hated mind games, and I still just desperately wanted a drink.

I could've had all the drinks I wanted if I'd stayed nice and quiet up in the suite.

That had started to sound better and better, despite how antsy I'd been to get out. I was out of my depth here. This guy had issues.

The cigarette had burned down to my fingers, and I really didn't have any other way to stall. On the other hand, now I had a reason to leave.

I dropped it and crushed it under my toe. "Well, I'm ready to head back up now that I've gotten a breath of air. Don't worry, I'm not planning on hanging out back here all the time or anything." His paranoia wasn't worth addressing, I decided. Especially since I had no idea how to address it in the first place. Better to get the fuck away from him as quickly as possible and never, *ever* be alone with him again. I'd bang on the door of the suite until MacKenna answered and chewed me out. Fuck, that had started to sound fantastic in comparison to this.

"I'll escort you." He smiled, and my flesh tried to crawl off my body and slither away in terror. Fucking gibbering gods, why did this guy freak me out so much? All of my instincts were screaming, and all he'd done was stand there! "After you." He waved a genial hand in the direction he'd come from, around the corner and presumably toward the door that had to be there.

Putting my back to him had my instincts not just screaming but jumping up and down. But I didn't have much choice. He could call MacKenna, or security, and have me dragged back up to the suite if he wanted. And while MacKenna was going to get woken up one way or the other, at least this way there might not be a public scene.

Nodding stiffly, I stalked past him and around the corner, the space between my shoulder blades itching the whole way, a weird buzzing that seemed to be spreading to the nape of my neck. I had to stand aside when I reached the door so that he could swipe us in. Why had he put me in front of him? And why had my head gotten so fuzzy? Had he...he'd done something. To me? What had he... My thoughts were coming more slowly, falling into my brain like blobs of Jell-O instead of flowing water.

That didn't make any sense. I shook my head and failed to clear it at all. The door hung open in front of me. I stepped through into some kind of utilitarian hallway, the flickering fluorescents above seeming to pulse at a rate I could actually see. Dim, then bright, then dim, and it made me so fucking angry. So *enraged*, I'd never been so furious, my vision clouding over with crimson red, my fangs dropping, and I had to kill him, so I spun around and growled, long and loud, echoing, and took a swing at his face, all weirdly big and small and close and far, that smile, those pale eyes...

My fist connected with a crack that traveled all the way up my arm and then around and around my head. He moved, falling back, hands coming up.

Something hit me like a wave.

I fell. The light went dim again, and then black.

Chapter 8

There Was a Gross Thought

Waking up sucked. Werewolves didn't usually get headaches unless we'd been hit with a sledgehammer or something, but the stabbing pain in my temples struck like a bolt of lightning the second consciousness returned. The newness of the sensation made it even worse, and I groaned, rolled to the side, and panted through a wave of nausea, head hanging over the side of the...bed.

Yep, in a bed. "My" bed, in fact, in MacKenna's suite.

I flopped back onto the pillows and nearly levitated right back up again at the sight of MacKenna leaning against the wall by the door, arms crossed over his chest and with a ferocious scowl aimed right at me.

"Fucking gods," I gasped. "The fuck, MacKenna. Give a guy some warning." He opened his mouth, but I drew another deep breath and continued with, "And maybe give a guy some warning his warlock's a fucking psychopath! What the hell did he do to me? Please tell me he's in custody right now."

The scowl went nuclear. "He said the same thing about you! What the hell did *he* do to *you*?" MacKenna raised an eyebrow, and his hands clenched as if his claws wanted to make an appearance. His eyes already had a faint golden glow, a definite warning. "You blacked both Walter's eyes and broke his nose and his cheekbone, Castelli. He had to knock you out so you didn't beat him to death."

I stared at him, my own fingers twitching, my eyes warming with their own glow. My gums itched. I wanted to drop fang and fucking attack him. Or someone. Walter. Fucking Walter? Uncanny valley mini-Ken-doll dude was named *Walter*?

"I wanted to know what he did to me before I punched him, not after," I gritted out. Because whatever whammy had hit me, it hadn't done a damn thing to muddle my memories. I'd been magicked. I'd felt it on my skin. And that overwhelming, uncontrollable urge to do bloody violence hadn't been organic. "He compelled me, or put some kind of spell on me, I don't know the terminolo—"

"Bullshit," he said flatly, pushing off the wall and looming at me. "Fucking bullshit. Why the fuck would he want you to attack him? Walter's been with me for years. I don't think he'd lie to me, but I know you would."

"I'm not lying, and I don't know either! That's why I'm asking you!" I forced myself up onto my elbows, needing to not be lying there like a fainting Victorian lady while he threatened me, but with my head throbbing and spinning too much for me to take more of a stand than that. "But he did. I felt the magic, like—prickles. On my back. Everything went blurry and all echoey. And then I attacked him. Out of nowhere, MacKenna. I wasn't angry." That wasn't strictly true. Walter had pissed me off. But not enough to try to kill him, especially since that could only have worked out badly for me.

Case in point, here we were.

MacKenna glared down at me, lips in a flat line.

But he didn't speak for a long time, leaving me in heart-racing, brain-exploding suspense.

"You're going to stay in this room," he said at last. "Not just in the suite. In this room. You open that door," and he gestured behind him, "and I'll have the cops here in five minutes. Walter asked me to have you taken away already for his safety, and I thought about it, so you'd better be fucking grateful to be here instead of there. You don't move. You understand?"

"MacKenna, you have to listen to me. That wasn't what I wanted to do. It was magic compel—"

"Shut the fuck up." His low, flat, uncompromising tone, and the brilliant flash of his eyes, was enough to cut me off at the knees. The words died on my tongue. "I don't have to listen to anything. Particularly not to you. I know you're a liar, and a selfish, self-centered one at that. I experienced it ten years ago, and again a few days ago when you cheated this casino and me, and I have no reason to believe a word out of your mouth. Stay. Here. Do you understand?

Yes or no."

Protests, complaints, and insults bubbled up, screaming for release. His words rang in my ears, and I went all dizzy again. "Yes," I muttered.

"Someone will bring you some food. I don't want to hear anything from you."

And with that, he turned and left the room, shutting the door without even bothering to slam it.

He couldn't lock it, either, since it only locked from the inside. But he didn't need to. For one thing, I could break it down in two seconds, and he knew it. And for another, even if I'd felt up to staging an escape attempt, it wouldn't work. He could keep me here if he wanted to, no cops required.

I crawled out of bed to the bathroom, did the necessary, and then staggered straight back to bed, head still aching like a bitch. Gods, I hated magic so much. Flipping the pillow to find the cool spot helped a tiny bit, and I curled up and tried to breathe through the pain.

And the seething, simmering anger at not being believed.

Although to my shock, anger didn't top my list of negative feelings.

I had a heavy, miserable clenching low down in my belly that felt a lot like…hurt. MacKenna's pungent assessment of my character kept echoing, over and over again, until it felt like falling down an endless well of dislike and disdain. *You're a liar. Selfish and self-centered. Experienced it ten years ago, and again a few days ago. Liar. Self-centered. Liar…*

Maybe he was right. Maybe everyone seemed to hate me for a reason.

But this time, I'd been telling the truth! Random violence wasn't me. Lying, maybe. Selfishness…well, okay, yes, but if you didn't look out for yourself, who would? My family sure as hell hadn't when the chips were down. Brook took over our family company and shoved everyone else out, and my parents, who'd always told me how important it was to have an alpha heir who kept up the expected lifestyle and displayed the right face to the world, cut me off the second they had to choose between my well-being and their own luxuries. Like they couldn't have funded both, even with less money coming in.

One private jet instead of two wouldn't fucking kill them, would it?

So if everyone else got to be selfish, why shouldn't I?

And I wasn't violent. I *wasn't*. That hadn't been me, except in the sense that Walter's magic had employed my physical body as an instrument of his will.

How could MacKenna believe that I'd attack a man who was no physical threat to me for no reason at all? Drunken seduction attempts and complaints about employees weren't on the same level as flat-out unprovoked murderous assault.

It took me a couple of hours of tossing and turning and marinating in my misery, my pounding headache, and my anger to circle back to the question MacKenna had asked and that I'd been too upset and distracted to focus on at the time: Why had Walter done it? What the hell did he have to gain? Discrediting me with MacKenna? Now there was a laugh and a half.

I flipped onto my back again, staring up at the ceiling and blowing out a long breath that I hoped would carry some of my confusion and frustration away with it.

It didn't.

Seriously, though. MacKenna already thought he'd met pond scum he liked better than me. And if Walter had managed to lower his opinion of me even further, what did he get out of it? MacKenna trusted Walter but not me, employed Walter for actual money but hadn't given me a dime—okay, unless you counted the comps when I first arrived, but whatever—and was obviously protective of him, which indicated loyalty, if not friendship.

All that I had was…MacKenna's dick. Did Walter want MacKenna for himself?

Now there was a gross thought.

MacKenna and Walter…ugh, ugh, ugh. Walter and anyone, frankly. But MacKenna and Walter? No. It made me sick.

But it also made sense. That look of pure hatred he'd given me as MacKenna told me he'd deal with me himself. The way he'd seemed too intensely invested in me and in my relationship with MacKenna.

He wanted what I had.

And gods, the irony in that. If that little fucker only knew…

The thing was, if I had it right, then Walter wanted me gone, but he wouldn't be earning any points with MacKenna by going about it like this. If he'd made me attack him just so that I'd look bad, he was lying to MacKenna, and I knew damn well MacKenna didn't like being lied to. And if I had it wrong, and he had some other agenda, then it couldn't be for MacKenna's benefit, could it? Or he'd have been honest about it.

I shouldn't care. If Walter wanted to fuck around and find out with the vengeful, grudge-holding asshole who'd blackmailed me and humiliated me and forced me to take his cock and his knot, then I ought to be cheering him on and hoping they screwed each other over.

But I cared. I grabbed a pillow and shoved it over my face and screamed into it.

That didn't help, and I lay there rumpled and breathing hard and hating myself.

At last I heard movement in the suite: someone coming in the door, footsteps approaching.

They knocked at my door.

Right on cue, my stomach gurgled and hissed at me, and I realized that at least half of my physical misery was simple hunger.

The girl who stood at the door when I opened it (wondering, as I did, if MacKenna would be enough of a dick to call the police on me for opening the door when he'd told me not to, even to get my food) gave me a wide-eyed once-over. Yeah, I probably looked like I'd been dragged backward through a hedge—and my werewolf nose confirmed that I smelled like it, too.

Fuck.

I thanked her and took the tray as quickly as possible, shutting the door and setting the food on the desk by the window.

Three covered plates, one large and two smaller, and a covered bowl. A strong, savory odor of lobster and salmon and a hint of chocolate rose from the tray.

My heart felt like it dropped down to somewhere around my ankles. I rushed back to the door and flung it open. "Wait!"

Halfway down the hall and about to escape this den of madness, the girl stopped short, visibly straightened her shoulders and took a second, and then turned to face me, customer service smile painted across her pretty face.

That killed any self-esteem I might have had left. Not even a real smile.

But I had to know. "Who ordered my food? Did the kitchen just choose at random?"

"No, sir. Mr. MacKenna ordered specifically off the room service menu. Is there something wrong? I can replace—"

"No, thank you, it's fine. Thank you. Nothing's wrong with it." Except that now I was more confused and upset and off-balance than ever. "Thanks."

I shut the door in her baffled face and slumped against it, breathing hard. Okay. Maybe I was imagining things. I pushed off the door and went back to the tray, edging closer to it as if it could bite me. Gingerly, I lifted off the covers. He'd ordered me salmon— only not the same dish I'd had the other day. It looked like it was stuffed with something that smelled like crab, and possibly brie. My mouth watered; it had to be one of the most luxurious foods I'd ever seen. And, of course, the soup was lobster bisque. The small plates held a salad and another flourless chocolate cake.

MacKenna had ordered this personally. He could've kept me on bread and water, or chosen things that he thought I'd hate. Instead, he'd gone for the most expensive items on the menu…and also the dishes I'd already shown I liked. Including dessert.

Or had he ordered them simply because they were the most expensive, and he was either running up my "bill" on purpose or mocking me for being formerly wealthy? If he wanted to do that, he could've ordered something super expensive he thought I'd hate. That's what I might've done.

Either way, I had too much to think about. Walter. MacKenna. The police. The fucking salmon and the motives behind it, for fuck's sake.

Freaking gods, I was losing my mind.

With no reason not to, I sat down and tucked in. Lobster bisque and chocolate cake might not solve my problems, but at least I'd feel like they had for a few minutes. My brother always thought that I was picky about food because I was an asshole who didn't care about other people's preferences in contrast to my own.

Well, okay. Sometimes.

But it was possibly the only uncomplicated pleasure in my life.

Sleeping: there were nightmares and anxiety dreams, or at best, sex dreams with confusing protagonists and unpleasant emotions. Sex: yeah, that was a whole other can of worms, because half the things I wanted, I could never have. I didn't want a high-powered female alpha (my parents' ultimate goal for me), or their second-best, a high-powered werewolf woman from a prominent and wealthy family. What I did want...well, I got drunk and gave anonymous blowjobs. Yeah. I didn't want to think about that.

More soup. Mmm.

Or travel. I liked traveling. Except that I could only go to places my mom thought were suitable. Las Vegas was borderline for her, but I'd escaped here as often as I could, because it was the closest I could get to seedy anonymity. People here didn't care what pack I belonged to. They only cared if I could pay for their drinks. It was honest, in its own way.

Getting high and eating what I liked. Those things I could just enjoy, without any baggage attached.

Except for now, because every bite reminded me that MacKenna was playing mind games with me and might still turn me over to the police.

Good times.

After the last bite of cake, I cocooned myself in bed again.

Fuck it. If anyone needed me, they could damn well shake me awake.

Chapter 9

Malicious, Petty Fun

MacKenna shook me awake.

I popped up like a Jack-in-the-box, shouting something incoherent—about my father and my brother, I realized as I blinked into his wide-eyed face. MacKenna took a quick step back, his hand falling from my shoulder.

"What time is it?" I rasped, rubbing my hands over my face. Gods. I had crud in my eyes and could barely focus them, and my heart pounded as if I'd been woken from a marathon, not a nap. At least the headache had gone away.

"Almost seven," he said. "In the evening, in case that wasn't clear."

The light of sunset through the uncovered window had tipped me off, in fact, and I glared at him, the only answer I had the presence of mind to muster. He chuckled, which only pissed me off more. MacKenna looked so handsome when he laughed. Too bad he was always laughing at my expense, or I might have enjoyed the view.

"Anyway, I'm taking a couple of hours from work," he went on. "Dinner. Fucking you. Good news, Castelli. You get to get out of this room for a while. Take a shower first."

And with that, he left again.

Fucking *asshole*.

I threw the covers back and lurched out of bed, stretching my back and scratching my stomach while I contemplated what tack to take with MacKenna. The nightmare I couldn't remember had left me edgy and fidgety, not in a great state of mind to make any decisions. Shit. I really couldn't afford to antagonize him any further, and frankly, I didn't have the energy or the will for it.

The last...two days? Fuck, I was losing track. Anyway, they'd drained me. Fighting back probably wasn't in the cards anymore.

So I went and took a shower. I washed extra carefully, admitting if only to myself that MacKenna had a point and that no one would've wanted to be in the same bed with me. I hadn't even wanted to be in the same bed with me. Washing my ass took concentration and teeth-gritting determination. I had to stick my fingers in there, or at least that seemed like the most logical way to proceed, anyway. When I twisted them, arm at a super uncomfortable angle, I brushed against—fuck, fuck, no, and I yanked my fingers out a little too roughly, leaning against the wall of the shower and closing my eyes for a second. My cock had gone half-hard at that slight touch on the right spot. MacKenna was going to light me up like a Roman candle with that huge cock of his. At some point, he'd start openly mocking me for it, and then...I didn't know what I'd do.

Everything from the night before swirled through my head, the parts that had gotten to me the most replaying like a highlight reel. His knot swelling inside me. Coming like a whore when he spanked me, for fuck's sake.

Gods.

I really had to find a way to hold my own against him. Exhausted or not, I couldn't let him walk all over me without even trying.

And then I remembered what he'd said to me.

I'm glad you didn't like it, actually. That makes this easy. You're just a fuck toy. And that's all I want from you.

If I'd been in a cartoon, I'd have had a giant lightbulb suspended over my head in midair.

That's all I want from you. I'm glad you didn't like it.

He wanted to humiliate me. He wanted revenge. And he could have that, he'd already gotten a damn good start, except...I could turn the tables on him in a way he wouldn't be able to argue with. What was he going to say if I transformed myself into his eager slut, whether or not he wanted it? *I'll call the cops if you come?* Or *No, stop, you're being a better fuck toy than I expected?*

Ha!

I finished washing up in a much better mood. It helped that the

Morrigan's branded shampoo smelled amazing and that MacKenna had mentioned dinner, the magic word.

It took an extra minute to dig through my luggage and find my best club clothes, wrinkling my nose at the faint lingering odd smell, but when I looked in the mirror after getting dressed…yeah, totally worth it. The jeans I'd shimmied into fit me like a second skin, super thin Italian denim that made my ass look round and bitable. And the gray V-neck T-shirt could've come off a Parisian runway. Actually, it had, now that I thought about it. Tight, nearly transparent, and perfectly cut.

I tilted my head and batted my lashes at myself. I was all icy-blue eyes, collarbones, and legs. Perfect.

Too bad I hadn't packed any eyeliner. I could give the motherfucker a heart attack.

As I sashayed out of my room and into the hallway, I was grinning. For the first time since Brook had dropped his "our father's not a real alpha" bomb on the family and cut off the flow of company money, I was actually having *fun*.

Malicious, petty fun that would almost undoubtedly have disastrous consequences, and indulged at the worst possible time.

But that was the best kind, wasn't it?

MacKenna stood by the window at the far end of the main room of the suite when I emerged from the hall, staring out at the Strip and sipping something from a rocks glass, suit jacket shed on a chair nearby and sleeves rolled up again to show those tattoos. Whiskey, it looked like he was having, and that was the faint scent I picked up, too. The table already held a selection of covered dishes emitting tantalizing smells, but it didn't look like he'd touched anything yet.

Waiting for me? So that we could, what, have an intimate meal together?

Fucking hell. I'd rather skip straight to getting fucked.

My grin fell away. Just as well, since I didn't want him to see it in any case, and he could probably catch a faint reflection of me in the window.

Strike that. He definitely had, because *I* could catch a faint reflection of *him*, and he'd gone very still, eyes fixed on—me. A second later he turned his head abruptly and took a deep swig of his drink, nearly draining it.

Yep. Score one for my slut clothes.

Suddenly dinner didn't sound quite so bad after all. Fuck him. He wanted to accuse me of assaulting his precious Walter out of nowhere, call me a liar when I defended myself, and lock me in my bedroom when he didn't have a use for me? I could make his life difficult too, damn it all.

"I'm hungry," I said, in a tone that implied I wanted more than food. "Is it dinner time?"

"Yeah." He cleared his throat before turning around. "Yeah, it's dinner time. They'll clear your dishes from earlier when they take this stuff away in a while."

That was such a random thought, not at all something I'd have imagined he'd consider—I mean, wasn't one of the perks of living in a suite in your own hotel not having to think about the logistics of dishes getting cleared?—that it had to be…his version of being flustered.

I'd flustered him.

Putting a bit of sway in my hips (and I'd never admit that I was imitating that slutty waiter) as I crossed the room to the table didn't come all that naturally; I wasn't used to using my body to attract men, and women didn't generally go for that kind of display. But MacKenna got visibly tenser as I got nearer, and as I sat and smiled up at him.

He took his own seat stiffly, clearing his throat again and abandoning his whiskey in favor of pouring a generous glass of the red wine sitting open on the table, picking it up and taking a drink of it immediately.

"Hard day at work?" I asked him. I even managed to sound sweetly sympathetic.

MacKenna choked, coughed, and put the glass down, shaking his head. "What?" he gasped. "Did I—what?"

"You seem tense." I kept my tone soothing and gentle, even though confining the malicious laughter in my chest had started to be a struggle. "Maybe I can help you relax."

And then I winked.

And MacKenna choked again, eyes going wide.

Without further comment, I started lifting the covers off the plates. I'd done enough for now. I wouldn't be able to keep a straight face if I kept it up.

While he gulped more of his wine, I revealed two steaks and sides, a couple of salads, and one single slice of cheesecake.

Okay, so I could keep a straight face for another round if I really had to.

I glanced up at him with my head tipped down, giving him the full benefit of an exaggeratedly sultry gaze through my lashes. "Oh, are we sharing dessert? That's so sweet."

MacKenna picked up his fork, his white-knuckled grip suggesting that it might be ending up in my neck instead of his potatoes.

"What the fuck are you playing at?" he growled. "Whatever it is, it isn't going to work. And the cheesecake's for you. I don't really have a sweet tooth. For you, or cheesecake. Fuck."

He looked down and stabbed his fork into his salad. The brick-red flush along his cheekbones made me hide a smile. Yeah, I was getting to him. But he didn't seem angry, precisely. More…off-balance. Yes.

"I'm not playing at anything," I said quietly. "That was sarcastic, I admit." He'd be even more off-balance and disarmed if I was faux-candid. I'd used that successfully before on all kinds of people: accountants, my mother, girlfriends. My brother never fell for it, though, the little bastard. "But I'm just trying to be nice."

He paused with a bite of salad halfway to his mouth. "You and nice aren't even in the same zip code," he said flatly, and stuck the fork in his mouth.

No, I would not feel hurt by that, damn it all. First off, I wasn't actually trying to be nice, so it wasn't like he was wrong. And second…well, I didn't care what he thought of me.

"Fine. But if we're eating dinner together, we have to talk about something. Telling me about your day at work isn't the worst thing, right?"

MacKenna swallowed and poked at the salad again, chasing a cherry tomato. My fingers twitched. Put it out of its misery!

"You don't give a fuck about my day at work. Besides, you wouldn't understand it. I doubt you've ever worked a day in your life, Castelli." He looked right at me, pinning me with his gaze. "If you want to make friendly small talk, how about you tell me why you were having a nightmare about your father murdering you and taking your alpha powers instead?"

My throat closed up and I gagged, choked, and sprayed my very first sip of wine across my steak and potatoes, eyes watering and lungs spasming. I set the glass down with a thunk and a slosh, wine spilling and staining the white tablecloth like blood.

Another choke, and a long, drawn-out wheeze, and I managed to get a breath again. I stared at him in horror, eyes still blurred. *That* had been my nightmare? How the fuck had he gotten that from whatever I'd been yelling when he woke me up? Unless…

"How long were you watching me sleep?" I demanded, voice scratchy and weak. I coughed again. "What the fuck is wrong with you?"

"You were shouting the hotel down. What was I supposed to do, Castelli?"

"Mind your own fucking business!" And suddenly, his use of my last name hit my very last nerve. "And call me Blake, Jesus. You think maybe I'm not that excited about being called by my family name right now?"

Silence fell for a long moment.

"Blake," he said slowly, and it sent an uncontrollable shiver down my back. "You going to call me Declan?"

"I'm not calling you anything," I hedged. I'd been thinking about him as MacKenna, and maybe I'd used his name out loud once or twice. But I didn't need to use a name for him at all. I really, really didn't want to. His first name felt heavy on my tongue, too heavy to let fall.

"Say it," he said, with a note of alpha command creeping in.

I couldn't look away from his eyes.

"Declan," I whispered, and they darkened even more.

His fork dropped to the salad plate with a clatter. "Dinner can wait."

My mouth went dry. I was starving, yeah, but…dinner could wait. My cock pressed painfully against the zipper of my jeans, which I'd put on without any underwear as part of my plan to be seductive.

Well, that had backfired on me, because seductive or not, it hurt.

Without even thinking about it, I got up and moved around the table. MacKenna—gods, Declan, he was Declan now, and something about that had flipped a switch in my brain and messed me up—kept his eyes locked with mine, and I still couldn't tear my gaze away. Dark eyes, compelling me.

I went to my knees beside him. He pushed back from the table with a scrape of chair legs on hardwood, turning so that he faced me, feet apart and thighs spread to make room for me. I shuffled closer, laying my hands on his legs.

The bulge in the front of his trousers drew my eyes away from his at last. Fuck, I needed to unzip my jeans and take my own cock out before it broke in half. But I couldn't—or could I? Why not? I'd been planning to unsettle him with my enthusiasm. So I'd wanted that enthusiasm to be fake. But he wouldn't know the difference, right? Following my plan and getting more comfortable could totally be compatible.

That was my story and I was sticking to it.

I let go of him, leaned back enough to relieve the pressure, and unbuttoned and unzipped my jeans, pulling the sides back and letting my cock spring free. It pointed up at me, shiny at the head and flushed dark red.

Declan made a funny sound in his throat.

My heart pounded. Time to follow the plan. I looked up at him again, finding his black eyes overlain with a gleam of alpha gold.

"See how much I want to suck your cock?" I asked, breathy not because I wanted to be, but because I couldn't seem to suck in enough air. No worries, because if this went as I expected, I wouldn't have room in my throat for air anyway. "Please? Declan?"

His eyes flicked down to my exposed cock and then back up, his chest rising and falling a lot faster now. A hand shot out and wrapped around the back of my head, fingers tangling in my overlong hair. And then he pulled, shoving my face between his legs. I toppled forward, catching myself on his knees but not resisting more than that. His still-clothed cock rubbed over my lips and my cheek, and I mouthed at it, wrapping my lips around the side of his shaft, prodding with my tongue, inhaling the scent of him, his arousal and lust and alpha magic.

I whined helplessly, working my hands up to try to get his trousers open so I could taste him, choke on him, moan around his knot…

Declan took a firmer grip on my hair and yanked me up,

exposing my throat, drawing a cry of surprise out of me.

"You're not getting off that easy," he said grimly, and then smiled, one of the ones that didn't reach his eyes. "So to speak. You want my knot stuffed in your ass, Blake?"

"Yes," I gasped, cock throbbing, and gods, I was so close I could've come all over the floor if he let me stroke it for just a minute. "Whatever you want. I'll take whatever you give me. Fuck me with that huge alpha cock, Dec—eep!"

He reached up with his other hand, faster than I could flinch from, and wrapped it around my throat. I stared up at him, wide-eyed with shock, hands flailing, as he tightened his grip with both, tugging my head back with the hand in my hair and increasing the pressure with the one on my throat.

Declan leaned down, eyes flashing. "Stop fucking with me," he growled, so low the vibrations sent tremors through me. "I don't know what you're playing at. But fucking stop it."

"I'm not fucking with you!" I had been fucking with him. I had to squeeze my eyes shut for a second against a wave of dizziness. I'd totally been fucking with him, hadn't I? His fingers tightened again, and my dizziness grew. "I'm not playing at anything."

Because I wasn't. Not anymore. Not with my ass clenching around nothing, anticipating the girth of him and the unbearable stretch of his knot, and not with my cock leaking and desperate, hanging in empty air begging to be touched. Not with my head pinned and my throat compressed and his black and gold eyes waiting to overwhelm me the moment I opened my own again.

I left one hand on his thigh, anchoring myself as much as I could, and let the other drop, wrapping it around my shaft. Yes, please, gods, let him let me do this…I stroked, and I whimpered, cut off as his fingers clenched convulsively around my neck.

My eyes flew open and met his again. I couldn't see anything else.

When he squeezed and stroked my throat, I did the same to my cock. My back bowed, the pressure forcing my chin up and nearly cutting off what little oxygen I had—and I spasmed, balls drawn up tight, and came all over my hand. Little explosions of white light filled my vision.

"Jesus fucking Christ," Declan breathed. "Fucking—fuck."

"So eloquent." Those two words took the last of my air. I slumped in his grasp, held up only by my hair and my throat, white flashes turning to spinning black spots.

I barely heard the rumble of Declan's laughter through the ringing in my ears. He let go of my hair and neck, and I started to topple, only to be caught under my arms and hauled to my feet like a sack of especially uncooperative potatoes.

Whatever happened next, it wasn't going to be my doing. And that was fine by me.

Chapter 10

I'll Give You Mine If You Give Me Yours

Declan manhandled me...somewhere, and I didn't care that much either way. The strong arm wrapped around my waist and the other hand holding me up with a firm grip on my ass were enough to keep me from falling over, and that was all that mattered. I let my head lean down onto his shoulder. He smelled like sex and alpha, with a tinge of that casino floor taint that followed you everywhere if you so much as walked through. It didn't bother me. The combination soothed me, made me feel safe. He smelled like competence and strength.

And then I did fall over, tumbling onto a soft surface that also smelled like Declan.

His bed.

My jeans came off, not without some cursing from Declan as he worked them down, and then his hands paused at my waist. "If you don't take this ridiculous shirt off yourself, I'm going to rip it off you," he said. "I'm not spending twenty minutes trying to extract you from it."

If it'd been any other shirt, I'd have let him. But seriously? Rip *this*?

I mustered the energy to flop over onto my back, blinking up at him as I clumsily worked the shirt up and over without bothering to sit up. It got stuck on my biceps. I wriggled around, finally emerging flustered and panting.

Declan had already produced a bottle of lube from somewhere, and he tossed it on the bed next to me, getting to work on his shirt buttons.

"Get yourself ready," he said. "I want to watch."

Aside from the showers I'd taken since the last time he fucked me, I'd never had my own fingers in my ass.

And that was what he meant. Lube, fingers, sliding inside. Twisting and stretching and making sure when his cock slid into me, he could go as deep as he wanted, opening me up the rest of the way, spearing me…

"You're getting hard again," he commented casually, and tossed his shirt aside.

Yeah, yeah I was. And his broad, naked chest wasn't helping. Fuck, I'd had good taste ten years ago. An image of Declan flashed into my mind: on his knees, maybe wearing the casino uniform, unfastening my pants and then taking my hips in his iron grip and pinning me against the wall, sucking every inch of my cock.

I moaned and fumbled for the lube, almost dropping it in my hurry to get it open *now*. It squirted all over my fingers when I squeezed too hard, and then I actually did drop it when Declan shoved his trousers and boxer briefs down in one go, revealing his cut hips and muscular abdomen and thighs…and that cock, aimed right at me.

I had three fingers stuffed in my ass within seconds, my knees spread, angling my hips up so that I could get deeper. It burned a little, but I didn't fucking care. The faster I could get myself opened up, the faster he could get inside me.

Tilting my hips also gave Declan a fantastic view. And his reaction left me even more breathless and wanting. He stared between my legs, eyes glowing, his hand gripping his cock like he was trying to keep from spilling then and there.

Not like I wasn't having the same problem. I couldn't contort myself into the right position and also touch my cock, but the motion of my fingers inside me, filling me up and not quite able to reach the right spot, drove me insane.

"Fuck, enough," he said roughly. "Turn over."

I pulled my hand out and started to roll, but it wasn't fast enough for him. He dived at me, grabbing me by the hips and flipping me onto my face, shoving my legs apart and kneeling between. This time I managed to get up on my elbows and keep my face out of the bedding.

Big hands pulled my ass cheeks apart, and then his cock pressed against my hole. It felt even bigger than it had before.

He thrust inside in one hard motion.

My nerves lit up along every limb and I thought I could feel every single one, as if I'd been transformed into one of those anatomy book illustrations showing the nervous system. I screamed, and he pounded me, and his fingers digging into my hips burned like brands, and I was saying—all kinds of things, uncontrollably, without a trace of the guile I'd planned to use when it came time for it.

Declan, please. Please fuck me harder. Gods, you feel so good, you're huge inside me, fuck me harder, please…

"Stop," Declan rasped, not stopping at all himself, his cock impaling me so hard I grunted and moaned. "Fucking stop it. You don't have to act like—*fuck,*" and he doubled his tempo, moving impossibly fast, not holding back his alpha speed and strength at all.

I was so close, so very very close, about to come with only the tip of my cock rubbing against the bed, and then…he stopped.

"No, don't, fuck," I whined, pushing back, trying desperately to fuck myself on him, to get that last bit of stimulation I needed to come again. Sweat ran down my forehead and into my eyes, my legs shook, my fingers ached with how hard I clutched the duvet. Declan held me in place. I could feel the effort it cost him, but he kept me from taking him in again. "Please, come on!"

He thrust in again, and I moaned my approval—and then he lowered himself down on top of me, crushing me into the bed with his full weight. His cock was buried in me, but he wasn't moving. And neither was I.

One of his hands loosened its death grip and slid under me, wrapping around my cock and squeezing hard enough at the base that it almost hurt.

Declan nuzzled my ear, hot breath brushing over the shell of it. "Knot my fist," he whispered. "I want to feel it."

My own hoarse, labored breathing filled my ears, rushing like a river, blood pounding beneath in counterpoint like the thunder of a waterfall. I stared at a loose thread on the duvet. A different duvet, I realized. I'd shredded the other one with my claws.

My knot. He wanted my *knot,* and knotting the empty air, or his hand, while he fucked me would be the final signal of my total submission to him, acknowledging him as the dominant alpha. There was a folk tale about that, part of shifter lore and custom. I'd found it in another pack's library when I was a teenager, and it'd given me a few really uncomfortable moments thinking about it in the shower.

Declan shifted his hips, grinding into me, putting nearly unbearable pressure on the nub of flesh inside me, sending sparks into my balls and my cock and up my spine.

"Knot, Blake," he said, and it was an undeniable command. "I'll give you mine if you give me yours."

Another thrust, another twisting squeeze from that strong hand, and I was spreading myself open as much as I could beneath his weight, tilting my hips to offer myself up.

"That's right," he purred, and the vibrations from his chest warmed my back, soothing me, sanding off the rough edges of humiliation and dying pride. "So good for me, Blake. You want my knot, baby?"

Baby? Did I hate that? I hated it so much, and I was so confused, but as the word left his lips I still squirmed and whimpered, trying to fuck his hand, trying to make him fuck me, caught between his fist and his cock and his rough-haired, muscular chest pinning me down.

"Yes, I want it." I swallowed hard. He didn't move. "Please, Declan. I want it. And I'll give you mine."

Declan mouthed my shoulder, flicking out his tongue, and thrust into me, so deep it took my breath away. "Here it comes," he growled, and thrust again, his knot starting to swell, stretching me open.

He came deep inside me in spurt after spurt, and I let myself go, let all of it go, all of my hang-ups about being the perfect alpha. My knot pressed into his hand as his come heated me from the inside. Declan let out a low, strangled groan, forcing his knot as deeply into me as he possibly could. It echoed my own knot, and it felt fucking incredible, allowing myself this part of my sexuality, of my nature.

"I want to bite you," Declan gasped, and my eyes flew open.

Bite me?

Fuck, his fangs sinking into my flesh, the sting of it mirroring the sharp, sweet pain of his knot inside me...

His teeth brushed over my neck, and I moaned and squirmed

and went hot all over. Bite me. It wouldn't take. Alpha/alpha matings required a mutual bite. He could bite me just like a claim, and it wouldn't do anything but leave a mark that'd fade to nothing within half a day.

I dug my fingers into the bedding and nodded, throat too tight to speak.

It was enough. With a deep, feral growl, Declan extended his fangs and bit down, hard.

His knot grew even more inside me, and so did mine, caught in his big fist, the lightning-bolt strike of his bite forming a circuit of pain and pleasure that coursed through me, our mingled alpha magic exploding like a firecracker.

I whited out, lost in a haze of sensation.

It felt like a long time before I drifted back into the real world, out of the red and gray mist of my blood pulsing into his mouth and his come pumping into me, my knot throbbing in his grasp as he massaged it, taking everything I had to give and then some.

Declan had turned us a little, letting the bed take some of his weight. But he still covered me from head to toe, one hand wrapped around my cock with the other arm around my waist, legs tangled with mine, chest pressed to my back. His tongue lazily traced the bite mark, sending fresh shivers through me with every pass.

"We're not bonded," he said quietly.

"I know how mating works between alphas." I tried to snap it at him, but it came out more of a whisper. "Why'd you want to bite me, anyway?"

A long pause, and meanwhile, he licked me again. Another shiver, and I clenched down on his knot. I could probably come again like this...or I could if I hadn't been completely drained of every drop of energy I had.

And every drop of come, too. Gods, I couldn't have made more if he'd paid me.

"Call it a kink," he said finally. "I've never wanted a mate, let alone you." Ouch, not that I didn't already know it. "Fucking another alpha's the only way I can knot and bite without any permanent consequences. That's a nice side benefit of this arrangement."

In my state of blissed-out enervation, I couldn't exactly argue with that.

Well, no. I couldn't exactly *disagree*.

But I could always argue, and I ought to if I wanted to keep any self-respect. I opened my mouth to do just that, and then I remembered I'd been intending to take the slutty fuck-toy thing to the limit, right? So I didn't have to argue after all.

"Mmm," I said instead, and wriggled in his arms a bit, snuggling impossibly closer—and uncomfortably aware that *mmm*ing and wriggling was coming a lot more naturally than arguing would have.

Declan went unnaturally still.

I wriggled again, just to be an asshole.

He slid his hand up from around my waist and cupped my pec, taking my nipple between his finger and thumb, starting to pinch and squeeze it, almost absently, like he was fidgeting instead of sending a whole new series of shockwaves down into the pit of my stomach.

"You want to tease me, I can tease you," he murmured in my ear. "You said you weren't playing games with me. But I know you are, darlin'. You won't win."

Oh, the hell I wouldn't.

"I thought I was your fuck toy and you didn't want me to enjoy it. So why are you trying to—ow, don't pinch quite so—fuck, Declan," and I trailed off in a moan, because he'd thrust into me, cramming his knot even deeper, and twisted my nipple in a way that doubled the sensation, and—

"Toys are for playing with, Blake. And I'm going to play with you as much as I want."

He didn't stop, rolling my nipple between his fingers, nibbling on the side of my neck right next to the still-throbbing bite, rolling his hips so that his knot rubbed on my sweet spot over and over and over again, until I wasn't writhing against him on purpose but because I couldn't help it, and my knot had started to go down but I was getting hard again, and that pathetic, keening whine was coming from *me*, gods damn it, and—he stopped. Everything. He went completely still, not thrusting and not jerking me off, putting his palm flat over my pec, my abused nipple throbbing against his skin.

I panted into the duvet and bit my tongue so I wouldn't beg.

I wouldn't beg.

No, I'd make him beg.

"Next time I'm going to ride you," I gasped. "Fuck myself on your cock and play with my own nipples and jerk off all over you. You can spank my ass until you knot me, bite me, fill me up and breed me—" I broke off in a scream as he jerked his hips back and tore his knot out of me, tugging on my hole in a flash of pain.

It had gone down enough for it not to damage me, but it burned, and I flailed as he let go and knelt up over me, shoving me onto my back.

I stared up at him, wide-eyed with shock.

His glowing eyes stared back, his lips curled in a snarl that showed his extended fangs.

Looming over me, tattoos gleaming and coiling around him, shoulders broad enough to blot out everything else in the room, fists clenched, he could've been that folk tale I'd read brought to life. I'd pictured someone very like Declan when I read it, and when I…thought about it later on.

And I froze like prey.

Somehow, I hadn't been afraid of him before, not even when he blackmailed me. Not even when he held me down and spanked me, or when he threatened me, or when he confined me to my room.

Now he scared me. My ass throbbed—not torn, but swollen and stretched and stinging from his abrupt withdrawal. And he looked like he was about to hurt me. The air around us quivered with his intent, with his alpha power, with the tension of my fright.

Declan's knot had shrunk, but his cock hadn't. He was as hard as he'd been when he started to fuck me.

As he lowered himself down, never looking away from me, somehow managing to prowl without doing more than leaning over, I realized he meant to do it again.

"Spread your legs, if you're so eager to get fucked," Declan said roughly.

I wasn't sure I'd survive it, honestly, let alone being eager.

But I spread my legs.

He braced himself on either side of my chest and lined up his cock.

The first thrust didn't hurt at all. He'd drenched my insides so completely, and knotted me so thoroughly, that I was as slick and open as I could possibly be. But the pressure of his long cock still had me breathless. My hands flew up of their own accord, locking around his biceps.

Declan grinned down at me, face only inches from mine. My cheeks burned. He didn't need to say a single word to tell me he knew how well he'd subjugated me.

That didn't he had to win, though.

Frightened or not, I never folded unless I knew I couldn't bluff my way out of something.

I flung my legs around his waist, wrapping them tight and holding him down, buried in my body, gripping his arms tightly enough to bruise.

"Is that eager enough for you, Declan?"

"No," he said, grin widening. "Not nearly." He thrust again, constrained by the way I had him pinned to me, but not losing much by way of force, and gaining depth. I groaned and tightened around him. "I think you can slut it up a little more if you really try."

I swallowed hard against the lump in my throat. That had been my plan, and it had been…working? Definitely working. That cold, indifferent mask he'd worn the other night had fallen away at last.

But now that he'd decided to fight back by demanding that I do what I'd *meant* to do to irritate him, any words I could've thrown at him felt desperate, and embarrassing, and I wanted to turn my face away and close my eyes and hide.

Alphas didn't get *shy*, for fuck's sake.

Today we did, apparently. First time for everything. Fuck my life.

"Fuck me," I whispered, and then winced. Gods. As dirty talk went, that didn't score many points. "I want your knot again." Oh, shit, I sounded so pathetic. Even though I actually meant every pitiful word.

Declan lifted a scathing, condescending eyebrow. Screw turning my face away and hiding. Spontaneous combustion might be my only way out.

He thrust again, slow and deep, stirring my insides more than fucking me.

"Nothing to say, Blake?" He leaned in even more, his breath brushing over my lips. It felt like a caress. Not quite a kiss, but adjacent. "About how you've given me what I want, and how it feels? I wouldn't have thought a real alpha would've—"

"Don't!" The word tore out of my throat and left it raw, my eyes filling, Declan blurring into a watery rainbow. "I am a real alpha!"

My wavering voice couldn't have been less of an alpha's firm tone if I'd tried. Gods, I probably wasn't an alpha, somehow. Maybe my father had been forcing our shaman to do something to me all these years, too. Or I'd somehow been tainted by his lies and subterfuge and posturing, given an example that I could never live up to—because it was false all along. Stunted and ruined. Made weak.

I jerked my hands away from Declan's arms and covered my face with them. Real alphas didn't cry. We didn't take other alphas' knots, or whimper and beg to be fucked. I still had my legs locked around his waist, his cock buried to the hilt in me.

Until Declan leaned up, dislodging both my legs and his cock and pulling out of me, leaving me empty.

The mattress dipped as he got up. I didn't move my hands. I didn't want to see the contempt I knew I'd find on his face, in his body language. The eagerness to get the hell away from me as quickly as possible.

I felt it when he left the room, because the heaviness in the air eased a little.

I ought to have gotten up and moved, gone back to my own room.

I didn't.

Fuck it. He could remove me himself if he wanted. I couldn't be bothered.

Chapter 11
Like You Care

Declan moved around in the main room of the suite for a bit. Eating his abandoned dinner? And maybe also mine? I couldn't muster more than the faintest sense of disappointment at the thought. Anger wouldn't come.

That dream Declan had seen me having, the nightmare about my father trying to steal my alpha magic, had filtered back to me in bits and pieces, the memory summoned by Declan referring to a "real alpha." My father had said those words in the dream as he cut my chest open and stuck his hand inside, fishing around for the source of my alpha-ness while I screamed in agony, immobilized somehow by the rules of dream logic.

What kinds of nightmares did my brother have, it occurred to me to wonder? He hated our father. He hated me. I'd done my share to make him hate me, probably. But he was so damn prickly. Teasing I'd meant in a friendly way when we were kids had made him go nuclear. And then I'd kept going with it after a while, only…not in a friendly way anymore.

He hated me for being an alpha.

And I was pretty sure my dad hated me for being an alpha, too.

They'd both despise me for the way I'd been acting with Declan, what I'd let him do to me, what I'd *enjoyed* having him do to me, albeit for totally different reasons. Our father would see it as a betrayal of the family. Brook would sneer at me for not living up to the alpha standard he thought I cared about more than anything, for not being the perfect alpha when he'd always been treated like shit in our family for not being one at all.

But it wasn't really my standard. It was our family's standard. And unlike Brook, I hated the family business. Working there had always been the only other way to be seen as useful.

Fuck. I hated all of it. And I kept seeing my father's grim, furious face as he tried to rip my magic out of my chest with his bare hands. Something about his face from the dream frightened me more than the action he'd been performing, and now that I'd remembered it, I couldn't see anything else.

Declan's footsteps came down the hall.

I hadn't so much as twitched, still sprawled on his bed naked and sticky like a slut and with my hands over my face like a scared kid.

What a horrifying combination.

Something clinked as Declan came nearer, and then his bare hip nudged my side as he sat down on the bed.

Curiosity won over embarrassment. And besides, I couldn't lie there in silence forever. I'd start screaming or something.

So I turned my head a little and peeked through my fingers. Still totally naked—distractingly so, in fact—he'd leaned back against the headboard, one knee up and the other leg stretched out. His muscular nudity held my attention so thoroughly that it took me a second to realize he was holding the plate of cheesecake.

Beefcake with cheesecake, a still life.

I let out a weird little giggle and then snapped my mouth shut, feeling my whole face going red-hot. Declan frowned down at me. "Are you all right?"

Yeah. Because I was acting like I needed the men in white coats, not because he cared.

I thought about it for a second.

"No."

Declan let out a long sigh, and then abruptly held out the plate of cheesecake and a fork. "This ought to help, right?"

I stared at him. Help? He wanted to…*help* me? With cheesecake?

"Why did you get that, anyway? Or the food earlier. The fancy salmon. Are you trying to run up my bill? I don't know if I want to eat it."

Declan's fingers clenched around the edge of the plate.

Dammit. No matter how drained and humiliated I felt, I had to do something about that. If he broke it and got shards of crockery in my cheesecake, I might lose my shit. So I scooted up on the bed—because fuck that new duvet and if Declan didn't want his own come all over it, he shouldn't have put so much of it in my ass—and snatched the plate out of his hands.

His grin as he let go of it didn't have the same edge that it usually did. His eyes softened, and they crinkled around the corners. In a better world, he wouldn't hate me, and I could lean against his chest and use him as an armchair while I ate dessert.

I hunched over and looked away, forking up a bite.

When I'd swallowed, I stared down at the plate. I was ravenous. Did I want the rest? I still couldn't decide.

"I'm not trying to run up your bill. And I shouldn't have said that, you know, a few minutes ago," Declan said quietly. "I should've connected the dots from what I heard earlier when you were talking in your sleep. But I was too focused on—tell me about the nightmare, Blake."

Now my hands were gripping the plate so tightly *I* might break it if I didn't watch out.

"Why are you being nice to me? I fucking hate it." I didn't, actually. But I knew the other shoe would drop, maybe in five minutes, maybe in half an hour. And that would make this little interlude of almost letting my guard down so much infinitely worse.

A long silence fell. My stomach churned, and even the best cheesecake I'd ever had failed to tempt me. So he'd ordered it just for me, because I liked it. And he'd brought it to me in bed. That made it dangerous rather than appealing, like Snow White's poisoned apple. A trap.

I glanced up. Declan had his eyes fixed somewhere off in the distance, maybe the opposite wall. Definitely somewhere that wasn't me. That telltale flush along his cheekbones had made an appearance again, too.

"I reviewed the security footage," he muttered. "After I chewed you out for lying to me. It can't have been Walter," he added, sounding so stubborn it made me want to shake him. "But someone used magic on you. I could tell when it hit you. You went from calm to feral instantly."

He'd seen it. He'd realized I hadn't lied—at least about the magic, anyway, even if he was still too damn stupidly loyal to stupid Walter to admit he had to be the culprit—and he'd left me alone in my room afraid and anxious and...*alone*. And then to come and get me for dinner without leading with that crucial piece of information?

"If that's your version of an apology, it sucks," I said flatly. "You were wrong. About me, about what happened. You assumed the worst even when I told you the truth. And by the way? There was no one else around. A huge empty loading dock, and there was no one."

"They must've disguised their presence with magic," he argued, still not meeting my eyes. "And it's not an apology. I don't have anything to be sorry for. You're a liar, and I treated you like one. The boy who cried wolf? You know that story, Blake?"

Fuck him. And I'd opened my mouth to say so when something else occurred to me. "And your precious Walter didn't notice the presence of another mage either? Is he that incompetent?"

Declan finally looked at me, cheeks even more flushed now, eyes gleaming. "You thought he was bloody competent enough to force you to attack him without leaving a trace. So which is it?"

"You're the one implying he's incompetent, not me! I don't think he is, which is why I know he's the one who put the spell on me. So *you* tell *me* which it is!"

"He was distracted dealing with you, and—"

"Dealing with me how, exactly? When I wasn't doing anything at all except standing there before he put his fucking magic on me!"

We both broke off, panting, both of us having risen to a shout, both of us leaning in until we were inches apart.

Declan stared me down, eyes glowing, and I could feel that mine were doing the same, fangs and claws itching to extend. His big body was rigid with tension, poised for fucking or fighting. But I wouldn't back down. Not now, not when he was in the fucking wrong!

At last he leaned back a little, shook his head, and glanced down, and I nearly toppled over from shock. *Declan* had blinked first? Were we in some kind of alternate dimension?

"Are you going to eat that fucking cheesecake, or do I have to?"

I yanked the plate out of his reach so fast it practically made a whooshing noise.

And Declan…laughed. Not at me. *With* me. He'd laughed at me enough by now that I could tell the difference immediately. My own lips tugged up helplessly, even though I was desperate to keep from smiling or laughing in sympathy with that infectious grin and those sparkling dark eyes. I couldn't give in that easily, could I? Let it go so quickly that he'd left me to think I was a prisoner with no way out?

"I guess I'm not getting any," he said. "I got it for you, anyway. I'm not—don't fuck around with me, Blake. If you order every single entrée on the menu on purpose to be a dick, I'm not going to be happy about it. But that doesn't mean—" He broke off and swallowed hard, his smile slipping away. "You need to learn a lesson," he went on after a moment, voice very low. "But that doesn't mean you don't need to keep your strength up if you're going to be any use to me. Making you my fuck toy's one thing. You deserve it. Starving you's another."

I let that sink in for a moment, looking at what he'd said from every angle before I responded.

And fuck it, if I wasn't going to talk, I might as well eat. I forked up more of the cheesecake while I pondered. Gods, it still tasted so good. Getting my adrenaline flowing with anger had burned off the heavy horror that remembering my dream had brought on, and my appetite had come roaring back.

Declan hadn't meant to say what he'd just said, I'd have sworn to it. He'd had other words on the tip of his tongue. And there was a lot of room between five-star gourmet meals and starvation; he could've had his staff bring me peanut butter and jelly sandwiches three times a day if he wanted to keep me alive without letting me enjoy it.

Maybe he wasn't quite as much of a hard-ass as he'd been leading me to believe, in short.

And I had no idea where that left me. Because the only way I could bear the way he treated me most of the time would be to assume that he was a bastard in general, and that I was in the right on some level.

But if Declan only treated *me* that way, lapsing occasionally into being his real self when I hadn't pissed him off so much, then that maybe meant…

That I deserved it.

I finished the cheesecake, but I didn't taste any more of it. It might as well have been a prisoner's bread and water after all.

"Feeling better?"

Declan's patronizing tone shredded the last of my already frayed nerves.

"Like you care," I snapped, glancing up from my plate to meet his eyes. If I'd been someone else, anyone else, he genuinely would have cared, probably. This...I'd freaked out. He wanted me fit for fucking. Ergo, food and a few minutes of downtime.

He gazed at me steadily, pinning me in place.

"You can explain what just happened," he said. "Or not. But if you choose not to, then you can't expect me to give a damn if it happens again. Next time I'll keep fucking you."

My chest ached as if he'd punched me in the sternum instead of saying precisely what I'd expected him to say: a variation on "No, I don't really care, and I'm only going to humor you so far."

I wanted to tell him. That was the worst of it. I truly wanted to. A faint possibility existed that he'd...take pity on me? And even though imagining it made my skin crawl, at least it'd be better than his hatred.

But I couldn't. If I told him the whole story about my father, about how he'd treated me and Brook, about his shaman and his lies and his pretense all those years, Declan might take his revenge on me a step further: he could make it public. As far as I could tell from glancing at the business news over the last couple of months, Brook had been doing a damn good job as the new CEO of Castelli Industries, now that he'd ousted the old regime. And as much as I resented his success, since I never could've achieved it, and as much as I hated the way he'd tightened up the purse strings and kept all the financial reward of that success away from me...I couldn't risk it.

I'd had a similar thought the other day when Declan blackmailed me. But then, I'd been focused on how humiliated I'd be if everyone in my life knew how low I'd sunk. Now I'd reached a depth of personal humiliation I hadn't thought anyone could plumb. And that made the thought of Brook's sneers, my father's incandescent rage, the board's grim-faced, head-shaking contempt—well, kind of distant and unimportant.

And that dream. I couldn't shake that dream, or the thought

that had come after I'd remembered it: What did Brook wake from, screaming or shaking or lying panting and sweaty in his bed, when he had his own nightmares?

Losing the company, probably. Losing what he'd worked for.

I doubt you've ever worked a day in your life, Castelli. Declan's words. True words. I never had. I'd never had to, and I'd never wanted to.

Brook and Declan wanted to work, and they were good at it, and I'd already ruined Declan's life once by fucking with his livelihood; I'd destroyed his efforts, even though I couldn't remember the details. The thought of doing the same to my own brother, bringing a scandal to light that he'd gone to incredible pains to cover up, even though he must have been aching to see our father suffer the public consequences of his actions…

I couldn't do it.

Brook would never know that I'd done this for him, and honestly I wasn't sure I wanted him to. He'd hate me even more for it, probably, simply on principle: he didn't want anything from me.

"Blake? Earth to Blake?" Declan's sardonic voice brought me out of it, back to Earth. I wished I really had been out somewhere beyond the atmosphere, past the moon, among the stars. A distant place where he couldn't reach me, where the lights of Las Vegas were just another faraway twinkle. Meaningless.

I blinked at him, taking in his frown and his cold dark eyes. No more pity there, only annoyance.

And that was good. I could deal with that.

"I'm not explaining anything," I said evenly. No more snarking and snapping at him. I didn't have it in me. Dealing with the revelation, slowly unfolding inside my stunned brain, that I wasn't actually worth a damn thing to anyone at all in the whole world, would be taking up most of my mental real estate for a while. "It doesn't matter to you. You should go ahead and knot me if you still want to. And I'll lie there and take it, because that's my job. We have an arrangement, right? So let's stick to it."

Declan's expression hardened and his jaw set tight.

"All right. Turn over and put your ass in the air for me, then. Since that's your job."

I had to hand him the cheesecake plate so he could set it on the nightstand first, which felt all kinds of horribly awkward, but then I rolled over, face down and ass in the air, like he'd told me. I didn't have to care, either. About any of it.

Ironically, I now appeared to be working for the first time in my life.

Wouldn't Brook be proud.

Declan fucked me, and I came, and so did he. But he pulled out before he could knot me, said, "We're done for tonight," and got off the bed. He hadn't wanted to be stuck with me for another half hour, then. Did I blame him? Not really.

The bathroom door shut and the shower came on.

I heaved myself up and went down the hall, gathering up my clothing and detouring to the dining table for one of the plates of steak on my way to my own room.

I showered too, and I ate mechanically, and I went to bed.

And I tried very hard not to think about anything at all.

Chapter 12
Win Win

Las Vegas tended to screw with your circadian rhythms. The past few days had been worse than most in that regard—and I'd thought there was no way I could top the time I spent three whole days and nights in the underground portion of one of the casinos with the fake cloud-dotted blue sky, progressively losing my grip on reality until I found myself staring up at the "sky," waiting for sunset. The Morrigan's casino host finally came to retrieve me. Not my finest moment.

But I woke up the morning after "dinner" with Declan, finally, at a relatively normal time: right about dawn, with rosy-gold rays spearing in through my window and the outside world looking like a real place, for once. I could even catch a glimpse of actual desert in the distance.

It made me long, bone-deep, for a convertible, a pair of sunglasses, and nowhere in particular to be.

Unfortunately I only had two out of three, and I doubted Declan would loan me a car.

Stealing a car might not help my current situation.

I still thought about it for a minute.

When I ventured out of my room and glanced down the hall, Declan's bedroom door stood open. He'd already gone out, then; if he'd been in there with the door open, I'd have heard his breathing.

The rest of the suite was empty too. Even the dishes from last night had all been cleared away. I'd always been a heavy sleeper, but even so…had Declan hired a team of fairies for his housekeeping staff?

There was something on the kitchen countertop, though—and my breath caught when I recognized my watch sitting next to a phone and a sheet of paper.

I read the note while I fastened the watch around my wrist.

> *Blake—*
> *This isn't your phone. Obviously. It has my number, Steve Franklin's number, and the line for the hotel concierge in it. Don't call any of us unless you need to. You can leave the suite, but stay in the Morrigan and be back by six. Don't try to gamble on credit and don't cause any trouble. You can charge reasonable amounts of food and drinks to the room anywhere in the casino or hotel. Don't test me on "reasonable."*
> *D.M.*

When I picked up the note, I found a keycard and a hundred dollar bill underneath it, and an examination of the phone showed me a basic smartphone model, out of date but functional. Declan hadn't disabled the internet or anything. I blew out a sigh of relief. Thank fucking gods, something to occupy my time. I could scroll the news and I could hang around downstairs, eating and drinking "reasonable" amounts. And the hundred bucks would keep me busy with penny slots—and I couldn't believe I'd sunk that low, but here we were—for a few hours if I wanted. Compared to sitting in my room going crazy and brooding over Declan and my family and my lack of anything resembling a plan for the future, it felt like overwhelming freedom.

What a difference a few days made.

Don't try to gamble on credit and *Don't test me on "reasonable"* had me shaking my head, though. What did he think I'd do, take over a high-stakes poker table and order every bottle of top-shelf liquor in the joint?

Not that he didn't have a point there. A few days ago, I would have.

I ran my fingers over the face of my watch, now the only really beautiful thing I owned. Why hadn't he sold it to cover my bar tab from when I'd arrived at the Morrigan? Whatever jabs he'd made about its value, it was worth at least ten grand even if he didn't bother trying to get the maximum for it.

The watch. The cheesecake. The…I was trying really hard not to think of the money as a kept man's allowance or a tip you'd leave a hooker. Giving me a measure of freedom, even if only very limited in scope.

Were his occasional gestures of kindness meant to torture me more, to keep me on my toes and unable to predict what his next move would be? Or were they, as I'd speculated last night, glimpses of his actual personality shining through the cracks in his determination to punish me as much as possible? Should I try to use it against him?

Well, for one thing, I was pretty sure it wouldn't work.

And for another…I traced the shiny face of the watch again.

For another, I didn't think I wanted to.

I crumpled up the note and dropped it in the trash, put the money and the keycard in my pocket, and left the suite. I could find a "reasonable" amount of breakfast downstairs and try to get out of my head a little bit.

Because at the moment, my head wasn't a place I wanted to be.

Maybe it never had been.

Ugh.

I let the door slam behind me on the way out.

***

"Anything else, Mr. Castelli?"

I startled and looked up sharply from my phone at the smiling waitress hovering over my table with a pot of coffee in her hand. I'd been miles away.

Decades away, more accurately. I'd found a website run by some insane Las Vegas historian with pages on each casino in the city, and I'd been halfway through a long essay on the Morrigan. Apparently Declan's paternal grandparents had immigrated from Ireland in the forties, with a large sum of money that the writer had no explanation for, and built the Morrigan from the ground up. Mob involvement and skeletons—both figurative and literal—were heavily hinted at. The fact that the damn writer kept talking about construction costs and issues with cement instead of going back to the mafia and the potential murders only had me more on the edge of my seat, albeit frustrated to the point of tearing out my hair.

This was Declan's background? For fuck's sake. And I hadn't even gotten to his parents yet, or to the part that interested me most: how Declan had ended up getting the Morrigan back. It made my family look normal.

"You can keep the coffee coming," I said, and reluctantly put the phone down so I could move my coffee cup into range of the pot.

Behind her, a group of laughing college-age guys passed by the entrance to the diner, which opened onto the casino floor. I watched them go by a little wistfully. For a second, as they moved out of sight, my eyes met those of a nondescript blond guy sitting at a slot machine almost directly across from the diner, one of the taller machines set in a cluster of three or four in a little circle. He instantly turned his back to me and bent over the screen, posture stiff.

Okay. Well, I wasn't his type? The feeling was mutual, buddy. Or maybe he thought I'd caught him ogling the waitress. Or the college guys.

But when the waitress had finished pouring my coffee and wiping up a small spill, departing the table with another smile, something felt…off. I glanced up from my phone without moving my head. The guy had half-turned again, a hand still on the slot machine but his attention clearly focused my way. And this time, there weren't any attractive women or cute college boys in between.

Maybe there was something interesting behind me. I forced myself to go back to the article I'd been reading, managing to make it through to where Declan's parents went bankrupt, as I'd speculated they probably had. I had to scroll back up again when I realized I hadn't given my full attention to anything I'd skimmed. Cocaine? Bad investments? Maybe both. They sounded nearly as awesome as my parents, either way.

Another glance up. The guy was still watching me. Or was he? He'd focused his gaze past my head again, but I truly didn't have anything behind me except for a couple of other people eating pancakes.

The back of my neck tingled and my fingers twitched. He probably hadn't noticed that I'd noticed, but that didn't make it any better

ELIOT GRAYSON

to have someone staring at me. Shit. Who'd be watching me? Had Declan assigned someone to keep tabs on me? But why the fuck would he? The Morrigan had cameras everywhere, plus I was always within eyeshot of an employee simply by the nature of how casinos were staffed. And this guy didn't look like someone you'd hire to watch your fuck toy, either. He had on khaki pants and a quiet plaid button down, like someone who worked in an informal office setting. Clean shaven. Boring shoes.

I took a sip of my coffee and pulled up a text message, entering Declan's contact and then hesitating. His note had made it pretty clear he didn't want to hear from me, but... Okay, so Walter had attacked me. I knew it, even if Declan wouldn't admit it. And now I had someone spying on me.

Two possibilities. One: Walter, and this guy, or possibly this guy on behalf of Walter, had it out for me because of Declan and thought they were helping him. Two: They had it out for Declan, and I was just a target because I was close to him.

Either way, it was Declan's problem, right? Because Declan had made me his problem. And I might be an alpha werewolf and everything, but that didn't mean I wanted to deal with this bullshit on my own.

I sent him a message telling him where I was and about the guy watching me, and I encouraged him to look at the security feed to see for himself. Brief and dry. No emotion, and no mention of Walter. After hitting send, I tried to soothe the queasy feeling in the pit of my stomach with more coffee, instantly regretting it. Too bad the restaurant didn't offer antacids as a side dish.

Reading more about the Morrigan was out, no matter how much I wanted to know what happened between Declan's parents' coke-fueled stock market shenanigans and Declan buying the place back. I simply couldn't focus, and I ended up scrolling random news sites to look busy. Declan didn't message back, the guy kept eyeing me in between poking at the screen on his slot machine, and my coffee got cold.

Fuck this. Part of me took sour pleasure in imagining how bored and annoyed my stalker had to be, sitting there forever while I did nothing but toy with a cup of coffee, but fuck this anyway. He clearly had a lot more patience than I did. I made a mental note: when

Declan eventually let me go, I could cross private investigator off my list of potential money-making possibilities.

I'd already signed the bill, so I got up, stuck my phone in my pocket, and sauntered out of the diner, hopefully looking a lot more casual than I felt. If this douchebag wanted to watch me, I'd at least walk around and make him work for it a bit.

On a—shit, I had no idea, and I had to pull my phone out to check—Tuesday morning, okay, Tuesday, I'd lost track of time completely, the casino wasn't exactly bustling. But the Morrigan attracted a certain type of local regular, people who had scheduled times during the week to go and sit at their favorite machines. I almost could've taken my stalker for one of them, someone who had a standing lunch break date with a cartoon lobster who liked to take his money while yelling cheerful advice, if I hadn't happened to catch him staring. Tourists weren't the Morrigan's bread and butter, unless you counted groups like that bridal party on a budget I'd seen the other night. That older woman there, eyes fixed avidly on a series of little oil wells spurting out gold coins. She kept this place open on a daily basis.

Since I'd charged my breakfast to Declan's suite, I still had that hundred dollars burning a hole in my pocket. Tuesday morning. Not exactly time for the high rollers to be out, and the Morrigan was on the lower-end side to begin with. After leaving the slots, I spent ten minutes cruising around the card tables until I found a likely-looking five-dollar blackjack table. Two other players, acceptable. Observing them for a couple of minutes told me they were playing close enough to correctly not to fuck up my game too badly.

I pulled my phone out of my pocket and opened up the camera, setting it to selfie mode. Not too discreet, but hopefully the guy watching me didn't have supernatural eyesight; I hadn't gotten close enough to scent him properly, and the casino's super ventilation system cleared out smells quickly, but I hadn't had so much as a whiff of anything magical or shifter from his direction. A quick scan behind me, tilting the phone to give me a view past each shoulder, showed me that Mr. Khakis had wandered over to observe a roulette table. That left me in his line of vision. Accident? I didn't think so.

Okay. Fine. I'd bore him by playing blackjack for a while, and maybe Declan would get his head out of his ass long enough to check the security cameras and verify my story.

Or maybe my playing blackjack would irritate Declan enough that he'd look more closely. Win win.

I took my seat at the end of the table, bought my chips and greeted the no-nonsense middle-aged woman dealing, nodded hello to the two guys at the other end, and started to play.

It'd been years—no, scratch that. I'd never played blackjack with a budget, or for such low stakes. And that made this unexpectedly fun and absorbing. Turning a few grand into a few grand more, or into zero, wasn't all that exciting. But playing five dollars at a time, with a limit of twenty hands if I lost them all? That got my blood pumping. It was a challenge.

After a few hands, I'd totally forgotten about my stalker, about Declan, about Walter. About anything except my absorption in the small pile of chips in front of me and in keeping track of the likelihood of the next card being what I needed to make the pile a little larger.

And it got larger. Slowly, bit by bit, with a dip down to thirty-five dollars in chips that had my heart racing way out of proportion to the loss. I mean, this was my fuck-toy spending money. Losing it meant nothing, aside from the fact that a hundred dollars was nothing in general. But when I got up to a hundred again I had to resist the urge to pump my fist in the air and whoop. And when the dealer started a new shoe and whole slew of small cards came out in the first few hands, hardly a high card in sight, I had to suppress a grin of triumph.

Playing that shoe, I more than doubled my money. Two splits and then a double down right at the end had me at two hundred and sixty.

The old me would've put it all on one hand, sucked down the last of my drink, and then gone to find someone to fuck.

But this time…I'd done something that I, Blake Castelli, disdainer of business and a hard day's work, had never done before: turned an honest profit. Well, mostly honest. I'd been counting cards.

That wasn't against the law, so I stuck with honest.

I colored up my chips minus a five for the dealer and stood up, the proud owner of two hundred and fifty-five dollars of my very own.

Sort of. If you didn't count the fact that a hundred of it had been given to me because I'd put my ass in the air.

Fuck it. I *was* going to count that, because I'd damn well earned it. And I refused to be ashamed of it, right now, coasting on the high of having made some money of my own. Fucking gods, was this how Brook felt making multi-million-dollar deals? Did he get a rush from it? I'd always thought he was boring as hell for wanting to spend his time that way, but…maybe he got a thrill out of it, and he wasn't so dull after all.

Maybe we could've had some things in common if our parents hadn't encouraged us to hate each other.

And there went my good mood.

As I left the table, the rest of the casino came back into focus around me with a whoosh of sensory input: the players' laughter and the dealers' brisk calls, the distant dinging of slot machines, the cool, dry air, the tinge of cigarette smoke and cheap booze and sweat.

And the clacking of the roulette wheel, where the guy still stood, a couple of chips in his hand and his eyes darting back and forth between his bet and me.

So, *so* not subtle.

Declan had told me not to leave the casino. Because he wanted to have me under the watchful electronic eyes of his surveillance system at all times, I'd assumed, and so that I wouldn't try to get away from him.

But it struck me to wonder if he wanted me in the Morrigan because he thought I wouldn't be safe outside of it. Now there was a thought, and it made the cold air in the casino feel downright chilly.

At the same time, claustrophobia hit me so hard I nearly doubled over. I felt trapped, confined within these labyrinthine walls and pressed on all sides by noise and people and furniture and *walls*, with some weirdo watching me and creepy Walter around here somewhere and Declan not answering my text. It was like the other night, when I simply couldn't stay in the building for one more minute and had to get out, and no rational thought about Declan's reaction or about the danger I might be in could overcome it. I needed the sky. I needed fresh air, or I might keel over.

A side exit let out on the parking lot forty feet away, and I made a beeline for it, dodging cocktail waitresses and weaving around card tables. I could smell the outdoors even through the pervasive gritty odor of the casino.

One hard shove, and the glass door swung open. I closed my eyes for a second, inhaled deeply...and the scent of Declan MacKenna hit me upside the head.

Oh, shit.

I opened my eyes resignedly. Declan stood leaning casually against a pillar right across from me, hands in his pockets, a not-a-smile curling the corner of his mouth.

Chapter 13

I'm Going to Eat You

Declan opened his mouth, probably to say something snide about how he'd told me to stay in the Morrigan. And then I would've had to argue back that I was on the Morrigan's property, thank you very much, not even all the way out the door, after which he might have reminded me that I'd been attacked on the Morrigan's property already, and then I'd have had to say something about how Walter was a lying little bitch...

Yeah, I didn't want to go there.

So I cut him off with, "If you were watching me enough to know where I was going, why didn't you message back?" Another thought hit me. "And how the hell did you get out here before I did? Do you have a teleporter, for fuck's sake?"

Declan shoved off the pillar with his shoulder, hands still in his pockets, his smile quirking higher. "You can't expect me to give away all my secrets, Blake. Or expect me to get distracted by your bullshit from the fact that I'm pretty sure I gave you a couple of very simple instructions to follow. Do you remember what those were?"

For a second, I saw red. His tone had veered perilously close to "reasoning with a toddler" territory.

"I haven't left the Morrigan," I hissed, taking a step of my own, fists balling at my sides. "And as for your other rules—"

"You were playing blackjack. And you're in the process of leaving the Morrigan. Don't get cute with me."

"You told me not to try to play on credit, and I didn't! I played that hundred you left me, and I won, by the way, so you need to take back what you said about me being shit at counting cards!"

I broke off, breathing hard, as I realized my mistake.

Declan sauntered another step nearer, still with that casual attitude that made me want to punch him right in the smirk. No alpha glow, no sign at all that I'd so much as annoyed him, let alone worried him with the message about the guy watching me or with the possibility that leaving the Morrigan might endanger me.

Even without him trying to be imposing, though, his sheer presence still blocked out everything else: people getting out of a car a few feet away, someone yelling in the parking lot. The smells of exhaust and cigarette smoke and of the sun baking the asphalt, hot and pungent despite the year winding down to late fall.

Declan eclipsed all of it, with his broad shoulders and the weight of his dark gaze, alpha magic and pheromones rolling off of him in waves despite how unmoved he seemed to be.

"So what you're telling me," he said, his voice a low rumble, "is that you took the hundred dollars I left you and used it to cheat. Here, at my casino. And then, once you'd collected your ill-gotten gains—"

"Card-counting is *not* illegal—"

"—you tried to leave!" he went on, raising his voice enough to run right over my protest. "Am I going to find a bottle of Scotch older than I am on your tab next?"

"I wouldn't even appreciate a bottle of fifty-year-old Scotch," I retorted, my voice coming out as sulky and bitchy as the words.

Declan's mouth dropped open, and he stared at me for a full three seconds. "Fifty-year-old—you little—how the fuck old do you think I am? You know what? Don't fucking answer that. Turn left and walk. And keep your goddamn mouth shut on the way."

The little bubbling flare of satisfaction at having needled him for once made me willing to comply, and so I turned left and started to walk.

The flash of his eyes and his looming presence didn't hurt, either. I didn't really think he'd shove me up against a wall and…do something right here in full view of his clientele, but you never knew.

Declan's hand landed on my elbow as he fell into step beside me, muscular fingers gripping not quite tight enough to bruise. Clearly he wasn't taking any chances on whether I might try to bolt.

I wouldn't, though. Not now that I was safe from whoever I

had after me.

My feet stopped moving like someone had flipped my off switch, and I came to a sudden halt, Declan's grip tugging me enough to make me stumble but not start up again. Horrified, I stared straight ahead, unseeing, caught around the throat by the force of that unwelcome realization.

I felt safe.

With Declan.

Because of Declan.

What the fuck had he done to me when he knotted and bit me? We hadn't bonded. That I knew for sure.

But he'd obviously done something to me. Changed me. Fucked me in the head. No way did Declan's presence make me *safe*, from anything—least of all from him, the blackmailing bastard.

And yet all signs pointed to my body and my unconscious mind disagreeing completely. My heart rate had dropped. The incipient panic had cleared away like fog under the sun.

"Blake, you with me?"

Declan's irritable tone snapped me out of my fugue.

"Yeah, I'm coming," I muttered, and forced my legs to start moving again, helped along by his impatient hand on my arm.

Fuck. It felt like walking through pudding, and my head had gone so light I wondered if I needed to tie it down to keep it from floating away.

"Not yet," he said out of the corner of his mouth, pulling me along the side of the building to what I saw was another of those discreet employee side doors. "But you will be in about fifteen minutes."

Shit, shit, fuck. Declan meant to take me upstairs and…I couldn't. Not now. Not after the morning I'd had, and after *this*. If he knotted me and held me in his arms, and gods forbid bit me too, the chances of my saying something stupid and pathetic and unintentional went to at least one-to-two odds, probably better.

Well, mathematically better. Worse in every other possible way.

"I didn't think you were the type for afternoon delight," I said, flailing for an argument that might change his mind. "I mean, don't you have work to do?"

"You're assuming I'm going to be delighted." My teeth

clenched together tightly enough to give me an aching jaw. Fucker. That had to be payback for the Scotch thing. He went on with, "I've already been at work for seven hours. I've worked more today than you have in your entire life. I think I'm owed a lunch break." He tipped his head down toward me and whispered, teeth bared, "I'm going to eat *you*, Blake."

The fuck did that…I couldn't bring myself to ask. I didn't want to know. I'd be finding out anyway. The biting? Was that what he meant? Had to be. Unless he'd added cannibalism to his extensive list of flaws. At this point, it wouldn't shock me too much.

Except that apparently I felt too *safe* with him to worry about it much.

Ugh.

I chose not to answer him, because any reaction would only be giving him what he wanted.

We entered the employee door in mutual silence as Declan swiped a badge he pulled from his pocket, and then he led me along another gray, fluorescent-lit hallway just like the one outside my holding cell or the one where Walter had attacked me.

Declan must have felt my shudder, because his hand tightened on my arm again.

"Service elevator's right around the corner," he said, his tone…kind? Not cutting, anyway, the way he'd been speaking to me a few seconds before.

He couldn't possibly understand how I'd been feeling remembering two of the worst experiences of my life, could he? Especially since he'd been more or less responsible for both of them. And if he'd been trying to comfort me…

Well, I didn't think I could deal with that.

The elevator did turn out to be right around the corner, and the doors opened immediately, for a miracle.

Declan didn't let go of me as we entered, keeping me pressed up against his side, and in the small enclosed space the scents of his magic and his desire nearly overwhelmed me, drowning out even the musty odor of the elevator.

By the time we stepped out into the service hallway of our floor, my head swam and my cock had perked up enough to rub against my zipper. I clenched and unclenched the hand hanging by my side to try to get rid of that sweaty-palmed tingling feeling. It didn't work. Declan's fingers wrapped around my elbow burned through the long sleeve of my shirt and made my skin feel like it vibrated.

I didn't know if I wanted to run away or run straight for Declan's bed. To get it over with, right? I wanted to get it over with so I could send him back to work and get another couple of hours of relative freedom—maybe I'd even make it all the way out the door of the casino this time and manage to take a look at the sky.

Sweat prickled the back of my neck and all down my spine, my palms growing clammier. My face felt horribly flushed.

Declan unlocked the door to the suite and pulled me straight through the doorway and the living area and down the hall toward his bedroom, all without slowing his stride.

"Strip," he said succinctly as we reached his bed, and finally let go of me to start tugging off his own jacket and tie.

The sudden lack of contact, of the heat of him even through that one place on my arm, jolted me enough that I started to obey him without even thinking about it. My buttons went quickly, my fingers seeming to have their own ideas about how much they wanted whatever he planned to dish out. I kicked off my shoes and toed off my socks, dropped my clothes on the floor, letting them pile around me, and then turned to find Declan standing naked to the waist, hands on his belt but not moving.

The look in his eyes as he stared at me was pure molten heat.

He might hate me, but he wanted me. Badly.

My spine and my knees seemed to go liquid all at once. I let myself collapse onto the bed, laying myself out like an offering, arms and legs spread. My cock hadn't quite stood itself up straight—it stuck out at an angle, indicating its interest clearly and looking goofy all at once.

Declan didn't seem to think I looked goofy. His eyes brightened, his alpha glow coming out to play. And for once, not because I'd pissed him off. This was all predatory intent.

I'm going to eat you.

In that moment, cannibalism didn't seem impossible.

And then he finally unzipped his trousers and pushed them down along with his boxer briefs, and I couldn't think about anything else. Declan completely nude took my breath away, all hard muscles and gleaming tattoos and rough hair, and of course the *piece de re-sistance*: that enormous cock, thick and flushed and straining in my direction.

Well, at least he'd be too aroused and ready to go to stop on the way to take bites out of me.

Except that apparently he had more patience than I'd thought, because once he'd stepped out of his clothes he put a knee on the edge of the bed, taking my ankles in his hands and pushing them apart—and then he didn't fucking *do* anything about it.

Instead, he stared down at me, eyes fixed on…not my cock, I didn't think.

Lower.

And another man gazing that avidly at my hole…it made me twitch, the thought of Declan scrutinizing that part of my body so closely.

Not to mention knowing what he had to be thinking as he did.

I knew how it felt to be inside someone. The heat, and the tight-ness, and the slick friction. How being on top of a partner, thrusting inside, fed the alpha part of my nature.

Declan was anticipating doing all of that.

And I was on the other side of it.

"I thought you were on a schedule," I husked through my too-dry throat. "Get this show on the road."

He grinned down at me, showing way too many teeth. *I'm going to eat* you. Fuck.

"That's the opposite of what I said. I told you I've already worked most of a full day, and I'm planning to go back for another before I knock off for the night. Looking for a way out, Blake?" He ran his hands up my legs, letting them settle on my inner thighs, thumbs almost brushing my hole.

"No!" I squeaked, and cleared my throat, feeling all the blood rush to my cheeks. The ones on my face, specifically, though maybe my ass was blushing too. I wouldn't blame it, the way he'd been star-ing at it. "No," I said again, consciously lowering my voice. "I know this is my work day."

The fingers on my thighs tightened bruisingly for a second and then released before I could flinch, almost before I noticed.

"Yeah, it is. And I think I also mentioned this was my lunch break. So spread your legs."

"They're already spread pretty much as far as they can—the fuck, Declan—what are you—fuck!" I threw my head back on a moan of mingled shock, horror, and a thrill I couldn't even find a name for as he ducked his head and buried his face between my legs, his tongue flicking behind my balls.

He ignored me, shoving one leg impossibly wider with one hand and cupping my balls in the other, keeping them out of his way as he—as he—fucking hell, he had his *tongue in me*, pushing past that little ring and delving inside. It felt nothing like a cock or a finger, far too mobile and slick and clever.

But thick enough to stretch me, and long enough to make me feel it.

He didn't have to urge me to spread any more; I did it on my own, kicking out and curling my toes into the bed, arms thrashing until my hands landed in the one place I didn't want them to go: Declan's hair. I wrapped it around my fingers, digging in and pinning his head in place, pushing my body up to meet him. He groaned, and the vibration of it against my sensitive flesh, tunneling into me, made me bite off a whimper and nearly cut through my lip with my teeth.

This was the last thing I wanted. To show him how much I— gods, how much I needed this, the pressure and heat building inside me, my cock so hard it hurt, but I didn't want to touch it, I wanted to touch *him*—

He pulled his tongue out and bit me, not hard, but a nibble along the edge of my slick hole, his fangs down and almost pricking my skin.

My whole body shuddered as I arched up, coming helplessly into the empty air, spattering my own stomach and chest. Heart racing and lungs laboring, I couldn't do more than lie there and quiver once I collapsed.

My hands were still buried in his hair. Could I let go? I needed to let go. My fingers didn't move.

At last Declan took the choice out of my hands, literally, lifting his head and dislodging me. My arms flopped down limp onto the bed.

I dared to peek at him under my eyelashes.

His eyes glowed down at me, as intent as they'd been before

he…ate me.

If this was cannibalism, then sign me up.

I managed not to say that out loud, thankfully. He'd have thought I'd lost my mind.

"I told you what I was going to do," he said. "You didn't know what I meant?"

"No," I whispered, too wrung out to be anything but honest. "It never crossed my mind."

Because Declan, alpha-est alpha in Vegas—not to mention how much he hated me—getting me off with his tongue in my ass?

No, that hadn't occurred to me. Cannibalism had truly seemed a lot likelier.

He grinned again, this time with a gleam of those fangs he'd dropped while he ate me out. And retrospectively, that ought to have terrified me.

It didn't. I just wanted it again.

"Turn over," he said. "I'm taking a long lunch today."

I rolled over onto my stomach, grimacing into the pillow at the mess smeared on my front and now on the bedding, and closed my eyes. He could do all the work of slicking me, and stretching me, and teasing me with his fingers, and fucking his cock in nice and deep, and knotting me until I couldn't take it—

Yeah, okay, my own cock had already gotten fucking hard again.

He could still do all the work.

And he did.

Chapter 14

What's Worse?

Declan's knot hadn't gone down at all by the time I blinked my eyes open and slowly came back to reality, lying on my side with Declan wrapped around me from behind. The bite he'd left on my neck throbbed in time with my heartbeat. I could feel his, too, syncing with mine and vibrating through my back.

And I felt safe again, which made me want to throw up and then run away screaming.

Well, he'd already made me scream. Running away was out. And it'd suck to throw up all over the bed and be stuck here.

Unfortunately, that left me with nothing to do but lie there enclosed in his arms listening to his steady breaths in my ear, savoring the heat of his body and the softness of the bed.

Ugh. *Savoring.* I really was, and it made me swallow hard against a wave of real nausea.

But it suddenly occurred to me that maybe Declan felt something similar. Pheromones. Hormones. Borderline mating-magic. I couldn't be the only one completely at their mercy, could I? He might not feel them as strongly. That didn't mean he wasn't mellower than usual—although he hadn't always been so mellow immediately after sex.

Still.

This might be my only opportunity to talk to him without getting my head bitten off, either literally or figuratively.

I cleared my throat and stirred a bit, and Declan's arm tightened around my waist. "So did you look at the security cameras earlier?" I asked, going for casual, even though my interest was anything but.

"Someone seriously was following me in the casino."

"I looked," he said after a moment. "I saw a guy checking you out. Lucky for both of you that you weren't interested, or there might've been trouble."

Checking me out? He so hadn't been! That had been...well, I guess it could've been stalking of the sexual-interest variety, not the dangerous variety. Could it have? Declan had me doubting myself, and I fucking hated it. I knew that guy had been following me. And he hadn't seemed like someone wanting to fuck.

Wait a second, though. Trouble? My heartbeat stuttered, and I really hoped Declan either didn't notice or put it down to irritation at his dismissive attitude.

The devil on my shoulder prompted me irresistibly. "You never said anything about being exclusive. Maybe I should've taken him up on—Declan, ow, the fuck!"

His fangs sinking into the still-raw not-a-mating-bite on my neck hurt like *hell*, it turned out.

"That hurts like hell! And where do you get off—"

A hard thrust, shoving his knot even deeper into my over-stretched body, had me breaking off in a ragged cry.

"This is where I get off," he growled in my ear. "Inside you. And no one else does that, ever." A pause, and I felt his heart give a quick one-two stumble this time. "Until I get tired of you and throw you out on your ass, and then it's fair game. But you're mine until I say otherwise."

Don't say it, don't say it...my mouth had other ideas. "So no one else gets to fuck me, but maybe he wanted me to fuck him. I'm an alpha, that's usually what people want from me. Is that on the table?"

He'd gone so rigid behind me that he could've been carved out of rock. Well, so much for talking to him while he was all fucked-out and mellow.

"What do you think is going to happen here, Blake? Best-case scenario. If you push me."

That was a damn good question, actually. I blinked at the wall across from me. It stayed stubbornly white, no answers magically appearing there. His arm around my waist could've crushed me, and it almost felt like it was about to. His fangs hadn't gone anywhere. My throat might heal quickly, but maybe not quickly enough if he tore it out completely.

The real answer, the one I didn't need any oracular walls to tell me, hovered tauntingly in the back of my mind. My eyes stung.

I want you to . . .

No, I couldn't even think it. I couldn't let myself. No one in the world gave a fuck about me, and Declan would be the last person I could think of who'd step up to start. He didn't care if I fucked someone else. He didn't care about *me*. He only wanted to control me. An alpha bent on revenge wouldn't have it any other way. Total dominance, until he'd crushed me down so small I couldn't fight back any more.

"Well?" Declan prompted, tone tinged with impatience. "The fuck do you think is going to happen if you piss me off?"

"I don't know," I said through numb lips. "Nothing. Forget it. I'll follow your rules."

The silence following that lame bit of bullshit had a baffled quality that almost made me smile. At least I could confuse him. That was something, right? Something adjacent to interest in what I had to say? I squeezed my eyes shut, hating myself with more intensity than usual.

"Yeah, you will." He cleared his throat. "You weren't interested in that asshole anyway, though. He's not your type."

Irritation twinged through me. Declan thought he knew what my type was? Fucking arrogant bastard! I bit my lip to try to keep in a snarl of annoyance, but it slipped through my teeth. "Not like it's up to you to tell me what my type is, but someone who wears pleated khakis wouldn't be anyone's type, or shouldn't be," I growled. "And blackmailing, neck-biting assholes like you aren't my type either!"

I tried to jerk away from him, at least from the waist up, to get a little distance before I fucking *exploded* and did something suicidal like reach back and whack him upside the head—and he moved his arm up around my chest, clamping me to him so firmly it knocked the wind out of me. His mouth closed around the muscle stretching from my neck to my shoulder.

And then Declan started to shake, his teeth vibrating against my skin and shudders going through his whole big body.

I froze, gasping for air, eyes wide with horror. Gods, was he having a seizure or something? Losing his grip on reality? Had Walter magicked him somehow too, and now he was going to flip out and rip me limb from limb? And yes, I'd take a couple of his limbs with me, but that didn't make the prospect any less terrifying.

He let out a weird, strangled sound around his half-mouthful of my shoulder. And suddenly it clicked.

Laughing. The bastard was *laughing*. At *me*. And trying to muffle it in my own skin!

"Fuck you! Fuck—fuck you for—I hate you so fucking much, Declan!"

He pulled his face away from my shoulder and laughed out loud, a low, rich rumble that shook me in a different way.

"Oh, fucking Jesus Christ," he wheezed after a long minute of me lying there with my face burning and my body stiff as a board in his grasp. "Shit. Blake. What's worse?" And then he was off again, cackling like a fucking madman. "The pleated khakis," he gasped at last. "Or the blackmail?"

Well, when he put it that way…okay, fine, what an asshole, but…I closed my eyes firmly, taking deep, even breaths. I wasn't going to laugh. I wasn't. No matter how infectious those low chuckles were, especially transmitted through his chest directly into me.

Especially not when I'd suddenly imagined Declan in pleated khakis looking like an admittedly really hot douchebag.

A spasm hit me. I choked and forced myself to cough to cover it, and that squeezed my muscles around his knot, and then his laughter broke off in a groan.

"Fuck," he said right in my ear, his hot tongue tracing the edge of it. "I don't think I'm getting soft anytime soon. But I'm not fucking you again until you answer the question." His voice took on extra resonance as he asked again, "What's worse?"

I wanted, desperately, to say the obvious: the blackmail, of course. Who wouldn't? But gun to my head…and I couldn't choke out the lie, not with that alpha command ringing in my ears and in my brain and in the empty space inside of me where a connection to another person ought to have been, wanted to be.

The blackmail. I formed the words with my mouth. No sound came out.

Declan shifted his arm, stroking his hand up and petting my

chest, running a finger around one of my nipples. It perked up almost painfully, and he scraped another circle with the tip of his nail on my areola. My cock stirred in answer. His hips moved slightly, just enough to punch a quick exhale out of me.

"Not answering's practically an answer," he said. "Unless you're being stubborn, not wanting to do what I tell you on principle. But I would've thought you'd learned better than that by now."

I had to deflect somehow. Dodge the question. Make him forget he'd asked it.

I clenched down hard around his knot, which really hadn't gotten any smaller. It didn't feel like an invasion anymore. It felt like it belonged there, a part of me, wedging me open and keeping me vulnerable in a way I couldn't even hate.

And fucking helplessly, hopelessly aroused, too. I couldn't forget that for so much as a second. Particularly not with that hand moving across my chest, tweaking the other nipple, plucking and twisting and making me writhe against him. My breath came faster, chest rising and falling. More rising than falling, pushing my nipple into his hand.

"I wasn't interested in him," I managed to choke out, "because he wasn't hitting on me. He was stalking me. Something you don't seem to be willing to admit." Because that might mean he'd need to take what had happened behind the casino more seriously? And the fuck, why hadn't he followed up on that? I'd started to feel like Declan meant to gaslight me; was I the crazy one? Declan seemed intent on making me think so. "I was attacked the other night. I was followed today. And you're blowing it off and distracting me arguing about whether or not I wanted to fuck this guy."

"Who's arguing?" Declan thrust lightly, swiveling his hips, his knot putting almost agonizing pressure on that sweet spot inside me and all my other overstimulated nerves. "What's worse, Blake?"

Gods triple dammit, I was the one who was supposed to be deflecting! "I'll answer you if you answer me. Oh, fuck, please don't—" He tugged my nipple hard, and I thrashed back into his chest only to be instantly pinned there as he let go with one final pinch and flattened his arm across my chest, hand wrapped loosely around my throat.

I subsided into gasping whimpers.

"Okay, I'll humor you," he said. "Maybe you were being followed. Maybe he didn't want to fuck you, and he had some other nefarious intent. You were attacked the other night, I'll grant you that. But this is Vegas. There are all kinds of crazies here. You can't assume anything at all. And I think you're getting paranoid."

Paranoid. Right. Which did not, thank you very much, mean that they weren't after me.

Definite gaslighting. What did Declan have to hide? A lot, probably, starting with his past and ending with the present. And it didn't look like I'd be getting any more out of him. Either he didn't care that someone was after me, or he truly didn't believe it. Either way, I'd never felt smaller and more insignificant—a real achievement, considering how my family had treated me my entire life. Brook always thought that getting praised for being an alpha had made me arrogant. It hadn't; my arrogance, such as it was, came from within. It'd done nothing but underline how inadequate I was to be called an alpha at all.

Just like Declan was underlining it now, with added italics.

"Your turn," he went on. "Answer me." His voice held a quaver of laughter and the depth of an alpha's command all at once, a combination that shouldn't have had me melting in his grasp and helplessly pushing my ass back onto his knot.

My head spun. "The pleated khakis," I muttered. "You absolute dick."

He let out the laugh he'd clearly been suppressing. "I knew it." He took my earlobe between his teeth and nibbled, rolling his hips again. His cock had gone so deep in me I didn't know if I had any internal organs left. The pressure throbbed through my whole torso. "You're unbelievable, you know that? Such a fucking snob, Blake. Nothing's good enough for you." Another thrust, this one so hard I yelped. Yeah, there went my lungs. I resisted the urge to look down and make sure I couldn't see the outline of him imprinted through my skin. "Except my knot. That's good enough for you, isn't it? That's exactly what you deserve."

Maybe it was exactly what I deserved. The hand on my throat tightened, cutting off enough air that I had to struggle to get a full breath.

Yeah, I deserved this. The blackmail. The knot. The vice-grip around my neck and the way I felt sickeningly safe in spite of it and the way he'd made me admit how shallow and pathetic I was. But I didn't deserve to be stalked and attacked and intimidated…by anyone but Declan. He ought to believe me. He ought to protect me—from everyone but him.

The sound of my own voice brought me up short.

I'd said some of that out loud.

I'd said some of that out loud. And Declan had stopped moving, frozen in place with his cock somewhere under my sternum, it felt like, and his hand locked around my throat.

Only my hoarse gasps interrupted the silence.

"You want me to protect you?" He sounded like I'd smacked him across the face after all.

"No, of course not, fuck. I don't know what you thought you heard." Fuck, fuck, I was panicking, and I sounded too high and too thin. "I don't want anything from you!"

Declan rolled us over so suddenly I was crushed into the mattress without any hope of catching myself, his full weight pinning me down.

"Good," he said roughly. "Because I didn't sign up for taking care of you."

Anything I might've answered got lost in a moan as he started to fuck me again, hard and deep, knot tugging painfully on the rim of my hole and then reaming me open again.

I probably came again while he fucked me, but it didn't even seem to matter. My body clenched around him again and again, every wave of pleasure-pain almost like an orgasm on its own.

By the time he finished, filling me with another burst of come, I could hardly breathe, hardly think, hardly open my eyes, hardly feel my extremities.

Declan held very still, his body rigid with tension.

His knot shrank down at least halfway, enough that when he tugged his cock out of me, it only made me wince rather than scream.

"You can control your knot?" I slurred into the bed. Damn him. Most alphas could only prevent themselves from knotting in the first place, not make it go down at will. He totally could. That explained his casual avoidance of my questions about it before. "You bastard."

That came out without much heat, since I didn't have a lot of heat—or any other kind of energy—left in me.

"Yeah," he admitted. And then, to my shock, he added, "I didn't think you'd want to be tied together again until it went down on its own."

He was right. I wouldn't have. In large part because of how much I did want to be, only without the hostility. I'd have given my right arm to be able to trade that sense of safety that made me hate myself, and him, for the emptiness that was swamping me with every passing moment.

Only I wanted it to be real.

Fuck. I wanted it to be real.

Stockholm Syndrome, or something adjacent? Probably. But that didn't make the hopeless clench of longing any easier.

As Declan left the bed and headed for the shower, the sounds of rustling clothes and the tap switching on telling me what he was doing, I buried my face in the bedding and breathed deeply, the mingled scents of Declan's body and mine, of sex and bitterness, making my head light and spinny. And I made myself a promise: I'd stop throwing myself at the brick wall and expecting it not to hurt.

No more pushing. No more questions. No more doing what I hadn't even consciously realized I had been doing until that moment: trying to get Declan to pay attention to me as a person, desperately hoping that he'd change his mind and see me as more than the spoiled rich kid who'd insulted him and then gotten him fired all those years ago.

Maybe that was all I was, and I didn't have anything else to offer. Or maybe I was worth something more than what he, and everyone else who'd ever looked at me, had seen when they did.

It didn't matter either way. I was his fuck toy, and possessiveness—natural in an alpha with a lover, even a blackmailed one he despised—couldn't be mistaken for anything more. He'd get tired of me, and that would be that. Walter might have it out for me, or he might not. Someone else might be stalking me...or not.

But I had to let it all go, or I'd drive myself as nuts as Declan seemed to believe I already was.

Fuck it. Fuck it all.

Chapter 15

Try Me

Letting it all go seemed easy at first.

I'd spent so many years showing—and allowing myself to feel—only the most surface of emotions: anger, entitlement, arrogance. Under the circumstances, I chose to temporarily trade those in for indifference, apathy, and resignation, but it was just as fake and just as likely to keep people from looking any deeper.

My family hadn't looked any deeper. Neither had Declan. Clearly, no one wanted to.

And it worked. When I didn't try to fight back, didn't bother arguing or demanding answers, Declan didn't go out of his way to humiliate or torment me aside from the rough, careless way he used me. He texted me at some point during the day to let me know when he wanted me available to be fucked, I awaited him obediently, and he fucked me. Sometimes he put me on my knees instead, or in addition to. I opened my mouth or spread my legs, and I moaned and cried out when he made me come, but I didn't talk more than I absolutely had to.

I took the hundred a day he left me on the kitchen counter, and sometimes I played it at the tables and sometimes I didn't. I very studiously didn't pay any attention to who might be paying attention to me, even though I was certain I could feel eyes on the back of my neck.

Sleep came with a side dish of unpleasant dreams, but I spent a lot of time sleeping anyway, simply because at least I didn't have to try not to think.

Because every time I let my brain turn itself on and start

functioning, I ached with the desire to go find Declan, grab him by the collar, slam him into a wall, and shout in his face. To tell him what that dream he'd noticed had really been about. To spill all my family's secrets in the hope that maybe he'd…pity me enough to do more than hate me.

Which he wouldn't. I'd already figured that out, and thinking more about it was only torturing myself. I knew he'd use what I gave him to expose my family, ruin Brook's attempts to keep the company profitable, and laugh at me as I begged him not to.

Yeah, no. So I slept a lot and numbed myself with cheap vodka and blackjack during the day.

That history-of-Vegas web page that might've held some of the story of the last ten years of Declan's life stayed open in the background of my phone's browser, but I didn't even bother reading the rest of it.

I couldn't care. If I did, I couldn't function.

Three weeks went by like that, with nothing interrupting the monotony of getting fucked, hanging out in the casino, and sleeping.

Not that getting fucked was monotonous. I craved it every second I wasn't getting it at this point, although I tried to convince myself it was only because everything else in my life had been so boring lately.

And eventually, inevitably, boredom won out over my determination to keep my distance and give Declan nothing at all that he didn't take.

It hit me like a slap to the face one afternoon as I sat at a blackjack table, slowly winning, my daily hundred now a hundred and forty. Forty dollars. Forty dollars minus tips for drinks, five vodka tonics, a cigarette I'd bummed from a fellow player, and the dinging and whistling of the slot machines in the next room echoing in my ears—a real downside of supernatural senses, because I couldn't escape the noise no matter where I went in the casino.

That was all I had to show for a whole day. Tinnitus, and a mild buzz that my werewolf metabolism would clear out within the hour.

I mean, I'd never accomplished much during the course of a day. I'd certainly never earned any money before, not even forty bucks, before I started playing to win with my tiny daily allowance.

But seriously. Fuck this. Indifference and apathy and a

determination to show Declan he couldn't get a reaction could only take you so far before you snapped. I colored up, tipped the dealer generously, and left the table, wandering without a purpose. Like I did everything these days.

Gods, I was so. Fucking. Bored.

And I missed Declan, like an itch under my skin.

Bored. I was bored, and that was all.

A group of retirees settled in at a blackjack table nearby, laughing and chattering. They weren't bored. The dealers and the cocktail waitresses and the security staff and the pit bosses, they all had something to do. They were busy. *They* weren't bored.

But I had nothing in the world to do but wait to get fucked.

Impatiently, if I was being honest.

Then again, patience had never been my strong suit. Instant gratification fit me much better.

On impulse, I flagged down a passing waitress who didn't have any drinks on her tray and didn't look particularly harried, and she stopped, offering me a genuine smile. That was new in the last two weeks. I'd been spending so much time down here tipping well and being otherwise unobtrusive that the staff had started to warm up to me. And with the way any community of people, including a casino, tended to gossip like wildfire, everyone knew by now that I was Declan's…I couldn't come up with a word for it that didn't make me feel like shit. That I was Declan's, full stop. They knew even if they hadn't interacted with me personally yet.

Though they hadn't really treated me any differently, no fear or extra care in the way they handled me. A reflection on the way I'd been behaving, or on the company culture Declan had instituted here? I wasn't sure.

"Do you know where Dec—Mr. MacKenna has his office?" I asked, with a smile of my own that I knew from experience generally got people to do what I wanted. "He wanted me to drop by, but I guess he expected me to know where to go."

Total lie, but if Declan got mad that I showed up without being invited, I'd take the hit. I hadn't yet seen him be anything but fair and kind to the staff. She wouldn't get in trouble if I made it clear to him I'd lied to her.

I'd expected her to demur, since handing out the location of the casino owner had to be a no-no, but instead, her smile only widened.

"Go through that door on the other side of the cashier, turn left to get to the service elevator…" I nodded my way through the directions, memorizing them as she went. "And have a great afternoon, Mr. Castelli," she said warmly, and headed over to the retirees.

I blinked after her.

She liked me. She actually *liked* me. That had been friendly, not fake-customer-service-friendly, and not even you're-fucking-my-boss friendly.

What the hell? No one had ever treated me like that in the Morrigan on my many visits before, no matter how much money I'd lost or how many expensive bottles I'd overpaid for. They'd bent over backward to give me whatever I wanted, including a fuck sometimes, but they'd never been…nice.

Maybe it really did come down to the way I'd been acting and not my connection to Declan. The first week or so of being here, before everyone knew Declan owned me, I'd been just another faceless gambler. No one special. Not a human being, an individual.

I'd hated being treated like that.

And some of those long nights when I'd already slept as much as my body could stand, I'd thought about how I'd always done the same to them. Anyway, I'd tried to be nicer when I came downstairs.

Gods. They'd noticed. Had I been that much of an asshole my whole life?

When the security guard at the door the waitress had sent me to nodded, smiled, and opened it for me without my even having to ask, I started to wonder if I'd somehow entered the Twilight Zone—or if I really, truly had been that much of an asshole my whole life.

Fuck.

No one stopped me on my way down the long, gloomy hallway or getting on or off the elevator. It dinged and let me out on the nineteenth floor.

It was a totally different world up here. Plush carpeting, walls painted a pleasant pale blue instead of that horrendous institutional gray, and nice wooden doors opening into people's offices. I headed down the hall, glancing out of the corners of my eyes as I did. Yep, normal offices, with desks and computers and people in business casual doing office-y things. Spreadsheets, maybe? Or email? Search me, really. They seemed busy and cheerful enough, though I couldn't imagine how. Working in an office like that had always been my worst nightmare.

The offices got bigger and nicer as I went along. I followed my nose. I could scent Declan on the air, very faintly, a pleasant whiff like a trace of woodsmoke on a winter night. Finally I reached the end of the hall and what would probably be one of the corners—it had way more than four—of the sprawling building, on the southeast side.

Yep, definitely the corner. The huge office had a desk for a secretary outside it, although it didn't have anyone sitting at it right then, and through the big interior window I could see through the office to its exterior windows: a view of the Strip on one side and the expanse of off-strip Vegas on the other.

My breath caught as I moved around the secretary's desk and took a step inside the doorway. Definitely Declan's office, because the mouthwatering scent of him had gotten richer and deeper, as if it'd permeated every piece of furniture. Even though offices in general made me twitchy—especially executive offices, where I'd been conditioned to expect various angry relatives belittling me—this one felt like home.

I closed my eyes and breathed deeply, letting my negativity melt away. So I'd wanted to avoid making myself more vulnerable to Declan than I'd already become, which meant avoiding him whenever I could. Whatever. The itchy, irritating tension I'd felt while wasting my time on the casino floor had gone, and the relief nearly overwhelmed me.

His scent grew stronger, and I felt that prickle of awareness I always had on my skin when he was near.

So it didn't startle me when his voice came from behind me. "What are you doing here?"

"I was bored." I opened my eyes and turned around to find him standing less than two feet away, close enough that his height advantage made me tilt my head up.

He raised an eyebrow at me, hands on his hips, appearing more bemused than annoyed. He'd shed his suit jacket and tie at some point and rolled up his shirt sleeves, and yet somehow he still managed to look like the boss and not like a slacker.

"Blow through your hundred bucks already?"

He brushed past me on the way to his desk, not pausing for so much as a touch. I turned to follow him, carefully wiping my expression blank to hide my disappointment. What had I been expecting, a kiss hello? He'd never kissed me. Not once. And I wasn't his mate. I didn't want him to kiss me, anyway.

He could've groped me or something, though, right? For fuck's sake. He could at least do me the courtesy of treating me like his whore, not an unwelcome copier toner salesman.

Declan dropped into his desk chair with a sigh, gaze immediately snagging on the screen of his open laptop. He clicked away for a minute, typed something, clicked something else, while I stood there disregarded and awkward. Right, because he either couldn't or didn't want to fuck me at the moment, and he didn't have any other reason to pay attention to me.

At long last he looked back up again. "You know, my grandmother used to tell me that you couldn't be bored unless you were boring. And then if I kept making a nuisance of myself, she'd give me something to do. I already gave you money so you'd have something to do." Translation: so I'd be safely out of his way. I swallowed hard, cold disappointment curdling in my gut. What else had I expected, though? This was exactly why I'd told myself I'd stop throwing myself at the brick wall that was Declan. Because it always hurt. "Do you need me to give you something else to do? Because frankly, I'm too busy to entertain you."

"I didn't come up here to be entertained." A lie, but maybe he wouldn't notice. Besides, "entertained" wasn't quite the right word. Soothed? Shit. Maybe I should admit to wanting him to entertain me. I hurried to add, "And no, I've been making money every day, actually."

Declan leaned back in his chair and grinned at me, eyes faintly sheened with gold. Genuine humor or a threat? Why not both?

"So what you're telling me is that you ripped me off for a suite, a line of credit, and an endless supply of expensive liquor. You're supposed to be paying off that debt by staying here. And instead, *I'm* paying *you* to take even more money from my establishment. Even after I told you how I felt about card-counting, particularly when done by you."

For the love of…*fuck* him. I lifted my chin and stared down my nose at him. "For one thing, you didn't believe me when I said I could count cards. That's your problem. And for two, a hundred dollars a day wouldn't get you photos of my feet on the open market, much less access to my ass. For what you've been doing to me, I'm probably already ahead. Even with the line of credit."

Declan looked at me wide-eyed for a moment, shook his head, and finally burst out laughing. "You know, I actually missed you bitching at me the past few weeks?" he said after he'd subsided—and then stopped abruptly, frozen, his mouth open a little.

As if he'd startled himself with the words that had come out of his mouth.

"I—I don't bitch," I stammered, too startled myself to come up with a better reply.

He scoffed. Actually scoffed. I wondered if he'd learned that from his grandmother, too. "Yes, you do. You bitch, and you whine, and you complain, and explain to me why nothing around you is good enough. But you stopped. About three weeks ago. Care to tell me why? Finally get a little humility, Blake?"

My turn to scoff. "If I did, it wouldn't come out like that. I know what I'm worth." The only thing was, I'd started to come to the uncomfortable realization that other people were worth something, too.

His eyes narrowed. "Then how would it come out?"

I fidgeted and strolled over toward the window, focusing on a golf course off in the distance to give me a reason not to look at him. "It wouldn't."

His chair creaked, and I could feel him coming up behind me by the hair standing up on the back of my neck.

"I think it has," he said softly. "I've been watching you."

My fists clenched at my sides. *Don't turn around, don't turn…*but he could probably see my expression reflected in the window, anyway, with his sharp werewolf vision. I could see his. His eyes, anyway, so bright.

"Watching me. To make sure I didn't try to rob you? Or attack anyone?"

A brief pause. "Of course." That sounded like a lie to me. "But I've seen enough to know you've been making yourself popular with the staff. Tipping well. Being friendly and patient when service is slow. I've heard about you, too. Good things."

His tone suggested that took effort for him to admit.

"I told you I'd follow your rules. And I wouldn't cause trouble."

"I know." He stepped closer. "But I didn't believe you. Are you actually bored? I thought all you wanted out of life was a drink and a fuck and entertainment. I fuck you every night, at least once. You could keep yourself drunk twenty-four seven without stepping over my limits on your spending. And you have a whole casino to mess around in."

True, true, and true, but…I could've made some retort about how I usually had more money to spend, or how no one was catering specifically to my every whim, or how I didn't want to *be* fucked, I wanted *a fuck*, and those were two different things. A couple of weeks ago, that would've been mostly true, and a couple of months before that, it would've been entirely true.

But not today. The real truth was, I'd never stayed in one place being entertained for long enough to get sick of it. I'd jetted off to Greece, or Hawaii, or Aspen, or the Morrigan, or wherever I could find pleasure for a week or two, and then repeated the process endlessly. I'd never had time to be bored, even though objectively, now that I'd sat with it…it was boring.

Maybe the people who worked in those little offices down the hall, sending their emails and then going home to microwave some dinner, would've given their right arms to be bored like that. Voicing any of my thought process aloud would've made me sound like such a douchebag.

But I kept coming back to thinking about Brook. He had the same privileged life I did, but he spent his time productively.

You could be rich but not useless.

I'd been both.

Now I was poor and useless. And that was incredibly dull.

So I didn't have a retort to make, unfortunately, and the silence lengthened around us.

Declan sighed deeply, as if the contemplation of my boredom and uselessness left him feeling equally bored.

"Okay, fine. You're not boring, so I'll skip that step." He didn't think I was boring? Be still my beating heart. "You want me to give you something to do? I will. But you won't like it."

I turned around at last and met his eyes. No alpha could resist a challenge, and I was alpha enough in that respect.

"Try me."

He raised his eyebrows. "Fine. Sit on the couch there, in front of the coffee table. I'd let you work at my assistant's desk, but she's particular about her stuff and she'll be back from vacation tomorrow anyway."

Work…at a desk? Or a coffee table, anyway? He wanted me to *work*? Well, what had I been expecting?

I sat down as bidden and watched as he opened a cupboard across the room and pulled out another laptop, twin to the one on his desk, and then dropped into the chair opposite me. He booted it up and typed something in, maybe a password, before he clicked a few times and spun it to face me.

The screen held a spreadsheet, some of the little boxes containing words and numbers and some of them empty. I mean, I'd never looked at one up-close before, but I'd seen them in the background on other people's computers. That had to be a spreadsheet, right?

I looked up at Declan, and my total bafflement must have shown on my face, because he shook his head and chuckled. "I told you you wouldn't like it."

"It's not that I don't like it." I didn't like it, but I couldn't admit defeat two seconds into his test, could I? Because this had to be a test. He'd throw this bullshit at me, wait for me to cry uncle, and then pack me off back to the casino to play low-stakes blackjack until he wanted me for the one thing I was actually good for, getting him off. "But what do I do with it?" I asked, more plaintively than I'd hoped to sound.

"It's a list of independent casinos, some on Native American reservations, some in Vegas, some in Reno, and so on. They're color-coded." I looked again, and shit, they were color-coded. At least, some of the boxes were different shades of blue and green and pink. That had to be what he meant. "There are customer demographics, numbers of slot machines per casino, numbers of different types of play tables…" He went on for a while, explaining what all the different columns were for and then directing me to a different tab with more categories and more numbers until my head started to ache. It probably only took five minutes or less.

It felt like five years.

"...So you're going to want to go online and look them up, make notes about how they're positioning themselves in the market, what they're emphasizing and what they're using as their main selling points. Compare that to the data and see what patterns emerge. Understand?"

Kind of. Sort of. Not really. I nodded at him.

Declan shot me a skeptical look. "Do you?"

What I truly didn't understand was why he'd give this to me, when I obviously didn't understand and would fuck it up immediately. I'd probably click on something and delete the whole thing.

I nodded again.

"Okay." That sounded equally skeptical. "Don't worry," he added dismissively, throwing it over his shoulder as he got up and went back to his desk. "This is only a copy, so no harm done if you fuck it up. The marketing department's working on it too. Maybe you'll come up with something they haven't thought of."

In other words, busywork. That no one would ever look at or use. And he couldn't have been clearer that he didn't think I'd come up with something his trained, skilled, trusted marketing people hadn't.

Well, okay then.

My eyes stinging, and the spreadsheet's ugly color-coding blurring a little in front of them, I turned back to the laptop and opened up an internet browser.

Chapter 16

Kind of Endearing

I woke up the next day just after eight o'clock, early by my previous standards but late by the standards of the company I kept these days. The cold coffee pot, holding only a few teaspoons of dregs, told me that Declan had been up and gone for hours. The usual hundred dollar bill sat beside it.

That felt a little bit like I'd been slapped. I'd sat there and worked on that stupid spreadsheet for three full hours the day before without even getting up for a glass of water. I'd only stopped when Declan stood, put on his jacket, and told me it was quitting time.

But apparently he assumed I'd be right back to blackjack and vodka today.

Well, fuck him.

I made a fresh pot of coffee, ordered some room service—an omelet, because I knew if I had any carbs at all I'd fall asleep with my face in the keyboard—and dressed in the closest thing I had to what the other people I'd seen in the offices had been wearing, black slacks and a blue button-down. I couldn't wear a suit. All of mine were designed to look natural on the deck of a yacht or at a wedding, not behind a desk.

And then I found my way to the offices, all the way downstairs, across the casino, into the back, and then up again.

Declan's assistant had returned, a nice-looking middle-aged lady who reminded me of a nanny Brook and I used to have when we were little kids. She waved me through, and Declan just stared at me for a second, sighed, and got the laptop I'd been using back out of the cupboard again without a word. Not so much as a *good morning*, the asshole.

Although he did look tired and busy, not too surprising since he'd been fucking me late into the night and then up at the crack of dawn.

And this time he bothered to give me my own login and password. Maybe that was progress?

I sat down equally silently and started to work. But the laser focus I'd achieved the day before eluded me this morning. Partly it was the sunshine pouring in through the windows, casting glare on my screen and reminding me that there was a world out there where people were living their lives blissfully spreadsheet-free.

But also, Declan kept getting phone calls, or maybe making phone calls, but either way he kept on talking to people. And while the words themselves were boring as hell, the sound of his voice…did things to me.

Even when he said, "I need those numbers by tomorrow morning," or "Call Steve, I think he already talked to Amy about that," his deep voice sent a little shiver down my spine, lodging in my still very faintly aching ass.

Gods, I shouldn't love that ache. I shouldn't crave being fucked again as soon as it faded, which it did quickly thanks to my body's supernatural healing. I was an alpha. And maybe that felt less and less important with each passing day away from my father's hypocritical lectures. But all of my family's fucked-up-ness aside, alphas usually didn't like getting fucked. We just weren't wired that way.

Well, apparently *I* was. His knot had been so thick inside me last night, opening me up and filling me until I couldn't move or speak actual words or do more than make sounds that seemed to drive Declan even wilder…

"Blake!" I startled and looked up to find Declan standing by the coffee table and frowning down at me. By his impatient tone, he'd already tried to attract my attention at least once. Had I really missed the actual, live, present-moment Declan standing next to me because I'd been so lost in daydreaming about last night's Declan pounding me into jelly?

Gods. I needed help.

"What the hell were you so focused on?" he demanded. "You weren't doing anything."

I could feel my face heat up like a furnace.

"Nothing. Just thinking about it. The spreadsheet. Thinking really hard."

"Right," he said, drawing the word out into several disbelieving syllables. "It's lunch time." His eyes took on a special gleam that I'd come to know intimately, and my heart sped up in anticipation. "We're going back to the suite for...lunch. Save that and let's go."

Oh, I could not possibly have saved my spreadsheet and closed the laptop quickly enough.

Declan actually smiled at me, which had my heart thumping even harder, and we turned to the office door.

My answering smile died a sudden death as Walter appeared in the doorway, soundless and scentless and creepy as always.

"Walter," Declan said, sounding distinctly uncomfortable. Jesus, finally he was getting it. And then he explained the tone by adding, "I forgot we were going to have a working lunch today."

A brief flare of mean satisfaction at having driven creepy, magic-assaulting Walter completely out of Declan's mind made me grin involuntarily, and by the look of pure death Walter shot me, he noticed.

Shit. He already had it out for me, even though Declan wouldn't admit it. And now I'd humiliated him. I went cold all over.

Alphas weren't supposed to be afraid. But Walter terrified me. I couldn't help it, and it was obviously an instinct I shouldn't ignore, given what he'd already done to me.

"A working lunch?" Walter said, a tinge of bitterness clearly audible. A date. He'd thought he and Declan had a lunch date. "We agreed you needed to spend less time working and relax."

Declan let out an equally uncomfortable-sounding laugh. "I'm sorry. It's been a busy morning and it slipped my mind. But I was about to relax, so I was taking your advice." He gestured at me.

That fell as flat as a deflated balloon. Walter stared at him in stony silence, his unnaturally expressionless face blank and smooth.

Fuck. Walter really did want Declan. I was certain of it now. And he wanted me dead, I was just as certain.

"Why don't all three of us go grab a bite?" Declan said, and I barely refrained from slapping him silly. Why were some men so incredibly dense when it came to this kind of shit? I wasn't exactly Mr.

Tactful, but—fuck's sake. "It'll be a good chance to—"

Oh, no, fuck no. I couldn't let him finish that sentence with the inevitable and horrifying "get to know each other," or possibly, "let bygones be bygones."

"It's fine," I put in, a little too loudly so as to make sure and drown out any other stupidity coming out of Declan's stupid mouth. "I have a few things I need to do anyway, I wasn't quite done. I'll stay here in your office for a while, okay? And catch up with you later." And though it made me want to gag, I forced out, "Enjoy your lunch."

If murderous, creepy Walter doesn't poison or roofie you. I managed to keep that part silent.

Walter stared at me as if I'd grown a second head, and he didn't seem to be placated in the least by my stepping aside to give him his Declan-time. Oh, gods, I'd just humiliated him a second time by acting like I had the prior claim. But what the fuck else was I supposed to have done? I didn't fancy my chances of making it out of lunch alive.

"I don't blame you for wanting to bow out of lunch," he said smoothly, with a hissing undertone like a passive-aggressive snake. "After all, if I were you, I might not be comfortable eating with someone I'd tried to kill, without even so much as offering an apology."

Rage boiled up in me, sudden and fierce, and my fingertips itched as my claws tried to surge out. He had the nerve to—after he'd hit me with his foul magic, after he'd *set me up*!

I looked over at Declan the way you would when you wanted to share your anger with someone, and remembered too late that he wasn't on my side here. He still believed some random third party had made me freak out.

Declan's eyebrows had drawn together in a deep frown, his eyes dark and troubled. He glanced from me to Walter, all the lines of his big body tight with tension. "Blake was under a spell when he attacked you," he said after a moment, turning back to Walter. "He's sorry for any damage he caused, I'm sure. But *tried to kill* implies intent. And that was lacking, Walter. You know that."

Walter's eyes sparked with anger, a faint flush spreading over his cheeks—the first sign of involuntary anything I'd seen from him.

"I don't feel safe with him, Declan." His voice took on a faint, irritating whine. "I told you that. Any decent individual would apologize."

"This matter's already been settled," Declan said with great and quelling finality, a hint of his alpha voice creeping in. "And if you didn't notice another warlock on the premises, then I'd say you bear some of the blame as our head of magical security." I rocked back on my heels, shocked beyond belief. Declan might not believe me completely, but he wasn't only taking my side…he was using my own logic, my own point about Walter's incompetence, to defend me! And when he took a half step closer to me, shoulder to shoulder, I was so grateful it made my knees weak.

I nearly missed Declan adding, "No one's apologizing. No one has anything to apologize for. And that's that."

Walter had gone so red I thought he might explode, his fists clenched at his sides. I almost empathized with him, having caught the sharp edge of Declan's cutting tongue more than once.

Almost.

But actually not at all, the little fucking bastard.

Walter didn't reply. And for once, I was smart enough to keep my mouth shut.

Declan said, "Blake, I'll see you later, since it seems I have a prior engagement. Walter, let's go." And with that, Declan inserted himself between us, blocking our view of each other and chivvying Walter down the hall.

Declan glanced back over his shoulder once before they turned the corner, his expression dark but unreadable, and then they were gone.

I stood there for a couple of minutes getting my breathing under control, fingers flexing, knowing that if I so much as moved a step I'd wolf out and put my claws through that big, shiny interior window. Thank gods Declan's assistant wasn't at her desk; she'd apparently already gone to lunch. Who knew what she would've thought of all of that.

When I was certain they were long gone and I'd gotten my shift under control, I headed down the hallway myself. I'd lied through my teeth about staying in the office and working. No way, not with how I felt like I might explode out of my own skin at any moment.

The suite. It was the closest thing to a den I had, and I'd go there and calm down. Wait for Declan. Have a drink.

And brood. Olympic-level brooding seemed called for.

Maybe several drinks.

***

Declan came home extremely early by his standards, a few minutes after five, shrugging out of his jacket and tie before he'd even gotten all the way through the foyer and tossing them onto a nearby chair.

I blinked up at him hazily. "Good day at the office, dear?" I slurred from where I'd slumped so deeply into the sofa that we'd basically become one. Several drinks had become…well, I had the bottle in my hand, and not a glass, so that more or less covered it. "Your head of mashi—magical security put the whammy on anyone today?"

That earned me a long, and long-suffering, sigh. Declan ripped at the buttons of his shirt as if they'd personally offended him.

"Jesus, Joseph, and Mary," he muttered, and headed for the bar. "Did you leave me anything?" he threw back over his shoulder.

"This is only my shecond bottle." I took another swig, just to make sure he didn't get any ideas about it—he could find his own. Fuck, I hadn't been this drunk in what felt like forever. It took *a lot* to put an alpha werewolf down. And I'd been trying to keep my wits about me lately.

Fucking Walter. I'd still been so angry when I got back to the suite that I'd needed to immobilize myself, or I'd have done something stupid. Stupider. Declan defending me had helped—at first. But then it'd only made me angrier, as I thought about it. He'd defended me without believing me, used my reasoning about why Walter had failed in doing his job without taking it to the obvious conclusion: that he'd been the one to magic me.

So as much vodka as I could pour down my throat seemed like a better alternative to storming off to find wherever they were having lunch, and giving them both a piece of my mind.

Mmm. Vodka. I wasn't angry anymore.

Walter had been, though. I couldn't suppress a ridiculous giggle at the way Walter had been so fucking pissed-off, and how dumb that had been of me to provoke him, and then I tried to take another drink and ended up spilling vodka down my front. I'd taken off my button-down when I got back, so at least it only soaked the front of my undershirt. Fuck it. I already smelled like a distillery.

By the time Declan came back to the sofa, glass of whiskey in hand, I'd sloshed another slug of vodka down my throat and moved on to laughing myself sick over how fucking stupid *he'd* been.

I'd managed to slouch across two of the giant cushions with my head tilted toward the arm. He dropped into the cushion by my knees, took a long drink, and then tipped his head back with a sigh.

"It's kind of endearing," I managed to mumble without slurring any of the words. Go me.

Declan rolled his head on the back of the sofa until he was looking at me, one eyebrow up. "Endearing. I can't think of anything that happened today that deserves that description. Unless you're talking about your bottle of vodka. The two of you look pretty happy together."

I blinked at him, probably looking like an owl caught out in the daytime, and waved the bottle gently. "We are." I grinned, and his face softened a little. Good. I was too drunk to deal with it if he got all annoyed with me. "But I meant you. So dumb. You must be so used to everyone wanting you you jush—just don't notice it anymore. It's still dumb."

"Used to everyone wanting me," he said slowly, an odd look in his eyes I couldn't begin to interpret. "Dumb?"

"Walter," I said, nudging his thigh with my knee. "He's gagging for it. He fucking hates me. I don't know why though, it's not like you like me." My tongue felt funny. I needed another drink. I managed to get the bottle to my mouth again, slurping some more and spilling just as much. "Whoops." The bottle wavered. "Hey!" Declan plucked it out of my hand and leaned forward to set it on the coffee table. "I was drinking that!"

"I think it was drinking you. Blake." He dropped back, turning to face me fully. "Walter doesn't...want me. You're drunk. You think he made you attack him, I know, but he can't have." A little note of desperation there, maybe? Gods, he was so close to seeing the truth. "He's my right-hand man, and you need to let this go."

"He wants you so bad." I tried to sit up, lunging for the vodka bottle. One of them, since it seemed to have split into multiples. I missed all of them, and I slumped back, still not sure which one was real. "Soooo bad, Declan. You're dumb. Trying to get us to eat lunch together, for fuck's sake."

The confused look on Declan's face mirrored his total lack of understanding from earlier so perfectly that I couldn't take it. My abdomen hurt from the tremors of laughter. I was off again, flopping onto the sofa and howling until tears came to my eyes, and then I wasn't sure if I was laughing or sobbing.

The cushions dipped and rose as Declan moved. His empty glass landed on the table next to the bottle, and then his hands were under my armpits and he was heaving me up. I flailed, but he effort-lessly tugged me upright and into his arms, my head landing on his shoulder.

I closed my eyes. Why was Declan spinning around in circles?

Oh, yeah. That was my brain.

He felt so warm and solid, and the scent of him…I inhaled deeply, shamelessly burying my face against his neck. Mmm. I wanted to get my arms around him. They didn't seem to be feeling coopera-tive, though, so I ended up leaning against him limply while he dragged me off somewhere, my feet shuffling along the ground and stumbling now and then with the effort of holding me up.

Declan held me up. Gods, I wished he'd keep doing that. He'd done it earlier, too, figuratively speaking. "You didn't make me apol-ogize." It came out all mumbled, but his alpha hearing would com-pensate. I didn't need to enunciate. Wasn't it ironic that enunciate would be so hard to enunciate when you were this drunk? I started giggling again, and choked out, "You don't believe me, so I thought you would. Make me."

He didn't answer me. A few more steps brought us…some-where, and then he slowly lowered me onto a soft, flat surface. That spun too, but at least it was spinning downward, soothing and suck-ing me in, instead of making me need to fall over. His bed, had to be. I could smell spice and heat and Declan in the bedding. I opened my eyes a slit so I could see Declan himself, all handsome and perfect, leaning over me.

My gaze landed on his mouth and stayed there. Those lips felt amazing on my neck, on my ass, anywhere he'd put them, really.

"Why won't you kiss me?"

I really hadn't meant to say that.

We both froze, staring at each other in equally startled silence.

"There's some things I don't want to take from you," he said at last. "Not many." He let out a low, shaky laugh. "But not that."

I licked my lips.

His eyes widened, tracking down and fixing on my mouth.

"You can. You own me, right? My mouth. You own my mouth."

The thought of him owning my mouth, right then and there, had my cock valiantly trying its best to get hard. But even an alpha werewolf couldn't manage an erection after nearly two full bottles of vodka in a couple of hours.

Fuck, but I really, really wanted to get hard and then have him own my mouth in every possible way. With his lips and his tongue and his teeth, and then with his fingers, stuffing them in, and then his cock, shoved in so deep I couldn't breathe. I moaned at the thought, rubbing myself against his bed and licking my lips again, getting them wet for him.

"Jesus fucking Christ," he muttered, shifting his stance in a way that told me *he* hadn't had any trouble getting hard, damn him. But he wasn't doing anything about it! I was right here, spread out on his bed, about as pliant and willing as anyone could possibly be. "Fuck. Ask me again tomorrow, Blake. I mean it," he added, tone hard and serious, looking me right in the eyes. "Ask me again tomorrow."

I started to argue, but the bed sucked me in too inexorably to resist. My eyes slid shut, and the last thing I saw was Declan gazing down at me.

Chapter 17

I Missed Your Voice

Since I'd never slept in Declan's bed before, I woke up confused, disoriented, and with a mouth that tasted like someone had murdered a particularly sandy desert and buried its corpse under my tongue.

Well, that last part didn't have anything to do with Declan's bed, to be fair.

I rolled over and groaned, throwing an arm across my eyes to keep the sunlight out, because *someone* had left the blinds wide fucking open when he got up and went to work.

I knew I'd be fine once I had a couple of glasses of water and a bite to eat; hangovers weren't really that much of a thing for werewolves without serious effort involving multiple illicit substances, and I hadn't been to a party that good in like, six months. But seriously. Close the damn blinds. Fuck.

It crossed my mind to find my phone, make some coffee, and send him a text complaining about the window.

And then I sat bolt upright, head in my hands, and let out another groan.

I'd slept in his bed. We hadn't even fucked. I could barely remember getting from point A to point B, point A being...my first trip to the bar in the main room of the suite, and point B being in Declan's bed, unfucked, thinking about bitching at him like we were an old mated couple.

I threw the blankets back and made a beeline out of his bedroom and into my own, switching the shower on as high as it'd go and barely taking the time to shuck my undershirt and boxer briefs before I dived under.

He'd taken my slacks off of me. I stuck my face under the spray without mercy.

He'd done that, but he hadn't fucked me. How unattractive had I made myself last night, that he hadn't even bothered to get me undressed all the way and get off? Walter wanted Declan to get rid of me. Declan trusted Walter, and he'd listen to him eventually, especially if I wasn't useful for the one thing Declan…

Walter.

Oh, fuck, *Walter*.

It came rushing back, and I leaned forward, letting my forehead rest against the shower wall and then thumping it there a few times.

Yeah, my being sloppy drunk probably hadn't gotten Declan's engine firing in the first place, but then I'd started telling him about how Walter wanted him and how he was dumb for not noticing.

They'd been working together for how fucking long? And while I found Walter incredibly repellent, objectively he had an extremely handsome face and a tight little body. Declan obviously liked him already. And he'd been completely oblivious before I came along and shoved it in his face. Maybe he'd never made a move because he thought he'd be taking advantage of the fucker, which given my circumstances was ironic in the extreme. But Declan didn't seem like a serial blackmailer, or anything—he'd made an exception for me, I was pretty sure.

Now I'd pointed out Walter's obsession with him, he'd probably spent his long, sexless night mulling the idea over and considering its merits. Someone he trusted, liked, and who wanted him. How could he possibly prefer me to that?

I let out a miserable moan as I realized I didn't even know if Declan had spent the night here at all. He could've poured me into bed and then waltzed straight back out the door and into Walter's bed instead.

But then why'd he put me in his? Because he'd planned to fuck me, clearly, before he gave it up as a bad job given my totally wasted state and my insistence on making pillow talk about Walter being in love with him.

Yeah.

I'd had better moments.

I left the shower as cranky and miserable as I'd entered it, but it wasn't until I'd stumbled into the kitchen, towel around my waist, that I remembered the last thing: I'd asked him to kiss me.

Fuck. I'd practically *begged* him to kiss me.

And he hadn't so much as touched me.

Well, didn't that put the rotten cherry on top of the crap sundae.

My phone—and fuck that, I'd check messages later when I had the strength for it—sat on the counter next to the coffee maker…which I didn't need to start. Declan had left it turned on and full. I sagged against the counter in relief. Declan had been here all night, then.

Unless he'd come back to get dressed after spending the night fucking Walter in every possible position and then made me coffee out of pity.

Enough. I couldn't handle this level of anxiety before I even drank any of the coffee.

Hitching up the towel with one hand, I grabbed the pot with the other to pour into the cup I'd pulled out of the cupboard.

A loud, insistent knock sounded on the door of the suite, and it startled me enough that the coffee sloshed all over the counter, dripping down onto the floor and spreading hotly under my bare toes.

I slammed the pot down and stomped, coffee-soaked feet and all, to the door.

This had better be good. And if it was Walter, I was going to deck him, and I didn't care if he turned me into a toad.

I yanked the door open, clutching the towel as it slipped a bit, and all but snarled at—the cute twinky guy who'd delivered my room service weeks before, the one who'd been so friendly with Declan, and vice versa.

That did not improve my mood.

He glanced up and down, went bright red, and swallowed hard. Okay, that mollified me a little. The guy couldn't help having good taste in men, and I stood up a little straighter, letting my abs flex.

So sue me. I was only semi-human, after all.

"Mr. Castelli," he squeaked. "Um. Sorry if it's a bad time? I have a delivery for you."

I blinked at him for a moment in total shock, wondering when the bad soundtrack was going to start…and then realized he was in fact holding a garment bag. Gods above, I needed to get a grip. And drink some coffee.

And take another shower, except—no, that faint, unpleasant odor wasn't coming from me. Delivery guy? Ugh, he needed a new cologne. Actually, it smelled a lot like the odor that had been on my luggage when I got it back from my previous suite.

"Did you pack my stuff? In my suite, before I moved down here?" I demanded.

"Uh. No? That was…um, that was Joe, I think. If there's something missing or damaged, I'm sure it was an oversight, and I'm so sorry. I'll get him on the radio right away—"

"No, no need, nothing's missing." Weird. Did the housekeeping staff use some kind of chemical, or…? I came up empty. Whatever. "Give me the—thing." I snatched it out of his hands, my towel nearly getting away from me, and stepped back to let the door thud shut in his face. Fuck, I'd been trying to be nicer. And he'd checked me out with the right level of appreciation for my toned upper body, which deserved a little courtesy. "Thank you!" I called out belatedly.

"No problem," floated through the door, sounding both baffled, understandably, and also relieved, probably to be getting away from the crazy, half-naked alpha werewolf.

I hung the garment bag in my room, put on some underwear, and went back to the kitchen, wrinkling my nose at the lingering smell. Maybe Declan needed to have a word with his staff about their hygiene.

Coffee finally achieved, I grabbed my phone and went back to face the weird smell and whatever was in the garment bag.

It turned out to be a brand-new tuxedo. A nice one, too: obviously custom-tailored and from a designer I recognized as one of the best. I had the feeling it was going to fit like a glove. How had…and then I remembered that I'd been coming to the Morrigan for so long that the hosts had all my measurements and clothing preferences on file. Declan—and it had to have been Declan who sent this—had clearly consulted the experts. More obnoxious than asking me, or thoughtful?

Obnoxious, definitely, especially since he hadn't even deigned to tell me I'd need a tux in the first place.

I tugged my phone out of my pocket, too annoyed to bother

worrying about whether he'd gone and knotted Walter stupid the night before.

Why do I have a tux?

A moment later my phone buzzed.

Because we're going out tonight. Be ready at 7. Best behavior, or else.

I typed out *Nice of you to give me advance notice, the fuck?* And then I thought better of it and hit the back button…except that my finger slipped and I hit send instead.

Gods damn it, today just couldn't go any more sideways—and then the screen lit up again. I stared down at it.

And stared some more.

You were too drunk last night to talk about it. Sorry. I meant to leave you a note this morning.

Declan had to be fucking with me. He'd say something scathing any second: about my behavior last night, about how useless I'd been. But no more messages appeared.

Damn it all to hell. Now I had no idea what to think.

I hung the tux right in front of the air conditioning vent to hopefully blow some of the smell off of it, and I settled in for a day of eating, mainlining coffee, and watching bad TV.

Hopefully that'd keep me from being too jittery about the night before, about tonight, about literally everything.

***

When Declan finally slammed into the suite at a quarter to seven, I'd been ready to go for a full hour. I tried to tell myself it was because I was afraid of what he might do if I delayed him; I knew, deep down, that I simply couldn't wait to have him see me in it, or wait to see him in his, or wait to find out what he had in mind for the night.

Maybe he'd be taking me on a real date. Maybe he wasn't angry about last night, or about the whole Walter thing.

Maybe he'd realized Walter was a snake and had fired him and thrown him out of the Morrigan with extreme prejudice.

Hope, it turned out, really did spring eternal.

Hope could kiss my lily-white ass.

Still. That didn't stop my heart from fluttering, lurching, and then dropping all the way down to my feet when Declan bypassed my room completely, ignoring me in favor of stomping down the hall to his own room. A moment later, I distantly heard the shower come on.

Standing around my room until he deigned to come and get me smacked of insecurity and of being his second-choice high-school prom date.

A drink. Several. Fuck it, I wouldn't have time to get sloppy drunk again.

Declan emerged into the living area of the suite ten minutes later looking like he'd stepped out of the pages of a magazine dedicated to the rich, gorgeous, and dangerous, and I nearly spilled my second martini all over myself. My fingers clenched around the glass a little too hard.

And my heart gave another treacherous flutter as he stood stock-still, staring at me with his mouth open, as if he'd started to speak and then…gotten overwhelmed by how handsome I was? I did look amazing, the bathroom mirror had told me as much. But I hadn't expected him to notice or to acknowledge it, even involuntarily.

"You look like you've recovered well from last night," he said at last. "And the tux fits." He cleared his throat.

Another flutter. I had to get it together.

"Yes," I managed.

"Please tell me that martini's stirred and not shaken." He moved at last, taking a few steps into the room and then stopping again, his hands twitching at his sides as if he didn't quite know what to do with them. "Otherwise you're ruining the James Bond effect."

James Bond? Yes, I looked damn good, but Declan was the one who could've filled in for whichever A-list stud Hollywood had picked for the role this time around. With his shoulders, and his stubble, and his piercing dark eyes, and the way the trousers hugged his muscled thighs…I snapped my own mouth shut. Drool would ruin my suit as much as a spilled martini would.

It took me a second for my brain to catch up. "He shook them, not stirred them."

"No, that was a change they made from the books, because they thought 'shaken, not stirred' sounded cooler than 'stirred, not shaken.' It's backwards."

That startled a laugh out of me. "You're such a nerd," I said without thinking. "Bond trivia? Really?"

A dark flush spread along Declan's cheekbones, and he turned away abruptly. "We should get going. Knock that back, we're late."

My stomach gave an unsteady lurch. I'd been teasing. Being…friendly. Without even meaning to be. And he'd taken it as an insult. Of course he had—when had I ever been pleasant to him? And I shouldn't want to be!

But I did, and I desperately wanted that moment back, that shining instant when I'd laughed at him and thought he might laugh with me.

"I was joking." The words came out without my wanting them to, small and plaintive.

Slowly, Declan turned back to me, eyes glittering. Those eyes. They caught and held me, and just that look was enough to have me breathing a little faster, heat pooling low down in my abdomen.

"It's shaken," I said, holding the martini up. "Not stirred. I don't think I'm Bond material." I swallowed hard, forcing myself to keep my eyes on his and not stare down at the floor in submission like an idiot. Unfortunately, I couldn't seem to lie or prevaricate when his eyes bored into mine like that. Some alpha I was. "I'm more like the Bond girl, only—not a girl. Pretty. Occasionally clever. Mostly useless unless someone needs eye candy."

The corner of Declan's mouth quirked, and he raked me up and down with his gaze, slowly, assessing. I fought the urge to squirm— or to throw the martini over my shoulder, throw caution to the winds, and get down on my knees. He still wanted me. No matter what I'd said or done the night before, he still wanted me!

"You're not a girl, I'll give you that," he said as he looked back up at my face.

That hit hard. I turned away quickly, hoping to hide how much, downing the rest of my martini at one go and setting the glass back down on the bar with a clatter. "I'm ready whenever you are," I muttered.

I didn't hear him move, but the heat of him at my back warned me he'd moved closer, hemming me in against the bar. I clutched the edge of it, closing my eyes, willing him to get the fuck away from me.

He didn't.

"Blake," he said softly. I counted to five. He still hadn't moved. A long sigh ruffled the hair on the back of my neck, making me shiver, and I jumped as a big, warm hand landed on my hip, sliding under the tux jacket to caress me through my shirt. "Shit. Blake, you are extremely pretty. And occasionally clever." I bit my lip and gripped the bar so hard there'd probably be dents, and my claws had started to creep out, poking into the wood. He'd need new furniture at this rate. Fuck him. Those were my self-deprecating words, *mine*. The first rule of polite society was not agreeing when other people criticized themselves! Had he been raised in a barn? He leaned in even more, his breath heating my ear. "And you're not useless. I've found a lot of uses for you."

James Bond had found the same uses for nearly every female character in the series, as I recalled. That didn't make them use*ful*. And even though I'd been so worried about him getting sick of me if I didn't make myself available to be used, I still wished, pathetically, that he'd see me as something more than an object.

I couldn't speak, couldn't move. If I did, I might cry.

Or I might spin around and try to claw his eyes out before he could see how much he'd hurt me.

"I've seen more of you the last few days, but you haven't talked much," he went on. "Except last night, and that was—anyway. You've hardly opened your mouth in weeks." His hand crept inexorably around my waist, stroking my stomach, the little finger teasing under my waistband. That touch was enough: my cock stirred, my ass clenching convulsively. I hadn't had him inside me for two days. And to add to that, he'd noticed. He'd noticed that I hadn't been speaking to him much.

Except for last night, of course. Fuck.

A little whimper worked its way out of my tight throat.

"I've opened it plenty," I whispered, unable to deal with anything to do with the night before. Addressing it directly might kill me with embarrassment.

"Only when I had you on your knees waiting for my cock. Last night, and today. It's the first time you've really talked to me in—a while."

He bent his head, lips brushing over the shell of my ear, until he could nuzzle under my collar and put his mouth against my neck, right where he always bit me. His tongue darted out, tasting, teasing, the heat of it arrowing straight down and into my aching cock.

"You don't like it when I talk." My claws buried themselves another quarter-inch or so into the bar, and my whole body quivered, so much tension with nowhere to go. "You tell me how much you hate me when we talk. Or you hate what I talk about."

Declan pushed even closer, and now I could feel his hardness against the swell of my ass.

My claws were never coming out of the wood. I'd have to stay here forever, which meant he'd need to fuck me bent over the bar.

Oh, fuck, I wanted him to fuck me over the bar *so badly*, and whether he hated me or not, I hated myself enough for the both of us. I pushed back against him, shamelessly rubbing my ass over his erection like a cat in heat. Declan let out a soft sound, his arm tightening around my waist.

"I might not actually hate you," he said roughly, reluctantly, as if the words were being pulled out of him. "I hate—fuck, maybe I do. I don't know. But it doesn't seem to matter as much. And I missed—fuck, Blake."

He bit down on my neck, releasing his grip nearly as quickly as he'd sunk his teeth almost through my skin, but it was enough to have me hanging limp between his arm and the bar, all my instincts telling me to submit. My head hung down between my shoulders, and I arched even more, practically begging him to get rid of the fabric between us and fill me up, complete me. My cock was trying its best to punch a hole right through my trousers, although—score one for the tailor. Even with its alpha strength, it seemed doomed to fail, and the constriction hurt like hell.

That edge of pain only took me higher, strung so tight I'd started to gasp for air. Sweat trickled down my spine.

"I missed your voice," he growled. "I missed—you."

That did it. With a moan, I pitched forward, held up only by his arm and my embedded claws, and came so hard inside my perfectly tailored tuxedo trousers that my vision went white, slamming into the bar and rattling all the bottles and glassware. My knees gave out. I hung there whimpering, supported by his strength, and when he bit at my throat and rutted against me I couldn't do anything but take it, tossed back and forth like a rag doll.

"Fuck," he said, jerking his mouth away from my throbbing skin, cock still hard against the crease of my ass, pressing on my hole enough to make me grit my teeth with want. "If I fuck you, if I knot you, damn it, there's no time. We're actually late." He let out a shaky laugh. "I'd give nearly anything to be inside you right now."

I blinked my eyes, getting a little focus and a little clarity.

"You can have the next best thing," I slurred. "Put me on my knees. I might need help getting my claws out of the bar first."

"No, not on your knees." He pulled back enough that I could sway myself upright, and then he wrapped a big hand around my wrist, massaging me until the muscles relaxed enough to let my claws retract. I winced at the sound of shredding wood, and splinters rained down all over the floor and the tops of my shoes. "Come on," he added, before I could start frantically apologizing for ruining his bar. "On the couch."

He led me there, arm wrapped firm and warm around me, but I stumbled as we reached the sofa, trying to go down on my knees in front of it and getting pushed into sitting on it instead. He didn't want me to suck his cock after all? My mouth watered, longing for the thick length of him pressing down on my tongue and painting it with his pre-come, pushing into my throat and filling me completely.

"But I thought—"

"No," he said firmly. "Not like that. I said not on your knees." He braced one of his own next to me, his hands working at his belt and zipper. "You almost fell over a second ago. Lean back and open your mouth for me, darlin'."

He'd only called me that a few times, and he'd always been mocking me, taunting me with an endearment that was anything but.

This time it almost sounded real. I let myself fall back, gazing up at him looming over me: jaw set, eyes blazing with something I couldn't name but that had my head whirling.

Declan braced himself on the back of the sofa with one hand, leaning down over me, his cock springing free to point right at my eager mouth. The air felt thick, filled with the scent of my own come soaking the front of my boxer briefs and now the scent of him, too, rich and spicy, and the hot bite of his alpha magic. The flushed head of his cock brushed my lips. I darted out my tongue and tasted him at last, moaning with the pleasure of it, reaching up to grasp his hips and keep him where I wanted him.

My tongue played around his cockhead, tracing the glans, pushing into the slit. Declan groaned and leaned down to wrap his free hand in my hair, the overlong strands slipping through his fingers. It didn't feel like coercion. It felt like a plea for more.

I gave him more, letting him fill my mouth, push into my throat, working my tongue over the underside of his cock and wrapping my lips around him to give him a tight hole to fuck. My claws tried to come out again, and I nearly choked when I lost my concentration on blowing him in the effort of keeping them in. I couldn't ruin his tux. It was the same designer as mine. That'd be a travesty, and then we wouldn't just be late, and Declan would be so angry, and…

He pulled back, letting me breathe my fill, and his fingers stroked over my scalp so gently I could hardly stand it.

"Don't be afraid. I'm not—stop thinking so damn much," he said quietly, voice hoarse. "Don't be afraid."

I glanced up at him through my lashes.

No, I wasn't afraid anymore. Not when I saw the way he looked at me, lips parted and eyes glowing faintly, as if my face was the only thing in the universe.

The very first night I'd been in this suite I'd sucked his cock right here on the sofa. Only then, he'd been sprawled at his ease and I'd been his unwilling supplicant, crouched on the floor terrified and furious.

When he pushed into my mouth again, I opened for him more than willingly, moaning around him and milking the head of his cock with the muscles of my throat.

It didn't take him long at all to come, with a low mutter of my name and a clench of the hand in my hair, almost hard enough to hurt.

Almost hard enough to make me come again myself, if my cock hadn't still been completely spent. But a spasming shudder went through my lower body all the same as he spilled down my throat, pulse after pulse of slippery heat. I swallowed and swallowed, but when he pulled back at last, he still left a trace on my lower lip.

Before I could lick it off, he let go of my head and brought his hand to my chin, gripping me with his fingers and rubbing his thumb over my mouth, transferring those few drops to his own skin. He let me go and reached for my neck.

Was he...yes, he was. Declan swiped his thumb down the side of my neck beneath my ear, right where cologne would go.

Scent-marking me.

I stared up at him, mouth open, not sure whether to be delighted or absolutely irate. Well, to be fair, getting that angry would've taken brain cells, which I'd currently run out of.

He grinned down at me, teeth a little sharper than usual. I could only be glad he'd kept his claws in. "Everyone at that party with supernatural senses is going to know you're mine." He sounded so smug he might explode. Glancing down at the damp front of me, he added, "And they'll know I keep you satisfied. Go clean up a little, but don't change your underwear. I want to scent you all night."

Oh, gods...I whimpered a little and managed to lever myself off the sofa as he stood back to make room for me. That was so gross—at least to the human part of me.

My more instinctive side wanted to tear off all of my clothes, even the scented ones, and put my ass in the air.

Fuck. Party. We were going to a party?

I wobbled to my feet and headed for my room, feeling the weight of his gaze on my retreating back the whole way to the door.

I could scent him on me, too.

Mine.

He'd said I was his.

Yeah. I couldn't really argue with that anymore. He owned me. And right now, I couldn't even pretend to hate it.

Chapter 18

This Won't Go On

Declan hustled me out the door the second I emerged from the bathroom, ushering me downstairs and into a waiting limo. A nice one: black, not too stretched, no neon lights or anything tacky, nothing I'd have to be embarrassed about riding in.

I tried to focus on how good it felt to be wearing decent clothes, going somewhere in a respectable vehicle, and for fuck's sake, actually leaving the Morrigan and going somewhere, rather than on being in an enclosed space with Declan and our combined scents of sex and alpha desire.

If I focused on that, I'd end up begging him to knot me in the car after all.

The limo pulled out of the Morrigan's driveway and into traffic on the Strip. It was Friday night stop and go. Maybe we had time for a fuck after all?

"Where are we going? Am I allowed to ask?"

"Not far," he said, putting paid to my hopes. "A few blocks. If I'd been going with Wa—colleagues I probably would've walked. I thought you might appreciate going in style."

I might've appreciated the chance to stretch my legs even more, but I couldn't help melting a little. A glance over at him out of the corner of my eye showed him staring straight ahead, not looking particularly melted himself.

If anything, he looked uncomfortable, awkward in a way I'd never seen him before, controlled and in-charge as he usually was.

And silent. Fuck, it was like pulling teeth to get him to tell me anything.

"What's the party?"

He sighed. "Nothing exciting, I'm sorry to say. Nothing up to your usual standards, so no half-naked Greek tycoons or piles of coke on the sideboard." That had a little bit of bite to it, and I turned, startled, to stare at him. He'd looked me up online and read the tabloids? Seriously? I'd done a bit of online research into his family, of course, but I hadn't thought he'd stoop to my level. "It's a stuffy cocktail party for slot machine manufacturers and vendors," he added quickly, as if hoping I wouldn't notice the specificity of what he'd said. "It won't be fun. It's business, and I find this aspect of what I do boring too. You'll just have to suck it up with me."

Well, those were my expectations well and truly set. What a bummer. Something snagged at my brain, though, and then it twigged.

If I'd been going with Walter. He'd been about to say that, and then corrected himself.

Walter was usually his date to these events, and he'd replaced him with me?

Did that have anything to do with last night? He hadn't mentioned this party to me previously, even though it had to have been on his calendar for a while.

How did I even begin to ask about that?

Obliquely. I had to approach indirectly, because every other time Walter had come up, Declan had been incredibly defensive.

"I'd think Walter would actually be the better choice for an event like this," I said as evenly as I could. Neutral. I had to try to at least sound neutral on the Walter issue, even though I'd never been less neutral about anything in my life. "I mean, I get replacing one employee with another when someone's busy or whatever, but I don't know anything about the manufacture of slot machines."

A long, heavy silence fell, and my stomach fell with it. He still didn't want to talk about it. I'd reminded him of all the stupidity that'd word-vomited out of my mouth the night before. Shit.

The driver of a car next to us laid on the horn, loud and insistently, making me wince. Someone shouted. More honking broke out. The limo crept forward a couple of inches, stopped, and then the driver changed lanes and gained us half a block or so.

"Look, regarding the employee issue," Declan said abruptly.

"That's not exactly what you are. But I'm not sure the current state of affairs is something I want to continue. I know you're not happy with this, and it turns out neither am I." He stopped talking, leaving me literally gripping the edge of my seat, breath held, heart pounding.

I'd known this was coming, but the reality hit so much harder than the sickening anticipation. Either Walter had convinced him to get rid of me, or he'd realized last night that I wasn't what he wanted. But this evening he'd come in my mouth, he'd rubbed his come on me, he'd called me his. I didn't understand.

No words came to my lips. I couldn't even form them in my mind, let alone reply.

"Nothing to say?" he went on when I stayed silent for long enough that we'd gone another half block, probably, and the honking had finally stopped.

I shook my head.

"Jesus Christ, Blake—fuck!" He sounded so frustrated, so angry, that my fight or flight response, enhanced in an alpha, rushed to tighten my neck muscles and tingle in my fingers. I couldn't move. I'd do something awful if I moved. "You didn't ask me anything today. Are you going to?"

Ask him? Was I supposed to? "I don't know, Declan, I don't—"

"Blake, last night you—dammit to hell." The limo pulled over and stopped, and then jounced as the driver opened his door and got out. "Look at me," he said urgently, and it wasn't a command I could resist. I turned and faced him, meeting his eyes, shocked by the blaze of gold there. "We'll talk tonight. After this fucking miserable event. I shouldn't have brought you, but we're here and it's too late for me to cancel now. There's a lot of money involved, and—it doesn't matter."

In other words, he didn't want to tell me anything about his business, because it was none of mine. I swallowed hard and nodded tightly. A whole seat separated us. Only a couple of feet, but it might as well have been a chasm. I could still feel the heat of his body against my chilled one, only not enough to warm me. Just enough to show me what I'd be missing forever when he kicked me to the curb later tonight.

"This won't go on, okay? I promise," he said, low and intent, eyes fixed on mine. "I should never have done this to you, any of it. Get through tonight, please, and we'll sort it out when we get back. We'll talk."

I'd imagined Declan regretting the way he'd treated me. Imagined it often, if I were being honest. Apologies, making up for it. Groveling, even.

But my fantasies had never included him regretting *me*, full stop. This was more like a nightmare, only I could usually wake up from those.

Anything I could've said or done—pleas to change his mind, throwing myself on him and tackling him into the seat, wild promises to be a better man and a better alpha and to be worth his time— became impossible when Declan's door opened, the limo driver standing there to usher us out.

***

If I'd been in a good mood when we walked into the party, happy and confident, it still would've been so dull I'd have wanted to claw my own face off.

Coming out of the last thirty-six hours of anxiety and anger and drunkenness, ending with Declan telling me he didn't want me any-more, it was pure torture—and made me want to claw everyone else's faces off.

Hundreds of expensively dressed executive types milled around in a giant ballroom in one of the more upscale Strip casinos, overus-ing the open bar and nibbling on subpar appetizers. I'd lost my ap-petite, luckily, and if I hadn't the dried-out shrimp would've taken care of the problem.

I couldn't tell what music was playing. It sounded painfully ge-neric, and the dinging of the sample slot machines against the walls drowned it out anyway. It all combined into a drone of background noise perfectly calculated to throb in my temples.

We circulated, weaving our way between moodily lit cocktail ta-bles, Declan shaking hands and saying a few words to seemingly eve-ryone. I nodded and smiled mechanically as Declan introduced me, but I didn't retain a single name, the faces blurring into a kaleido-scope of teeth and eyes and hair. I ran a finger under my collar a few times, trying to get rid of the itchy, not-fitting-in-my-skin sensation that had been building ever since we walked in the door. It didn't work, but I managed to keep it together, outwardly calm enough despite the sweat beading on my spine and under my arms.

At last we made our way to where the apparent host held court at a larger cocktail table that'd been draped in silver lame and lit with a pale-blue spotlight.

Gods. It was so tacky it distracted me from my panic and heartache for a full three seconds.

But then Declan stepped forward, a few other people moving tactfully aside, to greet a tall, smiling brown-haired guy in a flashy tux who looked to be presiding over the tacky table. The way they hugged made my vision go green with jealousy. Fuck, Declan's body language. Natural, if not super affectionate.

This guy was his friend. They'd probably never had sex, and they might not even be all that close, but they shared something Declan and I never would: comfort and ease.

I vaguely heard, "Mark, nice to meet you, Blake," over the buzzing in my ears, and automatically reached out a hand to shake. Mark turned to Declan and said, "I thought I saw Walter across the room a little earlier, and I assumed he'd come with you. Not as his date," he said hurriedly, turning back to me with the slight grimace of a man tasting his own foot. "But Walter usually comes along with Declan because these shindigs are too boring to bring an actual date to." He started laughing at the look on my face. "I know, it's my own party, but it's true. Not the liveliest. Just good for business."

Did that make me not an actual date either? Gods, what did I say to that? But his remark about his party seemed to demand a polite answer, so I managed, "I'm sure everyone looks forward to it. Sometimes you want the time and space to actually talk at these things."

Mark started laughing again as if I'd said something witty and engaging instead of bland. Ugh. Spare me from business networking. How did Brook stand doing this kind of thing constantly? There'd been a time when I thought I should've inherited Castelli Industries. When I'd believed that this kind of schmoozing wasn't "work."

If I ever talked to Brook again, I'd apologize, and I'd mean it. He deserved the money and the respect he got as CEO if this, and spreadsheets, were his fucking life.

"Declan, I like this guy, keep him around," Mark said heartily. "It's about time you found someone other than Walter to be your arm candy. Not that Walter isn't great," he turned again and leaned in, as if imparting a secret to me, "he and I were together for a couple of years. He was part of my decision to invest in Declan's buyout of the Morrigan, and he was right! But it got too awkward working together after the break-up, and he went with Declan as an advisor. Worked out great for everyone. Right, Dec?"

Dec. Fucking save me. I turned to look at Declan, who had an odd expression on his face, somewhere between uncomfortable and tolerantly amused. Well, the fucker should be uncomfortable, and not only because of the dumb nickname. I'd just found out more about his acquisition of his family's casino and about Walter and their relationship to one another from twenty seconds of Mark's babbling than I had in a month of living in his fucking pocket.

Because Declan had wanted it that way. He'd kept me separate, and now he probably didn't even want that anymore.

That sensation of needing to move, to get away, to get the fuck out of there, intensified abruptly to an almost painful pitch. My chest felt like it might crack in two, and the sweat might even be visible on my hairline now.

Declan was saying something to Mark, but I couldn't hear it. Just the dinging, and the buzz of chatter, and the clinking of glassware.

"I'll be back in a minute," I muttered, and slipped away. Declan and Mark both said something from behind me, probably about where they'd be or where I'd find the restrooms, but I ignored them and weaved my way through the crowd, not quite shouldering people aside but picking up speed as I went.

Out. I had to get out. Away from Declan, just *out*.

A doorway with a dimly lit exit sign led out of the corner of the ballroom. I made my way there, finding a hallway with both restrooms and a plain door with a stairway emblem next to it.

Perfect, thank gods.

I shoved the door open and rattled my way down three flights, my panting breaths echoing off the concrete walls. It felt like being trapped in a tomb. I couldn't, I couldn't...and then I reached the bottom and pushed open another door, all but falling through and letting it slam behind me.

The nighttime exhaust-tinged air of Vegas slapped me in the face, barely cool enough to soothe my burning cheeks and make my sweaty scalp tingle. I sucked in deep breaths, my heart slowing slightly but still tripping in an unsteady rhythm. The door had let me out in a sort of service alley, with a loading dock at one end and what looked like an entrance to a street—not the Strip, but I had no idea what side of the building I was on otherwise—down at the other.

I headed that way, hating the enclosure of the tall utilitarian walls all around me.

The alley let out onto a side street, still bright with neon lights and busy with drunken pedestrians, but not quite as chaotic as the Strip. My heart started beating faster again. And my cock was hard. Why the fuck did I have an erection? But I did, and I stared down at my own fly for a second in confusion. A group of stumbling, laughing tourists passed by, and when they were gone I saw a man standing by an SUV parked right across the sidewalk from me.

It was the guy who'd been watching me in the casino on the day I'd tried to convince Declan I had a stalker. His face hadn't made much of an impression, but his stance was the same, and the blond hair cut in a boring scruff, and he even had almost the same outfit on: pleated khakis and a button-down, this time black.

He smiled at me. It didn't reach his eyes.

And a bolt of pure lust shot straight down into the pit of my stomach, so crippling I nearly doubled over.

I knew damn well it wasn't real. I knew I didn't want him, I wanted Declan. Why the fuck was this guy even here? How did he know where I'd be, when I hadn't even known where I'd be? I wanted to demand answers, but more than anything, I desperately wanted to hightail it down the street, back around to the front of the casino, and race inside to the security of Declan's presence.

Instead, as if someone had me on a string, I stepped forward. And then again. My vision blurred. I needed to be closer.

Too late, far, far too late, it hit me so hard I almost staggered: this was the same as the night I'd left the suite and Walter had ambushed me behind the casino. And the day I'd seen my stalker, when I'd been desperate to get outside, itchy and panicky and irrational.

The smell. The smell on my luggage, the same smell on the tux.

Spell bags, or some other warlock contrivance I'd never have thought of. Walter. Stupid, stupid, stupid, that I hadn't realized. He'd done this to me, and I needed to resist, to run away, cold sweat breaking out on my forehead, my limbs weren't responding to me, I couldn't…

I walked right up to the man who stood waiting for me, wrapped my arms around his waist, and kissed him. It felt wrong, cold and fake, but my lips moved and my tongue slipped out to taste him, and I wanted to gag, but I kept kissing him, and he kissed me back with his hands on my hips pulling me in. I rubbed against him, kissing him, shoving our bodies together.

One of the doors of the SUV opened. The guy drew me toward it, hands still locked on my hips, and he turned us so that I was climbing into the back seat before him.

He followed, letting go enough that he could reach back and pull the door shut behind us.

My chest felt like it was going to explode with the force of the scream I couldn't form. His body on mine was fucked up and wrong and vile, and I wanted to buck him off, tear out his throat…

He lifted his head and broke the kiss. "We're good to go," he said, and the matter-of-factness of his tone hit me like a dash of cold water. I turned my head and looked up, shocked and frozen.

Walter smiled at me from the front passenger seat. "Good. Time to take a nap, Blake."

Everything went black.

Chapter 19

My Life Mattered

When I woke up, the SUV was moving—but I couldn't shift so much as a muscle. My head had gotten crammed against the door and my neck ached like a bitch. My arms lay limp, one dangling to the floor of the car and the other on my leg. I tried to twitch a finger.

No go.

I couldn't open my eyes, either, or speak. My autonomous functions weren't affected, though: I could still hyperventilate. Lucky me.

Kidnapped. I'd been fucking *kidnapped*, and the first thing Declan would do would be call me. No doubt they'd gotten rid of my phone. Then he'd look for me. He wouldn't find me. And then he'd probably request—and be allowed, professional courtesy and all that—to review the security footage of me leaving the party and the path I'd followed from there.

For a brief, shining instant, I almost felt relieved. Declan would look for me, he'd see the video and know—despair squeezed my chest into a tight ball.

He'd see me looking nervous and running out of the building as if I was late. And then he'd see me walking entirely under my own power straight to where the asshole I'd been forced to kiss was standing, smiling and waiting for me. Like he would've if we'd made a prior arrangement to meet there, in fact. Lastly, he'd see me making out with the guy, grinding against him and getting into the car totally willingly.

Declan would think I was cheating on him. And he'd meant to get rid of me anyway. He'd see this and wash his hands of me immediately, go right back to the party and drink until he forgot my name.

At least he wouldn't be going home with Walter, since Walter was here, with me, kidnapping and probably murdering me. That thought brought me less comfort than I'd hoped.

And speaking of. "He's awake." Walter's too-smooth voice, which paradoxically managed to grate on my every last nerve. "Sit him up. I want him functional for now."

As I felt hands on me, presumably fucking khaki-guy's, the magic binding me released a little bit too, enough for me to open my eyes and unkink my neck. Opening my eyes, my goal for the past several minutes, turned out to be highly overrated. I got a great view of khaki-asshole sneering at me, Walter turning around in his seat to glare at me with beady, focused hatred, and nondescript Nevada scenery going by out the window, partially illuminated by the moon. I couldn't see the driver except for the outline of bulky shoulders.

No other cars passed us, the road completely empty. We might've left Vegas on a highway, but we weren't on one anymore, that was for sure.

It looked like the kind of place you'd go to dump a body.

I shivered.

Walter chuckled. "Don't worry too much, *Blake*," and he gave my name a poisonous emphasis, as if he hated it as much as its owner. "You won't be frightened for long. Some alpha you are," he spat, and I flinched, in large part because he was right. Damn him to hell and back.

Of course, once I thought about the meaning of the other thing he'd said, I didn't care so much about not being a shining example of an alpha werewolf.

I cared a lot more about the sinister implications of "you won't be frightened for long." Would Walter be dropping me off at a spa to soothe my nerves? Ha. I figured I'd probably be frightened until I died, which wouldn't be long from now.

Oddly, confronting it directly inside my mind didn't make me feel any worse. Had I gone into some kind of shock? I only felt a dull throb of horror, not the shrieking panic I might've expected. It seemed inevitable, somehow. I didn't want to fight. I didn't care enough.

I stared blankly at Walter, now able to control my mouth and vocal cords but unwilling to reply to him.

Anyway, what did I have to say? *No, please, don't?*

Walter's horrible, creepy smile grew and grew as he watched me lie there, helpless and despairing. He was enjoying every second of it.

I blinked at him, his image wavering.

He might be *causing* every second of it.

This complete lassitude that was trying to take me over, this numbness in the face of my own kidnapping and imminent murder…this couldn't possibly be natural. Organic. This wasn't *me*. I'd reacted more strongly than this to getting denied a line of gambling credit, for fuck's sake!

What would Declan do if this were him? He'd be fighting. Plotting. Snarling.

Declan was a real alpha, though. The kind that my family held up as the true archetype, even though all of them—with the probable exception of Brook, who'd mated a low-class alpha with no breeding whatsoever who simply made him happy—would look down on him for his tattoos and his Irish heritage and his blunt way of speaking.

Not me, though—no real alphas here. I was pathetic.

But no. Fuck no. I hitched myself up in my seat as best I could, wiggling my hips to push myself more upright than khaki-fucker had left me. I needed to face this like a man and an alpha. Like anyone with something better than jelly for a spine, basically. Prove everyone wrong.

Prove myself wrong.

So what first? How to go on the offensive? Especially when, now that I'd identified and analyzed it, I could feel Walter's magic dragging me down like concrete galoshes of the soul, to wildly flail for an appropriate metaphor.

Gods. My brain kept going in meandering circles rather than focusing.

Part of the shitty magic too, no doubt.

I had to shoot my shot at some point, and the stretching silence seemed like a decent enough opportunity. Now or never. "Declan's going to come after you. Even if he doesn't come after me in time to stop you, he'll never forgive you."

Khaki-prick shifted in his seat uncomfortably, giving me a wary glance that told me he might be a little less sold on this plan than Walter was. At least someone in this car had some common sense.

Walter glared at me, black eyes glittering. "Mr. MacKenna's too good for you," he hissed. Mr. MacKenna? Like I wasn't worthy of hearing Declan's first name. What a fucking toolbag. "And he'll thank me eventually. He'll realize I'm the one who's been there for him all this time. I'm the one he needs. This will show him what a worthless slut you are."

I couldn't help laughing, even though it hurt my chest. The weight of Walter's magic sat on me like a pile of bricks, making everything hurt.

"I didn't do anything but what you made me do. And he doesn't want you. If he hasn't wanted you yet, he never will." Walter opened his mouth, but I talked over him, using every ounce of energy I could muster, every bit of willpower to combat the pressure of his magic and his fury. What Mark had said at the party had finally percolated through my brain, and I was going to use anything in my arsenal. Maybe it'd piss Walter off so much that he'd kill me more quickly, but maybe it'd throw him off his game instead. Give me an edge. "What, did you think you were trading up when you left Mark for Declan? Getting a hotter guy with even more money?"

The khaki-dick next to me laughed quietly, quickly cut off in a forced cough when Walter twisted further in his seat to shoot him a look of death.

"You're the gold-digger, not me!" Walter cried, rounding back on me, voice rising a whole octave. "You don't deserve what he's given you! You think you deserve—I deserve to be taken care of! Mark never wanted to take care of me the way I—" He broke off, panting, one fist resting on the center console and clenching and unclenching convulsively.

Fucking hypocritical bastard. Mark had probably dumped him for expecting to be a kept man, or maybe just for being a creep, and then Walter had tried to attach himself to the next rich guy who could give him a life of luxury. Gross.

The irony of it wasn't lost on me, though. All I'd wanted, a few months ago, was any way to get some money out of someone, enough to keep me in the kind of lifestyle Walter seemed to think the world owed him.

And now all I wanted was Declan. I would've wanted him even if he still had to wear a vest and a nametag to work every day.

But irony aside, it was working, my half-assed plan. I could feel Walter loosening his grip on me with every bit of self-control he lost. My arms and legs had real sensation in them, becoming limbs that I'd be able to move and not heavy, useless lumps. Even my mind had started to clear. Thinking didn't take as much effort now.

A little more. I only needed to piss him off a little bit more. "You won't ever have him. You know I'm right. Even if he doesn't care about me," which he probably didn't, but fuck, I had to save the pity party for later when and if I had the time, "he'll never get over a betrayal like this. And besides, he'll come after us. He's probably following us right—"

"How stupid do you think I am?" Walter demanded, his voice taking on that snake-hissing timbre again. There it was, that red blush in his cheeks, the tell for him losing his temper that I'd noticed the other day. Human eyes might not have caught it in the super low lighting, but I did. "I texted Dec—Mr. MacKenna from your phone." A slip of the tongue, there, and I felt some strength and power coming back to my hands. "I told him you were leaving, and I knew what to say to make him never want to see you again. Your phone is in very small pieces in the gutter. He can't track you that way. If he tries to hire someone with magic to find us, they won't be in time to help you. And once you're gone, the story will be whatever I say it is. You're nothing, Castelli. Nothing to him. Nothing to *anyone*."

Maybe true. Almost certainly true.

But I was something to *me*. My life mattered, simply because it was mine and the only one I had.

And if I lived…well, maybe I could convince Declan to give me a chance. A real chance, not the fucked-up blackmail-and-sex-and-occasional-spreadsheets limbo we'd been existing in. Or even just convince him to keep me around as his sex toy. I'd take it. Not too likely that it'd work, but if I held on to that faint idea of a future, it could keep me going.

Fuck it. I wanted to live, and that was enough for me.

The phone thing didn't surprise me, since I didn't think Walter was stupid and I'd already figured out that he wouldn't make a simple mistake like keeping my trackable phone. And I hadn't really believed Declan would be coming after me like a bat out of hell. The fact that he'd texted Declan pretending to be me shook me a little, though, since it made the idea of Declan wanting to follow me even less likely. Somewhere, deep down, I'd been holding on to a little bit of hope for a rescue. But I'd shaken Walter's cool, too, and that was something.

"At least he wants to fuck me," I said, letting my fangs drop a bit, snarling at him. My heart picked up its rhythm. My fangs. I could shift. Walter's hold on me had relaxed enough that I could use my shift! Keep going, keep pushing... "He was so desperate to get inside me the other day that he completely forgot about you. You don't even exist for him when I'm in the room. I bet he's never even thought about doing the things to you that he's done with me. A few days ago, I had his tongue in my—"

Walter let out a cry of incoherent rage, and fierce delight rose up in me, a burst of energy and power. I had him! He raised his arm, fingers flexing, and the air in the car took on a charged, staticky buzz, all the hair on my body rising as if I'd been rubbed against the world's biggest balloon.

He was going to hit me with magic. Maybe to kill me, maybe to silence me, maybe just to hurt me.

I had a split second to react.

My sense of smell told me that I was the only shifter in a car with three other humans. They were vulnerable in a way I wasn't.

Pulling on all of the strength I had, all of the determination, all of the magic inherent in my body and my genetics, I forced out the claws on my left hand, five razor-sharp six-inch dealers of death.

Khaki-douche shouted a warning to Walter, who reared back, his magic gathering in his hand.

But instead of going for Walter, I slammed my claws around the edge of the front seat and through the driver's shoulder.

The world exploded around me in a chaotic cacophony of screeching tires and screams and people flying through the air, the SUV spinning and jerking, Walter's magic surging past me in a messy wave of energy that singed me around the edges. My body got thrown forward, but I braced myself with a foot on the back of Walter's seat, kicking my asshole seat-mate in the process and connecting with something soft.

I hoped it was his balls. The way he shrieked suggested it, anyway.

Ignoring his cries and Walter's incoherent shouts and the thrashing driver, and his blood spurting everywhere—so disgusting, and I wanted to throw up, but I couldn't, I had to keep it together— I yanked my claws back out of him, nearly throwing up anyway at the sound of them scraping over his bones.

I twisted, kicking again, desperate for leverage, and tried to get a hold of the door handle. My blood-slick hand slipped and slid, my claws refusing to retract enough to let me use my fingers properly, and I scrabbled at it, panicking.

Fuck. This.

Alpha werewolves didn't need a fucking door handle, dammit. Door handles were for the weak.

I reared up and slammed my shoulder into the window. It shattered instantly, glass showering all over me and spraying everywhere, and I followed the motion through, grabbing the sharp edges of broken glass without worrying about my sliced-up palms and propelling myself out, swan-diving head-first onto the road.

My arms caught most of the impact, but my head still bounced painfully on the asphalt, an instant concussion blurring my vision and spiking pain through my skull. At least one of my arms was broken, and the other maybe as well. Small bits of gravel dug into my cheek where it pressed into the ground. Behind me, the screaming kept going, but I knew Walter would get it together any moment. He hadn't been knocked unconscious, and he'd probably used his magic to cushion himself from the impact.

Broken or not, that arm had to lift me up. It'd heal within half an hour or so, ditto the concussion. But I didn't have that long. I had seconds, probably. I let out a grunt of pain as I forced myself to my hands and knees and then staggered to my feet, glancing down to assess any other damage.

Not much, except to the tux. I spared exactly half a second to mourn it, because Italian wool deserved better.

And then I launched myself into a run, off the road, down the embankment, and skittering into the sand. Under the light of a half moon, scrubby bushes and spiky little plants dotted an endless expanse of sandy dirt, peppered with the occasional rock.

Almost no cover at all, and nowhere to go, with an enraged warlock right behind me and his magic still dragging me down, making my movements sluggish and my healing slower than usual.

Despair swamped me all over again. What had I thought I'd accomplish with this insane stunt? I could've waited until we stopped somewhere. Maybe Walter had some plan before, or in addition to, simply killing me. I could've turned them against each other.

Except that Declan's martini jokes and my ruined tux aside, I wasn't anything close to James Bond, who could suavely talk his way out of a situation like this. That sort of thing worked in movies. Not in real life.

No other choices left. I ran. Flat-out, with no destination, I ran like hell. A bolt of magic sizzled past my left shoulder and exploded a cactus, spines flying and spattering me in tiny agonizing stings. A moan tore out of my pounding chest, and I staggered to the side, picking up the pace again and pounding across the sand, dodging bushes and rocks, stumbling, a nightmare of fear and sweat and pain, shadowy objects in the moonlight. Another magical blast—and this time he winged me, the heat of it disintegrating the sleeve of my jacket and searing my still-broken arm.

That brought me to my knees, head hanging low, vision blurred to the point of uselessness. A rock pierced my right shin. A scorpion scuttled away from my legs and disappeared under a bush, small enough to take cover from the chaos, the lucky little bastard. My own hoarse breaths echoed in my ears. The dry, cold desert night had already sucked all the moisture out of my eyes and my nose and my throat, and I felt papery and hollow. But I couldn't stop now. I *couldn't*. Giving up would be worse than anything.

I forced myself up, wobbling and wavering but determined to face my fate without flinching. Walter wouldn't have the satisfaction of killing a coward.

I turned, expecting to see Walter raising his hands to deliver the final blow.

And he was, standing there halfway between me and the road. But he had his head twisted around, staring over his shoulder...at two more SUVs stopped right behind his, the headlights of all three shedding crisscrossing spotlights on the road.

And on a swarm of men, two of them taking charge of khaki-fucker, one of them opening the driver's side door of Walter's SUV, a few others doing whatever you did in a situation like this, one standing by the new vehicle and raising something up to his shoulder, and the other—Declan. My heart stumbled, expanded, clenched tight. The last was Declan, running faster than I'd ever seen an alpha move, headed straight for Walter with his claws and fangs gleaming in the moonlight.

Walter turned all the way, shouting something I couldn't catch at this distance. He raised his hands again—toward Declan. Fuck, he was going to—I forced myself to move, staggering toward him, but I'd be too late, he'd kill him, I'd rather die myself, and oh, gods, what a time to realize that—

A sharp crack rang out followed by a rolling echo.

Walter's right side jerked and he dropped to the ground with a gut-punched scream.

I shook my head, trying to clear the ringing in my ears and figure out what the fuck was going on.

The guy who'd been lifting something up: a rifle. He'd been aiming a rifle. Declan might have been depending on his own alpha strength, but one of his men, with a foresight and common sense I could've kissed him for, had brought along a gun.

As Declan passed him, Walter moaned his name.

Declan didn't even slow, changing his trajectory to avoid Walter, now no longer a threat, and instead barreling at me with single-minded focus.

I could see his face now, his expression: caught somewhere between joy and terror and fury, features twisted into something closer to his animal nature than his human one. No one had ever been more beautiful.

He'd come for me. I had no idea how he'd found me, how he'd followed us, but he'd come for me. I could scent him now, over the acrid tinge of the desert and the nauseating odors of blood and pain coming from me and now also drifting from Walter in the faint breeze.

I let Declan's scent surround me, ground me, and as I started to sway, Declan was there to catch me.

He skidded to a halt and wrapped me in his arms, tugging me into his chest and enclosing me in heat and safety and strength. My head dropped into the crook of his neck. I let my body go limp, trusting that he'd hold me up. Trusting in him completely.

He did, one hand sliding down to my hip, the other big and warm around the chilled, sweat-damp nape of my neck.

"Fuck," he said. "Jesus motherfucking Christ. Blake, darlin'. *Blake*." My name came out like a prayer, heartfelt and grateful. He buried his face in my hair and breathed me in, just like I was swallowing huge gulps of his scent and his presence, his alpha magic dark and heavy in the air, swirling around me and soaking in to soothe all my hurts. "You're bleeding. Do you need a healer? I could only bring an ex-army medic on short notice, but he can—"

"No!" I lifted my head, forcing him to do the same. Our eyes met. And held. I couldn't have torn myself away in that moment even if Walter had been about to explode the whole desert. No one had ever looked at me like that. Alpha gold had always been a sign of aggression, of hostility. Of something going wrong. Or at best, a sign of arousal and a different kind of aggression.

Declan's glow as he gazed down at me held nothing but the assurance that he could and would protect me.

And the expression behind that alpha glow…

"No," I said again. "I'm healing fine. Alpha werewolf here, remember? I need half an hour and a drink of water, Declan. I promise."

"Good." The sheer relief in that one word sent a shiver through me. He'd been afraid for me. And I didn't ever want Declan to be afraid of anything, but on the other hand—gods, he'd been *afraid*. For *me*. His expression changed, brows drawing together, and his eyes flickered to my mouth. "I'm sorry," he said slowly, and took a deep, shuddering breath. "I was waiting for you to ask me. A decent man would keep waiting. But I can't wait anymore."

Seriously? This was the second time he'd had something cryptic to say about me "asking him." What the fuck did he—

But I stopped caring about it when he leaned down, gently, coaxingly shifting his grip on my neck and tipping my head back.

And when he closed that small gap between us and pressed his lips to mine, I didn't care about anything else in the world.

Chapter 20

Ten Years Ago

No matter how many times I'd daydreamed about Declan kissing me, the reality far outstripped the fantasy—and how often could you say that about anything? His mouth took control of mine the same way his body had taken control of me so many times, opening me and tasting me and laying me bare for him to use however he wanted.

Which happened to be what I wanted too, so badly that I ached for it. His tongue teased between my lips and twined with mine as his arms tightened, gathering me so close that not a millimeter of space was left in between us.

Declan kissed me until I couldn't breathe, my lungs hot and laboring. All the pain and fear of the last few hours melted away, a much better and more natural kind of magic than the ones I'd experienced so far tonight.

I pressed against him, kissing him back with everything I had, trying to spread my legs and wrap myself around him and take him into me so that he'd never leave.

Declan tore his mouth away and lifted his head, leaving my lips tingling and throbbing, suddenly chilled and bereft. I moaned a little protest and blinked my eyes open.

He gazed down at me, eyes wide.

"I'm sorry," he said again. Sorry? He was *sorry*? At the first possible opportunity, I'd be giving him a piece of my mind about apologizing and showing regret immediately after giving me the best kiss of my life. "You're hurt. We're in the middle of fucking nowhere. And if I don't stop now, I'm going to fuck you on the ground right here."

At the best of times I'd have been all for it. Even the fading aches and stings of my injuries wouldn't have slowed me down.

But now that I'd tuned back in to reality, I had to admit that the distant sounds of Walter moaning in pain and Declan's men cleaning up the scene weren't the best aphrodisiac.

Walter's moans abruptly cut off, and I peeked over Declan's shoulder to see what was going on in time to catch one of Declan's guys carrying him away, slung limp over his shoulder like a sack of potatoes.

The scent on the air read like blood, not death, but he sure looked dead.

"Don't worry about him," Declan said, voice so low and grim it made me desperately glad I wasn't the target of his rage.

I looked back up at him to find his eyes still fixed on my face. Had he so much as glanced away since he'd reached me? I didn't think so, and I couldn't help smiling.

"What?" he asked, sounding actually worried about the answer. As if he cared what I thought and what I felt, as if he were really afraid I'd be angry about him kissing me. As if he cared about *me*.

His actions suggested he did. But I couldn't quite bring myself to believe it. Maybe he simply felt responsible, seeing as Walter—the man Declan had told me over and over again could be trusted—had kidnapped and tried to kill me out of jealousy.

"Why did you come after me? And how did you come after me? And I'm not worried about Walter, although I'm hoping the guy I clawed isn't dead. What are they doing with them? Won't they bleed out without a real healer?"

Declan's eyebrows went up. "You clawed one of them? I didn't exactly wait to check out the carnage." I nodded, and he grinned, sharp and predatory. "You rescued yourself, Blake. Fucking good for you. I wish I'd seen it."

I soaked up his praise, as thirsty for it as the desert sands around me were for a single drop of water. Not that I didn't notice he'd managed to deflect all of my questions, of course.

"I want answers, Declan," I said as firmly as I could manage after having my spine and my brain melted into goo by that kiss. "Stop trying to distract me by telling me how amazing I am?" I couldn't help the way that came out as a question, damn it.

"Yeah," he said, voice gone a little rough. "Yeah, you're fucking amazing."

He still held me so tightly I barely knew where he ended and I began. And he was standing here in this miserable desert, in the moonlight, with an unofficial crime-scene clean-up—cover-up might be more accurate—happening fifty yards away, and telling me I was amazing! But he still wouldn't—he still didn't—

"You were breaking up with me a few hours ago!" It burst out of me, practically a shout. "You told me you didn't want this anymore. I don't even know how you found me, I don't know anything! You're acting like you regret kissing me, and I don't—"

Declan cut me off by hauling me into another kiss, rough and insistent, a claiming more than a caress. When he pulled back, my bruised lips throbbed in the cold air, and my head fell back against his hand, my neck muscles turned into jelly.

"I'd never regret kissing you," he said, low and hoarse, eyes blazing gold. "Never. I regret not kissing you the moment I got you out of that interrogation room. I regret not kissing you ten years ago, kissing you and pinning you down and knotting you until you screamed my name." His arms tightened painfully, and he gave me a shake that almost rattled my teeth. "I was *not* breaking up with you. I was trying to tell you I want you to stay with me. For real. No blackmail. You really don't remember asking me to kiss you the other night?"

I stared at him, head whirling with too much information all at once, too many assumptions crumbling and reforming into a new reality. Declan, with his rumpled dark hair, the golden glow in his black eyes, jaw set, rigid with tension. Dangerous and strong and the alpha-est alpha I'd ever known.

He wanted me. For real.

And I…

"I asked you to kiss me when I was drunk, I remember that," I whispered. And then it finally twigged. "But you said no. You wanted me to ask you again?"

"Because you were drunk," he agreed. "And I told you to ask me again. It was fucking killing me all day. The second I woke up, I was waiting. Not that I slept much. And you didn't even mention it.

Even when I—I thought you were blowing it off because you regretted it."

"You want me." I had to say it aloud in order to believe it, and even then it sounded so unlikely. "For real. You want to—like a, a lover?"

The smile that got me lit up the whole desert—or at least it did for me. It reached his eyes, making them sparkle, and brought out...fuck. A dimple. He had a dimple in his right cheek.

It didn't make an actual sound, of course, but I swore I felt and heard something crack in my chest.

I had it bad.

In fact, I loved him.

Fuck, I really loved him. I hadn't even known what love felt like, and maybe that was how it'd crept up on me.

But this had to be it, this expanding feeling in my chest, the spinning of my head, the way his arms around me felt like the home I'd never realized I needed.

"Like a lover," he said softly, leaning down and brushing his lips over mine in the gentlest possible tease. "Like anything you want. As long as you're mine. As long as you choose to be mine, you can have anything you want from me."

I only wanted him. The words stuck on my lips, though. If I dared to trust him that much—it felt like falling, spiraling down, dizzy and disoriented. Except that I already had him holding me. Maybe he wouldn't let me fall after all.

"I only want you."

I stretched up, pressing my mouth to his, kissing him rather than being kissed.

He took it over within half a second and had me bent over his arm and ravaged.

And that was more than fine with me.

A loud throat-clearing interrupted us, how long after I didn't know. A little whine left my throat as he lifted his head and broke the kiss. I'd gotten one leg wrapped around his hips, my straining cock desperately trying for enough friction.

It couldn't possibly be enough, not when I was ready for him to bend me over and plow me into next week, sand and spiky cactus plants and scorpions and an audience of hard-bitten bodyguards be damned.

I blinked up at Declan as he turned his head, looking as flushed and dazed as I felt, and glanced over. "Yes?"

I gave whoever was standing there a lot of credit for not turning tail and scurrying away at that extremely unwelcoming syllable.

"Liam's got them both stable enough for now," said a deep male voice. "But we need to call in a Medevac, and you should be long gone before they get here. We'll say we found them like this. If one of those assholes tries to claim otherwise, I'll take care of it."

I leaned my head into Declan's shoulder and let out a sigh of relief. If they were calling a Medevac then everyone was still alive. Okay, so I maybe wouldn't be losing a lot of sleep over Walter's fate. But the driver—well, he'd been perfectly happy with the idea of leaving my corpse to rot in the desert. On the other hand, I didn't want to be a killer. Not even in self-defense.

Declan sighed. "We'll be there in a minute."

Crunching footsteps receded, leaving us alone in the quiet of the night again.

Another sigh, and a kiss to the top of my head that had me smiling into his shoulder like a moron.

"Come on, let's get you home," he said.

Home. I was already there, of course. But the suite, with a soft bed and room service—werewolf healing took a fuck-ton of energy, and I'd just about reached my limit—and oh, gods. A shower. A hot shower.

So even though my legs protested against any movement at all, I didn't resist as Declan led me back toward the road, one arm still holding me protectively right against him. I'd go wherever Declan took me, and if that was toward steak and lobster bisque, so much the better.

With every step, a little jolt went through my heart, surprise and joy and disbelief.

He's mine. He wants me. I love him. He wants me!

"This isn't just because I almost died, right?"

Declan hugged me closer, shuddering. "Don't mention that ever again if you want me to stay sane," he said. "And no. Remember? On the way to the party? I was trying to tell you. Now stop worrying and focus on not falling down, unless you want me to carry you."

I very very much did not want Declan to carry me in front of all of his tough-guy security team, so I settled for elbowing him in the ribs and picking up the pace a little.

It wasn't that difficult, actually, because recrossing the ground I'd run over, panicking and hurt and alone, only this time with Declan at my side, felt like victory. Saying I'd rescued myself might be an exaggeration; I'd have been dead if Declan had been only another few minutes behind us. But I'd tried. I'd done my best, and I'd bought the cavalry some time, and I'd caused some damage.

So I held my head up high as we climbed up the embankment onto the road. And I preened a little as someone—presumably Liam—looked up from where he was holding a bandage and kneeling over the prone form of the driver to say, "You really did a number on him," in a tone of admiration.

Probably not the best attitude for a medic, but whatever. Worked for me.

Declan ushered me into one of the cars with heart-melting care, settling me as if I'd been a hundred years old and also made out of fine china. The quick kiss he dropped on my mouth as he ducked back out to consult with his men had my heart racing all over again.

My broken arm had finally mostly knitted together, the sharp pain subsiding to a dull ache, and the concussion seemed to be fading too. The tiny wounds from flying cactus spines had healed. Adrenaline comedown was a bitch and a half, but that'd fade eventually.

I leaned back in the comfortable seat, closed my eyes, and let everything go.

***

It took a little under two hours to get back to the Morrigan. I felt like it should've been several times that long, given how remote the location of my almost-murder had seemed from all the lights and bustle and noise of Vegas. Declan tugged me over to his side of the car and tucked me halfway into his lap, and I dozed there the whole way home, stumbling out in a daze when we finally stopped behind the casino near a discreet service door.

The same one Walter and I had used the night he attacked me

the first time, in fact. I tried not to show it, but I shuddered a little. Declan pulled me closer and hustled me to the elevator, throwing a few words of instruction over his shoulder to the men who'd escorted us home.

I didn't care about any of the details. My feet felt so heavy, ditto my head. Everything. Enough to outweigh how happy I was, even.

Happy. What a weird feeling. "I'm happy," I mumbled, swaying into Declan's grasp, knowing he'd hold me up.

He chuckled. "You'll be happier in a second."

The scents of salmon and steak and soup and chocolate and garlic potatoes hit me as we walked into the suite, and suddenly I cared about the details.

I cared *deeply*.

My stomach let out a fearsome growl worthy of an alpha werewolf at his angriest.

It took me about ten minutes to demolish literally everything edible in sight, including the array of desserts—every single one on the menu, I thought, and maybe a couple that weren't on the menu at all.

I looked up from the ruins of the table to find Declan leaning one hip on the edge of it, smiling down at me. "You need me to order another round?"

Guilt hit me nearly as hard as my sudden, overwhelming contentment. Declan had made the effort to arrange a feast for me from the car, and I hadn't even left him a bite.

"I'm sorry, some of that was for you, I didn't—"

He pushed off, leaned down, and tugged me up out of my chair. "You really think I ordered two different kinds of cheesecake for myself? Blake, you're healing. Come on. Shower."

"Shower" turned out to mean "shower with Declan." He followed me into his bathroom, and the moment he had the water running, he started to undress me with a concentrated focus I didn't think had much to do with wanting to fuck me, given the way he checked every inch of me for lingering injuries.

My jacket hit the floor first, and then the bowtie. I stood mute and still, soaking in the gathering warmth of the billowing steam, Declan's hands working on me. Petting my shoulders, stroking down my arms and examining the fading bruises left behind by the break, and muttering something about ripping Walter's guts out and strangling him with them.

I smiled to myself.

Yeah, I really wouldn't be losing sleep over Walter, even if Declan carried out his threats.

He unfastened my watch and set it aside on the counter, the light glinting off of the shattered face. "Shit, I've had that watch for years," I mumbled, knowing it was such a small thing in the grand scheme, but…that was the last remnant of my old life. The only possession I'd retained that had any intrinsic value.

"That watch saved your life, actually," Declan said in an oddly restrained tone. "I, ah. Put a tracking device in it before I gave it back to you. That's why I gave it back to you." I stared at him, half in fury and half in…awe at his forethought? But what a sneaky asshole! "I'll buy you ten more," he added quickly, as if trying to stave off my anger. "As many as you want. And I won't put trackers in any of them, you have my word." That didn't really make me feel less offended, but when he lifted my wrist and kissed it, that took the wind out of my sails.

"I don't need ten. I don't need any." He looked up from where he was bent over my arm, lips caressing me, and raised a skeptical eyebrow. "Okay, one or two. No Rolexes, though."

He shook his head and laughed, his breath heating my skin and raising the hair on my arm, and then let me go, starting to work on my shirt. It peeled down and drifted to the floor. Declan moved closer, his breaths the only sound except for the shower. His fingertips traced my ribs. "Blake," he whispered. "Blake."

As if that was the only thing he had to say, the only thing that needed to be said.

Declan knelt, undoing my belt and fly, the zipper slowly sliding down. I hadn't been conscious of becoming aroused. Too exhausted, too overwhelmed, too shaky, too stunned by eating and healing.

But as he slipped his hand into the gap of my open trousers and ran his fingers over my length, I hardened, the blood rushing to my cock making me lightheaded.

Declan leaned in and nuzzled me, breath hot through the cotton of my boxer briefs. I lifted a hand and ran it through his hair, my own breath catching. I'd knelt for him so many times. I wanted to do it again, and soon. But I'd been on my knees for other men before. Giving a blowjob turned me on, even when it wasn't the man I loved. Declan didn't have a single submissive bone in his body. If he wanted to be on his knees at my feet…that was for me. *Only* because of me.

"I should've just done it," he murmured, and it took me a moment to realize what he meant.

"I wouldn't have appreciated it," I said. With regret, because I knew it was true. I wouldn't have valued him at his real worth ten years ago. I'd been so stupid.

He glanced up, eyes sparking with desire and something predatory that sent a shiver down my back. "I'd have made you appreciate it," he growled, and then he tore my underwear down and swallowed my cock all at once.

I staggered and practically doubled over, curling down around him in an effort not to come instantly, the hot, eager suction of his mouth overwhelming me. Steam curled around us from the running shower, the air thick and heavy with moisture and with two alphas' pheromones, with Declan's powerful, rich alpha strength winding around me. My lungs labored and my cock pressed into Declan's throat, his hands on my hips holding me up as much as keeping me where he wanted me.

My balls drew up hard and tight, my stomach clenching. So close, his tongue dancing over the underside, my cockhead throbbing against the roof of his mouth.

Declan pulled off completely. I let out a cry of frustration.

"This is what I would've done to you. Gotten you so close. Gotten you fucking begging for it." I whimpered, not even able to beg. I would have then, though, if he'd given me what I asked for—his version of it, anyway.

I'd clearly had no idea what I'd been inviting when I propositioned him.

He was shoving my remaining clothing off, my cock bobbing neglected in front of his face. I lifted one foot and then the other, and he'd gotten up and manhandled me into the shower before I could blink.

I slumped against the shower wall, the heat of the water shocking, the wall cold, my legs near giving out…and then Declan was there, pressed against my back and even hotter than the shower. His cock pushed between the cheeks of my ass, so hard and thick, the head nudging my hole. I moaned and tried to arch my back to take him in. He could fuck me raw, I wanted it, I wanted...

"I'd have done it ten years ago." He pulled his hips back. "Slammed you up against the wall. Spread your legs and fucking reamed you." He thrust again, pulling my cheeks apart and rubbing his cockhead over my clenching hole. "You'd have taken it, Blake."

"I would, I'd have taken it then, I'll take it now, please—"

"No," he said, and pulled back again, arm looping around my waist, resting his chin on my shoulder. "Not now. Ten years ago, yeah. But—not tonight. I want to," he went on, voice dipping low and hoarse. "Believe me. But I almost lost you. I almost—" He broke off in a groan, kissing my shoulder, arm tightening around me. "I almost lost you," he said quietly, and I felt a minute tremor go through him, as if he'd only in that moment taken the time to think about it.

I put my hand on his forearm, petting him, soothing him, torn between horror that he'd been put through that much fear and worry and a totally, shamefully delighted exultation that he'd cared enough.

Fuck, I could be forgiven for it tonight. I'd be the better man tomorrow when I hadn't been kidnapped.

Tonight, I could savor it.

"You have me," I said. Declan leaned against me, still rigid with tension, fingers digging into my waist. He drew a deep, shuddering breath. Gods. There was only one thing I could say that'd reassure him, that'd make me as vulnerable as he was to me right then. One thing I'd been hoping not to say until he said it first—if he ever did, which I wasn't counting on. I squeezed my eyes shut and gathered all the courage that'd let me dive through the window of a car earlier that night, plus a little, since that hadn't been nearly as scary as this. "I love you."

I thought Declan had been tense before. As soon as the words left my lips, he turned into granite.

"You love me." His flat tone gave nothing away.

My heart twisted into a miserable, hard little ball.

I shouldn't have said anything. So stupid, and now he'd change his mind—

"There's no fucking way," he said, with an edge of bitterness.

"You're grateful to me, and you need me because you don't have anyone else. And you want me," he growled. "I'm going to keep you so well fucked that you'll never stop wanting me. But you can't possibly love me. Not after the way I've treated you. You don't need to lie to me to make sure I take care of you, Blake. I will. No matter what."

Of course. Of course he thought I was lying. My hand clenched on his forearm, fingers digging in so hard it had to be painful, but at least I kept my claws in check.

I didn't want him to take care of me.

Okay, yes, I fucking wanted him to take care of me. But more than that…I wanted him to trust me the way I'd chosen to trust him.

And maybe that was more important than my pride.

"I do love you," I choked out. "Whether or not you can love me, I do. Love you." The shower hammered down, nearly drowning out the words if he hadn't had a shifter's enhanced hearing. I was so glad he was behind me and couldn't see my face; if I'd had to meet his eyes to say this, I'd never have been able to get it out. I knew I was stumbling over my words anyway, repeating myself, unable to convey the clarity I felt inside. "Maybe I deserved what you did. And—I've seen you the way you really are. And I love you. So if you can't love me, that's all ri—"

"Jesus fucking Christ, Blake!" He spoke so loudly it made me wince. "Fuck." He wrapped his other arm around me and pulled me all the way against him, pressing his face into my neck. It muffled what he said next, but not enough; he wasn't the only one with supernatural ears. "Of course I fucking love you."

His sincerity, the truth of it, rang in every word. It echoed inside me, resonating, filling me, expanding me so much it felt like I might vibrate out of my own skin.

Telling him I loved him hadn't felt nearly as momentous as repeating his words back to him, feeling the weight of them on my lips and in my soul.

"You love me," I whispered.

Declan mouthed at the junction of my neck and shoulder, the place where he'd bitten me so many times. So many false starts, so many half-formed bonds, so many agonizing moments when that sense of connection had faded into nothingness and left me hollow and alone.

"Yeah, darlin'. I love you. I mean it. If you don't mean it after all, don't tell me. I don't think I'll survive it."

I couldn't help laughing. Declan, insecure? How could he possibly—but he'd stopped moving, his mouth still. "I'm sorry, you just—you really are stupid about this kind of thing, Declan."

"Too stupid to deserve you." He punctuated the words by kissing me right where a mating bite would go. A real mating bite.

"You know, the next time you bite me, I'm warning you. I'm going to bite you back."

Declan sucked in a deep, hitching breath, his hips surging forward as if he couldn't help himself, his hard cock riding the crease of my ass. Gods, I'd almost forgotten about my own, but it was just as hard.

"Let's get you washed up," he said, suddenly sounding like a man on a mission. "Because the things I want to do to you, I can't do in a shower stall."

I smiled and pushed off the wall, reaching for the soap.

I could get on board with that. And I'd make him tell me he loved me again and again, preferably while he knotted me, and claimed me, and owned me—and really forced me to believe, without the slightest shadow of a doubt, that he meant it.

Chapter 21

A Lucky Man

If I'd really tried, I might've been able to look at a calendar and count how many times Declan had laid me out on his bed, naked and waiting for him to take what he wanted.

But I didn't need to count to know that it'd never been like this.

He settled me on my back, head carefully placed on a pillow, kneeling between my legs and leaning down to stroke a hand through my hair and down my cheek, coming to rest across my throat. Instead of a threat, it felt like safety.

All right, a little bit of a threat.

But that only had my cock perking up, getting harder every second that he pinned me down, glowing eyes fixed on my face with an intensity that would've had any sane man running away screaming.

Or spreading his legs.

I went with option two, letting my knees fall open to give him full access, my arms relaxed at my sides. Touching him—I wanted to, and I would. But right now I knew what he needed from me, and that was complete surrender, allowing him to re-stake his claim on me. I'd been taken from him. He needed to take me back. I was alpha enough to empathize.

I lay passive and still as he ghosted his other hand over my chest, made me let out two hitching gasps in a row with a soft tweak to each nipple, and trailed his fingers down my stomach and to my inner thigh, his eyes following the path of his hand. His fingers tightened slightly around my throat as he slid the other hand under my balls, two fingertips tracing my hole. I had to tip my head back to get a full breath, lengthening my throat and making myself as vulnerable as one alpha could to another.

Declan's chest rose and fell faster as he gazed down between my legs.

His cock stood up even harder than mine; I didn't care that much about how mine ached for a touch when my eyes landed on his, tall and thick and flushed, impossibly larger than the tight little hole that was currently resisting one of his fingertips.

He'd plow me open with it. And I'd love it, that feeling of being stretched into a sheath for him. A shiver went up my spine as he nudged the tip of his finger slightly deeper.

That was enough to have me begging.

And begging more, as he replaced his fingers with his mouth.

And begging incoherently, babbling out how much I loved him, as he claimed me all over again, washing away the feeling of Walter's magic and the desert sand and my own pain and fear far more thoroughly than bathing could ever have done.

At last he stiffened, groaned, and filled me with wet heat, his knot swelling and locking us together so tightly I couldn't shift a muscle below the waist. The burn of the stretched skin of my rim crested like an endorphin rush.

"You didn't bite me," I slurred in his ear, eyes drooping closed. At this rate, I'd fall asleep before his knot went down.

He kissed my throat, I trembled and clenched around his knot, and we both groaned, Declan's breath hitching. "I'm not biting you again until I'm sure you want it," he said, and cut off my gathering protest—I did want it, right now, dammit!—with a quick kiss. Declan lifted his head and looked down seriously into my eyes. "I want to make you happy for a while. Prove I can do it forever."

Well, what could I say to that? I loved him so much it hurt, and I said that, and then he kissed me again, and more, and rolled us over so that I could drape myself across his chest and close my eyes and droop into a contented slump, like a big cat.

He'd proved it in the last five minutes. Fuck, he'd proved it when we got back to the suite and he'd had more than one kind of cheesecake waiting. That showed a pretty damn fundamental understanding of how to keep me, Blake Castelli, happy for life.

I must've mumbled something to that effect into his broad chest, because he petted my back and said, "I'll tell the hotel pastry chef to work on a few more varieties. You can taste-test them. Maybe that'll be part of your job around here."

Job. As in work?

That had my eyes popping open again. I'd thought I wasn't his whore anymore, but his...love.

Also...

"Job?"

Declan shook with laughter under me, jolting me up and down and tugging his knot uncomfortably, and I swatted weakly at his shoulder, too tired to put much force behind it. It still would've bruised a normal human, but he'd barely notice, damn him.

"No spreadsheets," he said, running his fingers through my hair. My eyes started to close again. Damn him twice for knowing how to soothe me even in the face of a threat of gainful employment. I mean, I'd been bored as hell hanging around the Morrigan playing blackjack for pennies. But I wouldn't be trapped in the casino anymore. I could go wherever I wanted...except that Declan would be in the Morrigan.

Which meant I wouldn't want to go anywhere else.

And that took the wind out of my mental sails.

"No spreadsheets," I repeated. And that was great. I appreciated the prospect of a totally spreadsheet-free future, unless maybe I had the chance to set one on fire. The marketing department was thoroughly, and probably to their great relief, entirely on their own. But the problem...my throat tightened. Declan loved me, right? He already knew how useless I was for anything but sex and loved me anyway. Surely he wouldn't change his mind about me if I was honest. "But I don't actually know—how to do anything. Anything else. I mean, I don't know how to do spreadsheets, but the couple of days I spent in your office means I know more about them than probably anything else to do with running a business."

"There's no hurry, Blake," Declan said, still stroking my hair, in a tone so mellow that I thought he might never be in a hurry again. About anything. "We'll figure it out. You won't be bored, I promise. I'll make sure you're happy. But you don't have to do anything you don't want to do."

That didn't sound so bad. I squeezed his knot and made him groan and clutch me tighter, and then smiled into his chest. Fuck, I would *never* get tired of that.

"Brat." His hand came down on my ass in a stinging slap, and I yelped and squirmed, finally subsiding back onto his chest again.

His steady heartbeat almost lulled me to sleep, but I'd hit that point of tiredness when my brain simply wouldn't shut down all the way. I stared at the wall. Declan's hand stroked up the length of my back, and then down again. My eyes still wouldn't close, despite how heavy my lids had been a few minutes before. It might've had something to do with my evening of near-murder, running for my life in the desert, clawing someone's shoulder down to the bone, being blasted with magic, etcetera, now that I thought about it.

My brain-to-mouth filter *had* apparently shut down for the night, though, because when I started talking, what came out was, "Next time I tell you one of your employees is trying to kill me, you should believe me." The spreadsheets flashed through my mind. "Next time it's probably going to be the marketing department."

"Jesus, Blake." His hands stilled, one wrapping around my waist and the other at the nape of my neck, holding me tightly. Underneath me, his chest expanded and then dipped as he drew in a deep, shuddering breath and blew it all out in a gust. "Never again. Fuck." He kissed the top of my head. "I'm sorry about the marketing spreadsheet. I wanted to keep you busy with something so complicated and boring you'd go away and stop hanging around my office distracting me. And then you—you actually tried." Another kiss. "I couldn't believe how hard you tried."

Bask in the warmth and admiration in his tone, or bridle at the condescension of it?

No, too tired to bridle at anything. And besides, he kind of...well, condescension wasn't all that unreasonable. He'd worked his way up from nothing, from a professional setback I'd dealt him, to own this place. Meanwhile, I'd barely recognized a spreadsheet when he put it in front of my face.

"I really was bored."

He let out a low chuckle. "Obviously."

"Oh, shut up. Seriously, though. I wanted to..." *Make you proud. Get your attention. Prove I was worth more than my ass.* "...help you. Spend time with you." That sounded a little less pathetic, anyway. Sort of. Fuck.

"I wanted to spend time with you, too," he said quietly. "So much that I couldn't get anything done with you there."

That was nice, but— "Can't help but notice you haven't apologized for the really important part of this, Declan. Not that I'm angry!" I lifted my head, suddenly frantic to make sure he understood. His troubled gaze met mine. "I'm not angry. I get it. What Mark said, Walter had been supporting you, or pretending to, before you even got the Morrigan back, right? But I was telling you the truth the whole time."

"Yeah," he said, jaw tight. "Yeah, you did. But remember how I compared you to the boy who cried wolf, before? You get that, don't you? I am sorry. You have no idea how much I regret not dealing with him before he took you. But from my point of view, I had a liar telling me not to trust someone who'd never let me down. I had a lot of doubts about it, though," he added, as I started to protest. "I did. Once I'd started to realize you weren't exactly what I'd thought you were. The doubts simply didn't build up enough to change my mind until it was almost too late."

I'd have preferred a little more groveling, but all right. I couldn't help thinking about when Walter had confronted me and Declan had told us both that no one had anything to apologize for. That the matter was settled.

Declan would never be anything but carefully even-handed, and I simply had to get used to it.

I loved that about him, anyway. I loved everything about him.

"Fine," I said grudgingly, and rested my chin on his chest, peeking up at his face. "At least you figured it out in time to come for me. I honestly thought you might shrug and let me go. Walter did a good job of making it look like I was there of my own free will. He had spell bags in my clothes, I think. To make me go outside where I'd be vulnerable, and to make me—with his partner in crime." I shuddered, the visceral memory of how it felt to kiss that fucking asshole henchman of his coming back to me with irresistible force. "Gods, that was gross."

Declan petted me, soothing me, rubbing a circle at the base of my spine. His knot had started to shrink and slip out of me. It should've felt unpleasant, but instead I simply basked in the stickiness, letting the intimacy of it calm me more than Declan's touch, even. He wasn't getting up and going to the shower, leaving me alone.

"Better? I could feel your heart racing." Declan smiled at me. "Blake, I never would've bought that you were kissing that motherfucker of your own free will. Believe me."

"But how did you know? I mean, my body language—everything. I couldn't control any of my actions at all."

Declan's smile grew into a grin. "Didn't take Sherlock Holmes to figure it out, baby. Just someone who knows you. I looked really damn closely at the security footage. He was wearing pleated khakis, and on top of that, he had a cheap shitty haircut. You would never."

I couldn't help bursting into laughter, leaning in to kiss him, savoring how it felt to choose to do it rather than being magicked and manipulated. Declan's lips distracted me for a while, long enough that when I finished thoroughly tasting him, I'd calmed down enough to settle with my head on his shoulder, content to let everything else go.

This time I'd turned to face the window instead of the wall. The lights of Las Vegas shone in with distant blinkings and flashings, like the world's largest slot machine, the moonlight having to compete to be seen even this many floors up above the Strip.

In the morning, the sun would shine straight in on my face, and dollars to donuts Declan would've already gotten out of bed and gone to do something productive.

"I love you," I said. "Even though you never bother to close the blinds. And you're a morning person."

He laughed and held me impossibly closer, snuggling me into his chest and into the cradle of his hips, enclosing and protecting me.

"Then that makes me a lucky man, darlin'," he said without hesitation. As if he believed that down to his very bones.

I closed my eyes, sinking into the warmth and safety of his embrace. I'd let him believe he was the lucky one, but I knew better.

Or maybe we were both luckier than we deserved.

Epilogue

You Don't Want a Choice

"Mr. Castelli," Laura said, and smiled warmly. "Go right in. He's never too busy for you."

"You know it's Blake." She shook her head, laughed, and went back to typing.

I hadn't yet given up on trying to convince Declan's assistant that I didn't deserve any particular formality; after nearly four months of trying, though, I'd started to fear it was hopeless.

I set the double latte I'd grabbed on my way at the edge of her desk—if she insisted on calling me Mr. Castelli, I'd at least make sure she said it with affection—and stepped into Declan's office.

He glanced up from his laptop and then immediately back down again, which I knew meant "I'll forget what I was typing if I don't do it right now." At first that'd hurt my feelings. Shades of being treated like an unwelcome and disliked inconvenience at Castelli Industries, of so many times I'd been called on the carpet in my father's office only to be ignored until he deigned to notice me. But I knew it wasn't the same thing—not even close.

I'd finally, haltingly, told Declan about my father, one night a week after Walter tried to kill me. I'd woken up screaming and thrashing from a nightmare involving both my father and Walter. Declan hadn't taken no for an answer. After I'd told the whole story, not hiding any of my own culpability, I'd had to physically prevent him from booking a plane ticket to Boise to beat the shit out of my father personally.

I'd been tempted, not going to lie, but I'd stopped him. Mainly because of Brook and how much another scandal would fuck him over. One of these days I knew I wanted to try to reach out to my brother, but that could wait.

Unlike me. I wasn't good at waiting.

I wandered over to the window, hands in my jeans pockets, trying not to look impatient.

Declan had given me a new watch the day before. Not for any particular occasion, just because. I'd taken it back this morning to fix the slightly loose clasp on it, and the manager of the store had asked me which item I needed help with. A few pointed questions later, and I found out Declan had also picked up a ring.

And he hadn't told me about it.

Of course, maybe he'd bought it for himself—and maybe pigs would fly, because Declan never spent that kind of money on frivolous things for himself.

And maybe he wanted to wait to give it to me.

But waiting…again, not my strong suit. His chair creaked, and I turned. Definitely not waiting.

"Mmm," Declan said, pulling me into his arms and nuzzling my throat. "I missed you."

It'd been three hours since he kissed me goodbye and left for work.

And I'd missed him too.

"That's why it's time for lunch." My arms snaked around his waist. Fuck, he felt good. Solid and warm and perfect to weigh me down between my legs…keep it together, Blake. "Right now."

He nibbled the side of my neck. "It's ten."

"Okay, brunch, whatever. Fuck, Declan that's—it doesn't matter that it's ten, we're not going to be eating anyway."

He chuckled and lifted his head, smile widening into a wicked grin that made my breath catch. "Speak for yourself."

My heart sped up even more. "I have plans for my mouth today, too, actually."

Declan raised an eyebrow. "Brunch, huh?"

"Brunch." I pushed my hips into his, tipping my head back in submission.

His eyes darkened and started to glow all at once. "I'm convinced," he growled, and started pulling me toward the door. "I'll be back when I'm back, Laura," he said as we passed, and she sighed the sigh of the long-suffering.

I couldn't help thinking about the time Walter had appeared right as we'd tried to leave Declan's office for an early "lunch," and everything that'd brought on. Fucking Walter. He wasn't there to stop us this time; he'd been moved, last I'd heard, to a maximum-security magical/supernatural prison after trying to murder his cellmate in the last facility. And I genuinely hoped I'd never have another update.

I forgot all about Walter as Declan tumbled me into the elevator, kissing me like he'd been starving for me. I felt the same hunger, but I couldn't relax into it the way I normally did, when I simply let him take control and let myself go.

"What's the matter?" Declan pulled back and pinned me against the wall of the elevator. "You're all twitchy."

A ring. He'd bought a ring, even though he hadn't bitten me at all since he'd rescued me and brought me home. Apparently he didn't believe I was happy enough, or something?

Or he'd changed his mind.

But he'd bought a ring.

Fuck it.

"You bought a ring," I blurted out, my cheeks going red-hot and my palms starting to sweat. "I went to get the watch clasp fixed and talked to the jeweler. And you bought—a ring."

"No," Declan said slowly. "I had a ring resized. Two, actually. This one was my grandfather's, it was too large for me. I also had my grandmother's resized. Picked that one up months ago. That one was too small."

I blinked at him, letting all of that settle in my brain.

His grandfather's ring had been too large for *him*, which meant that the one he'd picked up months ago was intended for someone else.

He hadn't bought a ring. He'd collected the matching one to the ring he'd had for me for…

"You've had my ring for months?" I demanded, voice rising to a pitch too high and loud for the elevator. We both winced as it echoed. That didn't slow me down. "You haven't bitten me! You haven't even asked to bite me! You haven't—did I do something?" Sudden, crippling terror hit me like a blow. "I did something, didn't I? You

198

got the ring, and then I—was it when I kicked that guy out of the casino? I know I didn't have any actual authority, but security backed me up, so—mmph!"

Declan's hand over my mouth didn't stop me from trying to keep arguing, but it did silence me.

"They wouldn't have helped you if you hadn't been right, and I gave you the authority immediately after that, remember?" He didn't remove his hand, so I nodded grudgingly.

The guy I'd tossed out had been such a dick, hitting on the cocktail waitresses in a way that didn't quite catch the negative attention of the eyes in the sky but that made them visibly uncomfortable to someone close enough to notice. And Declan had made me a part of the security team after that—well, maybe more like a mascot. But he'd told them, and me, that I could eighty-six anyone who acted like an asshole.

He'd refrained, kindly, from pointing out his obvious reason for giving me this job, and that much authority: literally no one in the world was more qualified for determining how much douchebaggery from a casino VIP was too much douchebaggery to be tolerated.

It might've also had something to do with wanting me to stop trying to get him to give me a job at Lucky or Knot, the strip club he owned downtown. Either way, "security mascot/rich asshole wrangler" worked for me as a job title, even though Laura kept refusing to order me any business cards.

I'd stopped trying to talk, so Declan removed his hand and replaced it with his mouth, pulling back after he'd completed the process of short-circuiting my brain. Gods, his lips.

I blinked my eyes open.

The elevator dinged, and the door rattled open onto the hallway of the service corridor on the bottom floor, our route to the other elevator that'd take us up into the hotel tower.

I opened my mouth.

"Hold that thought," Declan said, and dragged me out.

I managed to keep my tongue bitten until we got up to the suite, anxiety keeping me silent. He'd only addressed one part of my concern: that it might've been that one incident that put him off the idea of marrying me. Mating me.

Gods, Declan had wanted to mate me.

Fuck. And he'd changed his mind.

By the time the door of the suite thumped shut behind us, I'd started to hyperventilate so badly my vision blurred.

"Fuck, Blake." His voice took on a tinge of worry. He gave me a shake, hands gripping my shoulders tightly. "Blake!"

His eyes blazed gold, jaw set and brows drawn together. I took a deep breath, focusing on his face.

"Blake," he said more quietly. "You haven't done a damn thing wrong. Why would you think you had?"

His total confusion at the idea went a long way toward calming me down, but he still hadn't explained anything!

"No! No, of course there's nothing. Declan, I'd *never*. I would never." I broke off, panting and closer to tears than I'd have liked. I'd been so confident, so determined to give Declan a piece of my mind, tell him what I wanted from him. But even if he hadn't re-thought his desire to mate me for any particular reason, knowing that he'd been waffling about this decision for such a long time made me feel so small, so insignificant. So unworthy.

Declan stared at me for a long moment, mouth in a hard line and eyes raking me over, obviously assessing me for…I had no idea what he might be looking for, actually.

"I was trying to give you a choice this time," he said at last, releasing his hard grasp on my shoulders and stroking down to my wrists, taking my hands in his. "I wanted you to be the one to suggest taking the next step, because I'd walked all over you before." The corner of his mouth quirked, not quite a smile. "But I was a fucking idiot, wasn't I? You don't want a choice, do you?"

Put like that, it made me sound so incredibly pathetic. Weak and needy and dependent.

But he was right. I didn't.

I didn't want a choice. I'd always choose Declan, always. But if he left the choice up to me I'd never stop wondering if he'd truly wanted me. I hadn't even realized I felt that way until he put it into words, somehow knowing me better than I knew myself, as he so often did.

Agreeing aloud felt like more than my alpha pride could take. Instead, I shook my head slightly, and Declan let out a long, slow breath, as if he'd been more worried about my answer than he wanted to let on.

"Then I won't give you one," he said, very low. "Come on, sweetheart. Come with me."

We went to our bedroom at the end of the hallway, and I knew to start stripping my clothes without even being told. I'd turned into Pavlov's alpha werewolf, undoing buttons and zippers and kicking off shoes the moment Declan got that look in his eye.

Lately Declan had been taking more time with me, kissing me, touching me, bringing me to simmering delight before he finished me off, as if he wanted to make up for all the times he'd had me without any of that—and as if I didn't want him no matter how he pleasured me, gently or roughly or anything in between.

This time he didn't try to be gentle.

The moment I had my pants off, he shoved me onto the bed so hard I bounced when I landed. He was between my legs instantly, three slick fingers stuffed into my hole so suddenly I cried out, the other hand in the center of my chest, holding me down and at his mercy.

He bared his fangs at me, eyes glowing like stars. "You're mine, Blake. Mine, all mine, and no one else's."

He didn't make it a question, but I knew he wanted an answer anyway. "Yours," I gasped, pulling my knees back to try to alleviate the sting of how quickly he'd prepped me. "All yours."

Declan thrust into me without any more back and forth, forcing his way inside and showing me without further words that I belonged to him, that he owned every inch of me.

A lot of inches. Fuck, it took a lot of inches to hold him.

I never quite got used to it, panting with the effort of being stretched open so wide and deep every single time.

Declan braced himself on his arms and started to fuck me, a hard, steady rhythm that pounded the breath out of my lungs with every forward motion and tugged on my hole with every withdrawal. He had me on the point of coming within what felt like seconds, my knees clamped around his hips and my hands raking over his back, trying to keep him closer, drag him impossibly deeper.

And then he stopped, right as my balls drew tight and my cock started to spasm. I let out a high-pitched moan of pure frustration as he took my chin in his hand and made me look him in the eye.

"Knot for me," he said. "I'm not fucking you the way you want me to until I see it."

"Oh, gods," I gasped, my hand flying to my cock, face going from orgasm-flushed to burning. Most of the time, Declan didn't demand that I knot for him. Even though I'd done it before…it still rode the edge of too much, too humiliating. Too degrading, even. It highlighted how imbalanced our dynamic was: one alpha with all the authority, and another with almost none.

That we both wanted it that way didn't matter so much in moments like this.

He had to force me to knot, though usually he didn't.

Today he had to. He had to demonstrate, beyond the shadow of a doubt, that every part of me belonged to him.

I frantically stripped my cock, twisting under the head and squeezing at the base where the knot would form. Declan shifted his hips minutely, pressing his thick girth into exactly the right spot, and I spurted come all over my hand and my stomach, curling up into the pleasure of it.

The base of my cock swelled, the knot forming instantly. I wrapped my hand around it. Gods, so hypersensitive. I almost couldn't bear it.

"Play with it," Declan said hoarsely. "Show me how good it feels to be my bitch."

That toppled me over an edge I didn't even know I had, my orgasm hitting again in a second wave that tightened every muscle and left me whimpering, squeezing my knot and coming again all over my chest.

Declan started to fuck me again, this time slamming into me like a man possessed. I had to brace myself on the headboard to keep from having my head shoved through it as he pounded me up the bed. Every stroke took me higher, feeling like that poised, about-to-fall moment before I came, only over and over again until I writhed under him, quivering, every muscle rigid.

At last he stopped, shuddering, as his knot grew, thrusting one last time to firmly lodge it inside me. He came hard, hot and deep.

"You said you'd bite me back the next time I bit you," he growled. "Going to keep your promise?"

"Yes, Declan, yes—"

He curled down, set his teeth into my skin, and bit.

I threw my head back and rode the crest of pain, the way it sent tendrils of fire down all my nerves, magic rather than mundane sensation. My whole body lit up, gold and rich purple and some color I couldn't even name that didn't seem to exist as something visual but only as a flavor of Declan's alpha magic.

Every other time he'd done this, that magic had faded after a few minutes, dissipating when those tendrils weren't met by equal and opposite alpha power.

This time, when he released me, he tipped his head to the side and bent down to place his neck in reach of my mouth. My canines dropped instantly. I bit down without hesitation, piercing his flesh.

The taste of his blood in my mouth hit first, salty and rich, pleasing to my animal instincts but nauseating to my human ones.

But that vanished immediately, overwhelmed by the taste of his magic and the burst of my own that flowed out of me to reach out for his, twining with it and melding with it and forming—a bond. A mating bond, knitting us together permanently, making us one.

I let go of my mouthful of him, my head falling back.

Mated. I could feel him without touching him, almost see him when I blinked my eyes closed. Permanently there, in the edges of my senses and at the border of my soul.

"Fuck," Declan gasped against my shoulder. "Fuck, that's— Blake, you're even more beautiful than I thought. The way you feel."

I clung to his upper arms and squeezed as hard as I could, turning my head to press a kiss to his temple.

"I know," I whispered. "I mean, you too. I love you."

He lifted his head, gazing at me with eyes so much softer than I usually saw them—than anyone else probably ever saw them. "And I love you, Blake. You seriously don't even know." He reached over and fumbled with the nightstand, fishing around in the drawer until he came up with something small and glinting. "Left hand."

I held it up between us, and Declan slipped the gold ring onto my ring finger. It had a faint pink sheen to it, some kind of rose gold, and an even fainter tracery. Something Irish. I fell in love with it instantly, and I knew I'd be driving every member of the casino's staff nuts showing it to literally everyone, sometimes twice to make sure I hadn't missed anyone.

"I'll put mine on later," Declan said. "I can't reach it from here."

His eyes kept flicking from the fresh mating bite on my neck to his ring on my finger, as if he couldn't decide which he loved the most.

"I'll put it on you myself. I may not want a choice about mine, but I want to choose for you. Can I?"

Declan leaned down and kissed me so softly, so gently, that I sank back into the bed, lightheaded with how much I loved him.

"You own me too," he said quietly. "Always."

I put my arms around him and drew him down to rest his head next to mine.

Always worked for me.

The End

Thanks for reading, and I hope you enjoyed Blake and Declan's story!

Blake's brother Brook's HEA with his hired alpha can be found in *The Alpha Contract*, the previous book in the Mismatched Mates series. For their cousin Drew's romance with his human mate, check out *Lost Touch*!

Acknowledgments

My first and most fervent thanks have to go to Amy Pittel this time. Amy's never-ending (and possibly teeth-grinding) patience with the process of my writing and her beta reading this book left me weak with gratitude. We both lost track of the number of versions of this book she ended up reading. Thank you, Amy!!!

Thank you so much to the lovely Alessandra Hazard, who also read a couple of different versions of several chapters of this book, plus the whole thing end to end! As always, this book is much better for your advice. If anything quacks, it's not your fault.

A special shout-out to Bobbie Gail! She thought of Lucky or Knot, possibly the most brilliant name for a Las Vegas shifter strip club ever. Bobbie, you're a genius. Thank you!

I also need to thank my Las Vegas braintrust, Melissa M., Sa R., Stephanie H., and Sam Burns. They're the ones to ask if you ever need to know where to dump a body in Nevada. (I am implying nothing in particular with this statement.) And they were very generous with their time and knowledge! Any errors are mine.

Get in Touch

I love hearing from readers! Find me at eliotgrayson.com, where you can get more info about my books and also sign up for my newsletter or contact me directly. You can also find out about my other books on Amazon, or join my Facebook readers' group, Eliot Grayson's Escape from Reality, to get more frequent updates. Thanks for reading!

Also by Eliot Grayson

Mismatched Mates:
The Alpha's Warlock
Captive Mate
A Very Armitage Christmas
The Alpha Experiment
Lost and Bound
Lost Touch
The Alpha Contract

Blood Bonds:
First Blood
Twice Bitten

Goddess-Blessed:
The Replacement Husband
The Reluctant Husband
Yuletide Treasure

Portsmouth:
Like a Gentleman
Once a Gentleman

Santa Rafaela:
The One Decent Thing
A Totally Platonic Thing
Need a Hand?

Beautiful Beasts:
Deven and the Dragon
Corin and the Courtier

Brought to Light

Undercover

The Wrong Rake

Made in the USA
Monee, IL
31 January 2025

10379481R00121